'And her own mother, in the secret life we do not see, was a child too. I come from a line of children without end.'

J.M. Coetzee, Life & Times of Michael K

# 1.

On our last morning in New York, I slide the mattress down three flights of stairs and leave it on the sidewalk, propped up against a tree trunk. The A4 note I've taped to the white fitted sheet reads: *No bedbugs. New-ish (3 years). Help yourself.* It's February. There are mounds of mud-streaked snow at irregular intervals on the concrete, and the crystallised remains of the chemical salts they throw down to melt pathways through the ice. For all their filth, I know I'm going to miss these winters. This upside-down world of winter in February and shadows that fall to the north.

The apartment looks as it did the day we moved in: bare walls; ashwood veneer floors; and tall, narrow sash windows overlooking naked trees and an overcast sky above Brooklyn. I have been distributing house plants to friends over the past few weeks, and smaller items of furniture, like the bronze drinks stand and the antique wooden chair I bought because it reminded me of my grandmother. I tried to sell a few of the nicer pieces on Craigslist, but mostly people wasted my time. I've been leaving the functional furniture on the street in tranches these last few days. The side table. The TV stand. Even the TV. I never saw anyone stop to look at these items, but the people who wanted them must have been watching. The furniture disappeared every morning before sunrise.

Last night Adrian tried to distract Frasier, our pug, while I packed the last of our clothes into the grey-green suitcase Frasier knows from every time we've left him behind. Adrian pulled the excited faces, he made the excited noises, and he threw Frasier's favourite rubber ball down the empty hallway, but none of it worked. Frasier wouldn't leave my side. When Adrian and I finally tried to get some sleep on the mattress on the living room floor, Frasier refused to be held. He paced the unfurnished room. He made small whimpering sounds.

I thought maybe we would put down roots here, too.

I wheel our luggage and Adrian carries the crate with Frasier in it to a busy corner. I hail a cab by lifting my arm into the cold air and shouting, 'Taxi!' It would be quicker to request a ride on my phone, but I'm not leaving New York without flagging down one final cab the way they do it in the movies.

Cape Town looks dry from the plane. I try to point this out to Adrian beside me but I'm conscious of speaking very slowly, and slurring my words. I'm heavily sedated, with beta blockers and sleeping pills and booze. Some homeopathic calming chews as well. I take combinations that are not recommended, in doses that are not recommended. A delicate balance: not so much that I'll kill myself, but enough to keep the plane whole, to stop the engines from exploding and engulfing us all in flames as we plummet to the earth. Enough to unclench my jaw, to keep my teeth from shattering in my mouth. 'It looks like the Middle East,' I say, avoiding the term 'aerial footage' which comes to mind but would prove difficult for my tongue in this woozy fog.

'You've never been,' Adrian says and smiles at me.

I wave away his doubt. Things are worse than I realised. The vegetation is dead. The mountains are brown. The sky a terrible greyish-white, like sun-bleached bones.

There are notices all over the airport about the drought. A countdown clock measures the days until the city runs out of water. The taps have already been switched off in the airport public toilets. Little blue bottles of waterless hand sanitiser wait by the basins.

I read apocalyptic predictions in our Uber on our way into the city. CNN, BBC, *The Guardian*, *The New York Times*. We're all over the global press. Mixed in with the dread, and the exhaustion that follows the adrenaline when we touch down on solid ground, is a strange sense of accomplishment: the world is paying attention to our crisis. Our ignored continent, where no one cares what happens, where tragedy is supposed to be part of the brand. This time, we're a canary in the coal mine. This climate chaos is coming for you, these articles imply, and so *this* African suffering matters.

'It's a strange time to move home,' the Uber driver says to me. 'Cape Town's in trouble.'

He's Zimbabwean, I'd guess, from his accent and the music playing on his sound system.

'How's it been?' I say.

'You will see, you get used to it. The politicians say they will send in the army when they switch off the taps.'

Shacks glide past my window. Slums stretch to the distant mountains. Sheet metal, canvas, cinder block, wooden crating – homes built from anything that can be found. Packed close together, holding one another up. Emaciated goats search in vain for grass along the concrete fence that keeps these settlements from spilling over onto the verge, where children play soccer in the sand. We pass beneath a pedestrian bridge encased in steel mesh, like a long metal cage. It used to be a problem, I remember. People on bridges throwing bricks onto the freeway below, shattering the windscreens of cars racing to the airport. All those passengers bound for Europe and America and Asia, for gap years and ski holidays and shareholder meetings. Honeymoons and cheeky little getaways. *Decided to treat myself,* they'd caption, posting to Instagram from the departures lounge. Or: *Time for a little adventure. Why not?* I can see why they need the metal cage.

'Why did you come home?' the driver says.

It sounds like a real question, warm and interested, not an accusation of madness – how could anyone choose *this*? They are usually white, the people who inflect it like that, and I tell myself they are usually older than me, too. Some people assume that our moving home means we failed to make it in the world because they think the world is other places. But then there are those who ask the question out of nervous optimism. They want to believe South Africa is going to be okay, and they want to believe that my moving home means I do, too.

'He wants to have a child,' Adrian says from behind me.

I catch his eye in the rear-view mirror and hold his gaze for what feels like minutes. Eight years together and still I cannot read this expression of his. His hazel eyes are green in this light, and intense. Does he hold it against me that our time in New York was cut short, or is he trying to protect me?

The driver glances between Adrian and me, aware that something is going unsaid. 'Hey, you guys are funny,' he says. 'Normally the white people who talk about kids are the ones who want to leave.'

I laugh and shake my head in a way that I hope conveys we're not those kinds of white people.

'That's amazing, man,' the driver says, genuinely delighted. 'Congratulations. So your girlfriend is pregnant?'

I try to catch Adrian's eye again, but he's looking out of the window.

'I'm going to adopt,' I say.

Whatever the reason Adrian said 'he' instead of 'we', it's easier just to go along with it. It's tiring to have to surprise taxi drivers with our sexuality, with our marriage. We both pass for straight most of the time, if we're sober and in the company of anyone but our closest friends. We both probably seem pretty straight right now. It was something I was proud of, once. To be gay and ordinary seemed revolutionary when I was younger. Proof that I wasn't despicable and effeminate, showy or bitchy or shallow. Now, it just makes me sad that I got so good at passing. I don't even remember what parts of myself I cauterised.

'You know, children are a lot of work,' the driver says, laughing and shaking his head. 'Too much work for one person. You must meet a nice girl.'

'I know plenty of nice girls,' I say, trying to sound light-hearted and non-committal and maybe like one of the boys. Anything to move the conversation on, but it's cowardly and suddenly I can feel tears stinging behind my eyes.

I open the window a little. The car fills with the roar of the outside world, and the heat of it. My eyes dry out, but the stinging won't go away. It's the most feeble membrane keeping all of this mess inside me and I don't even know if I'm angry or sad, but at any rate I'm very unstable and that terrifies me, again. To feel so unstable so quickly. I almost tell the driver everything: that I tried to come off my medication in New York and it was a mistake. That I wept in a client meeting when the marketing director shot down my idea, and that my boss found me lying on the carpet underneath the boardroom table with tears streaming down my cheeks, twice, even though I didn't think I was sad, didn't know what was making me sad. I got so angry I had to leave the apartment sometimes so that I could scream, unheard, in the noise of the city, standing on a bridge over the BQE with the traffic rushing beneath me. I punched a lamppost and broke my thumb. I got myself fired and lost the visa that had come with the job and what's more, I'm a big raging homosexual and this beautiful man sitting behind me with the sandy-blond hair, short beard, the olive skin and the ever-changing eyes is my husband. But I don't want all the warmth to go out of this driver and our conversation. I don't want a low rating on the app.

Adrian leans forwards and rubs my shoulder, and it probably tips the driver off, because straight guys don't touch each other like this, but it's okay – the driver is maybe surprised but he doesn't look angry. I put a hand on Adrian's hand. He's pulled me back from the precipice again.

'Do you have kids?' Adrian asks.

The driver tells us about his son and wife in Harare. The boy is ten and very good at maths but all he wants to do is play soccer. 'They will join me when my son finishes primary school. God willing,' he says. 'It's getting more difficult for Zimbabweans here.'

I watched the most recent xenophobic attacks on my laptop in New York. Spaza shop owners pulled out of their shacks and beaten, set on fire. Houses burnt down. The violence was right here, in these townships racing past my window – against Zimbabweans, always, and against Somalis and Nigerians, against immigrants from any other African country. It's never the Germans who are the victims of this mob violence. It's never the Brits. Maybe that was the parting gift of the colonial era: turning our black and poor against the 'foreign' black and poor. I think about Trump and his wall. Brexit, which is going ahead. The arc of history is supposed to tend towards justice, and yet here we are slipping backwards towards nationalism and big-otry, and it seems unstoppable now, like we're trapped in a novel set just before the Holocaust and this time, we know how it ends.

'I'm sorry,' I say. 'It must be so difficult. I hope you managed to stay safe.'

I almost say, One of my best friends is Zimbabwean. It's true, and I want to show we're on the same side, but it would sound too much like 'some of my best friends are black'.

We take the upper of two arteries that lead to the city centre. Spectacular views of the downtown high-rises and the bay beyond. Even in the drought, the sea sparkles. District Six is still a wasteland, just as it was when I left, just as it's been since the 1970s. Dead grass and mounds of rubble and burning trash. The mosques and churches stand among empty plots, saved from the bulldozing that took place all around them, the houses razed and the families who lived here dragged to the outskirts of the city because they weren't white. It's 2018, twenty-four years since the transition to democracy, and only a smattering of homes have been rebuilt.

Our route descends, at last, into the city I remember. The city I dreamed of as a child growing up in Johannesburg. Cape Town had its magnificent mountains, its white sandy beaches. It had fynbos and hiking paths. It had centuries of architecture, not like Joburg's short, brutal life as a mining town turned economic powerhouse, where beauty was an affectation. This imagined Cape Town had a more tolerant, liberal attitude towards race and sexuality. A long history of racial mixing, a creolised society. Gay people lived their lives out in the open here. It was a softer and kinder place, I thought. A longed-for escape.

We pass the old bubblegum-blue Art Deco block of flats that I must have walked past a thousand times in my life and it hits me at last: the American adventure is over. We are home. This is the neighbourhood where I lived for many years before New York, but it's bone dry and I swear it's got poorer. Sleeping bags under the overpass, homeless people at every intersection with cardboard signs that read

*HUNGRY Plz Help*
*No Job No Food*
*God Bless*

There's a joker with a sign that says *I bet you R10 you read this* and then, at the next traffic light, the most heart-stopping sign of all: *You can avert your eyes but I'll still be here.* The man holding this sign doesn't cringe and smile like the others. He doesn't cup his hands or do the strange bouncing, imploring bow. He meets my gaze dead on.

'I don't know how I'm going to do this,' I say to Adrian.

The driver glances at me out of the corner of his eye. 'It's the next left?' he says.

The beggar doesn't even try to catch his attention.

The house is just as I remember it, but dirtier. It must be the drought that makes it look so run-down. Dust mottles the peeling white walls. Dead plants in the front yard. It's an old terrace house, built in the 1840s, and tucked into an oak-lined lane that no one knows about, almost too narrow for cars, just off a busy side street near the centre of town. I bought the house a few years ago with the money my father left me when he died. It has high ceilings, shuttered sash windows and original wooden floors. The sunlight is soft and dappled through all the oak leaves in the lane. It's a quiet cocoon, and I loved it the moment I first set eyes on it. It was going to be my forever home, the place I raised a family, but walking in now, after the cramped apartments of New York, I struggle to remember the person who fell in love with this place. It's too big, too grand. I'm too young to have a house like this.

There's human shit at the base of the oak tree that presses against the perimeter wall. The shit has splattered on the wall and barbed wire

14

that encircles the trunk of the tree now – new since I left. The tenants must have laid it out. They've installed electric fencing atop the perimeter wall, too. There's electric fencing on every house in the lane. Security cameras on poles. Armed response warning signs on every property.

Frasier remembers the house, which surprises me. He was a puppy when we left. He claws at the sage-coloured front door, sprints inside when I open up, and spends the next ten minutes sniffing along the skirting, smelling how things have changed, and sneezing. He runs in joyous, random circles.

I wish my feelings were as uncomplicated as his.

I turn on the lights in the bedroom and nothing happens. I try the lights in the living room, the kitchen. In all the house, only one lightbulb flickers to life. How did the tenants live like this? I imagine them sitting in the living room, watching the sky turn purple through the old windows, then black. They don't move. They don't stand up or go out or do anything but wait for the darkness to consume them.

'I'm going to get lightbulbs,' I say.

'Do you need me to come with you?'

'I'm fine.'

'Get some stuff for dinner, too.'

It's a short walk to the nearest supermarket. Left onto Vredehoek, right onto Schoonder. The street names strike me as they never did before. The strangeness of Dutch names in a city in Africa. New York has them, too – Gansevoort Street, Harlem, Brooklyn; there's even a theory that 'Yankee' comes from an old reference to Dutch New Yorkers, whom the colonial New Englanders joked were always called Jan or Jan-Kees – but indigenous culture was so thoroughly replaced with settler culture in America that you don't even notice the blood on the names. Dutch is no more out of place here than English is; it's from an equally tiny country, equally far from its original home, but

15

my consciousness formed in English and that makes it almost impossible to see English expansion and dominance for what it was. Just as brazen and bizarre as the Dutch, as the Portuguese. Who did the Europeans think they were, filling the world as if it belonged to them? And yet it's so easy to believe it was inevitable, the only possible history.

The same homeless people sit on the corner, just as they did years ago. The old matriarch among them. She reigns from her upended plastic beer crate in an ankle-length skirt and thin, beige cotton jersey. Her face is round and flat, skin the colour of oak. She smiles at me as I walk past her on my way to the supermarket. She has a collection of household items lined up on the red earth in front of her: three pairs of old shoes, two romance novels, a set of silver candelabras clouded black. I assume they were given to her by other pedestrians on their way to the shops, small items for her to sell. Beside her, sitting in the dirt, is a man with a deeply lined face and two younger women, close to the kerb, breaking off bits of baguette and feeding the crumbs to the pigeons. They watch me as I go by. Not one of them speaks.

The car guards are more vocal, more pushy. They follow me for sections of the street, overly friendly, making their presence known. 'Everything's good,' says the fresh-faced young man in a reflective yellow vest, falling into step beside me. 'Everything's fine.' He peels away when I move beyond his kingdom into the territory of the next car guard, who smiles at me and points to the cars as if to say, you see, I protected yours. I try to appease them with a brief smile, but I'm determined not to give them any money, not when I don't have a car yet and I plan to walk this route many times a week. 'It's okay,' says the car guard when he sees I'm not stopping to give him any cash, 'you can get me something in the shops.' It isn't a question, and I smile to make it feel less like a threat. I walk faster than is comfortable. I take a different route on my way back from the shops, walking three blocks out of my way to avoid the car guards, but I feel even worse when I return to the corner where the homeless people sit. They don't ask me for anything. They look through me, through my bags laden with food and lightbulbs and toiletries, into the distance, resigned to their role in this grotesque play.

New York's poor didn't make me feel like this. I wasn't a symbol of privilege there. I wasn't a symbol of anything. I was ordinary, or lower. An immigrant. There is wealth in New York that's unimaginable here. Beyond the reach of our middle class, even our elites. 'Learn to speak English,' someone hissed at me once, after I'd taken the trouble to give him directions, and I loved how it stung. I had to say my ideas three or four times at work before anyone heard them. They just assumed: he's from Africa; he can't have good ideas. Our apartment was tiny. We stood in sweaty crowds on the hot subway platform, waiting for the same grubby trains as everyone else. I was pushed and ignored. I was no one worth following down the street.

Beggars in Brooklyn elicited nothing in me but a clean-burning, uncomplicated sadness that made charity so easy. They had fallen on hard times, or the system had broken them, but it wasn't my system; it wasn't this system that gave me everything I have. Here, on Schoonder Street, all I can think is: I did this to you. My ancestors did this to you. And maybe beneath all the reasons white South Africans emigrate – the economic projections, the crime, the corruption, the considerations of the kids – is the simple urge to escape this feeling of culpability and complicity. I could give everything I own to these homeless women, to these car guards, and it wouldn't make a difference. It's a drop in the ocean. Impotent against centuries of dispossession. There is no way to atone for this.

Why we emigrate.

My chest is tight when I get home, but I know it's not a heart attack. I've been told so many times by so many doctors that it's not a heart attack. My heart is fine, for now. I try to force a few slow deep breaths into my lungs. I install the lightbulbs by candlelight. When I turn the power back on, the house is beautiful again. As I remember it, my forever home. It was the place I was going to raise a family and my god, I need that now. A place to feel grounded and rooted and safe. A child to pour my love into, to protect and nurture. To help another human being grow, instead of watching the world fall apart around me.

Adrian opens a bottle of wine and pours two small tumblers. He hands one to me and we toast to new beginnings. It's velvet on my tongue.

'I just want to finish unpacking,' he says. 'I'm almost done.'

I follow him to the guest bedroom and stand in the doorway as he lifts the last of our winter coats from his bag. He's unpacking the heavy woollen clothing and jackets into the wardrobe in the guest room, presumably to save space in ours. We won't need them again. No arctic blasts in our future. No snow on the sidewalk. He closes the wardrobe and raises his arms in triumph – 'All done!'

I imagine a baby's cot in the corner, beneath the empty bookshelf. I imagine her cooing in here in the early-morning half-light. I can see her in this bed when she's a little older, nestled in beside me. I'll read her books in isiXhosa, because her birth parents will be Xhosa and I'll be fluent by then – I have to be. I want her to be comfortable in any group. She'll move between worlds with ease, fluent and loved and secure in herself. But these are always the dreams of parents – to fix what is broken in themselves.

I'll read her some of my favourite childhood books, too. The uncontentious ones that haven't been cancelled. *Where's Spot?*, *The Very Hungry Caterpillar*, *The Wump World*, so she falls in love with nature early on. Wumps look so much like the dassies she'll see sunning themselves on the rocks on Table Mountain and she'll love dassies because they'll remind her of home.

She'll have that smell my brother is always telling me his kids have. That warm, clean, slightly sweet smell that babies give off. Milky and innocent. I press my lips to the top of her head and breathe it in. My chest feels, for a second, a little less tight.

# 2.

Sibs wears a royal-blue blazer, white blouse and cotton slacks patterned with white, black and emerald-green geometric shapes. She angles her face down, smiles at me side-eye through the metal pedestrian gate. Her hair is natural, buzz-faded on the sides and dyed a rich auburn colour that complements her huge, clip-on rose-gold earrings. I open the gate and her lips crack into a wide smile of bright pink lipstick and brilliant white teeth. She opens her arms towards me and steps up off the street. 'I'm so happy you're back,' she says. We hug. Only then do I see the little girl behind her, obscured by the wall.

'And who is this?' I say, dropping to my haunches. The girl must be almost three, with that big-eyed, solemn expression only babies and toddlers can pull off. Dark skin so smooth she looks as if she's been polished. A tiny nose.

'This is Buhle,' Sibs says.

'The name fits,' I say, and wink at her. 'Just like her mom.'

Sibs laughs and claps her hands. 'Ah, you haven't forgotten isiXhosa. That's good. We must continue our lessons.'

I smile and recite a few of the lines I remember. How are you? Where have you come from? The weather is warm today. Sibs never gave me lessons, but she encouraged me when I attended night classes. We performed these same opening lines every time she came into work, a robotic exchange that made me feel, for the first few recitations at least, like I was at the vanguard of integration.

'Seriously though, Sibs. You look absolutely amazing.' I make a show of looking her up and down.

She laughs again and extends her arms, flips her hands, makes the gestures of a celebrity posing on the red carpet. I get the sudden sense that this is true. That this is the real Sibs, the iconic diva, well known for her portrayal of the role of the domestic worker in the version of South Africa where nothing changed after '94. She has a great eye. I remember this about her. She always arrived looking stylish. In a parallel universe, she's a fashion blogger, maybe a clothing designer or buyer. She throws these looks together effortlessly, rather than building them up from hidden gems in discount bins in harshly lit mass-market retailers that smell of chemicals and sweat. She doesn't get dressed in a shack without running water. Her rose-gold earrings aren't plastic, but real gold, bought online on impulse.

'You know me, mos,' she says. 'It's not a crime to look good, hey?'

'It's so good to see you.' I close the front door behind Buhle. 'How did you know I was back?'

'I know one of the other ladies who works on the street.'

Now that we're inside, off the street, she's nervous. She rubs her hands over her hips and won't meet my eye. I offer her some tea, ask her if she'd like milk for Buhle. I don't have anything childproof, only glasses and ceramic mugs, but Sibs extracts a little plastic sippy cup from her bag. She seems relieved to have a task to perform with her hands. I fill the cup with milk and then, remembering how my brother microwaves the milk for his kids, ask her if Buhle would like it warm.

'Are you okay, Sibs?' I say.

She forces a smile. 'No, I'm fine,' she says, but she won't look at me.

I busy myself with making tea. I like making her tea. It's a small act of hospitality that puts some distance between myself and my parents' generation. They would never have offered their domestic worker tea.

Sibs - came back

The maid in my house growing up made me tea, even when I was a teenager and really should have been doing that for myself. She made me dinner every night, and laid a single place setting at the dining-room table. She wouldn't join me, even when I asked her to. She wore a light-blue uniform with a white collar and a little white apron and we called her Patience, even though Patience wasn't her name.

I hand Sibs a mug of strong, milky tea. Three sugars, I remember.

'I want to ask,' she says, barely glancing at it, 'can I come back?'

I had hoped this wasn't coming, but why else would she be here? Adrian and I decided we wouldn't get a domestic worker when we moved home. We discussed it in New York, righteous with the clarity of distance. How feudal it is to have servants. 'We can clean up our own mess,' Adrian said, and I agreed. We'd been doing it for three years in Brooklyn. Vacuuming Frasier's fur out of the rug. Scouring mildew in the grouting of the shower and piss-splatter from under the toilet seat. We had latex gloves and bleach-stained cleaning clothes. I was ashamed at how novel it felt in the beginning. Not new, exactly, but something only students did. A blast from the past. 'We shouldn't be able to afford a cleaner,' he said and he's right. He works in EdTech and I'm in marketing. We're not billionaires or landed gentry. 'The system is broken,' I said, depressing myself at the thought of all this exploitation, all these millions of people desperate for this kind of work, for any kind of work.

Sibs didn't finish high school, I remember, and even if she had, so many of the schools in the rural Eastern Cape, where she's from, are almost as bad as not attending school at all.

The microwave pings and I remove the sippy cup of milk. 'I'll have to ask Adrian,' I say, but when I turn back to give her the milk and I see her eyes, I know I can't make her wait and I can't say no. It's not enlightened to wash our hands of the system if all that does is deprive

not enlightened

22

Sibs of an income. The system makes Adrian and me uncomfortable. It shouldn't be like this; this shouldn't be her only option, but *should* is meaningless.

'Of course you can come back,' I say, relieved that Adrian has already left for work. 'Once a week, again?'

She nods. 'Or even more,' she says. 'I lost my other jobs. The one lady, she emigrated. And the other one, she said I was stealing and they fired me. But I wasn't stealing. You know me, I've never stolen anything. You can check your wallet, or even those little jewels – those rings. She left them lying around everywhere. I never touched them. I bet you she hid that pair of shoes that she said I stole.'

'That's terrible, Sibs. I'm sorry. So how many days are you working now?'

'No, this will be all.'

'Oh god.' I remember how out of control I felt when I lost my job in New York. Like someone had pulled the plug out and my life was circling the drain. That wasn't even real poverty I was circling. And I wasn't dragging a daughter with me.

'Okay. We only really need once a week,' I say, 'but I'll pay you for two.'

'No, twice a week is fine,' she says. She grins, pressing her lips between her teeth to show me she's half-joking. She knows she's pushing her luck.

'There's not enough to do for twice a week!' I say and she laughs. 'Maybe when we have kids.'

'Okay.'

I do a quick Google search on my phone for the average domestic worker salary in Cape Town. I offer Sibs double the going rate.

'I'll ask if any friends need the help,' I say, even though I'm probably not going to. They all have domestic workers already, and besides,

I need to rekindle these lapsed friendships, dormant after three years away. I can't start out by guilt-tripping people.

From her tote bag Sibs retrieves a simple cotton house dress, yellow with white daisies on it. 'Can I change in your bedroom?' she says.

'You don't have to start today. You have Buhle here. You can start next week.'

'She's fine,' Sibs says and then, glancing at the fruit bowl, 'Can I give her a banana if she gets hungry?'

'Help yourself. I have to get ready – you can change in the guest room.'

I close my bedroom door and strip down. It's cold in this old house with its rattling windows, and the water restrictions make it impossible to warm up in the shower. I push the grey plastic bucket over the drain, position it directly beneath the shower head and turn on the tap. The longest flow of water is wasted, ten to fifteen seconds, as the water heats up, falling straight into the bucket. Once it's warm enough, I step into the flow, feet on either side of the bucket, and let it run over me for five glorious, skin-tingling seconds. I turn off the tap and lather myself in soap. I rinse off with another short burst of hot water, ten seconds to get the suds out of my armpits and groin. I slide the bucket, now three quarters full, to the edge of the shower to let the spillage drain. I towel myself off. I'll use the grey water to fill the toilet cistern and, once I've replaced all the drought-dead plants in the yard, to keep the new ones alive.

When I step out of the bathroom, I see Buhle's head poking up over the far side of my bed. She's about the same height as the top of the mattress, so all I see are her eyes and hair and forehead. She watches me, silent and impassive, and my first impulse is to call Sibs to fetch her, but Sibs must have let her in. Buhle can't use door handles yet, can she? She's too young. And I don't want to make Sibs

24

feel awkward for having let her in. I smile in a way that I hope isn't creepy, and I try to retrieve my underpants, jeans and button-down shirt from the cupboard as quickly as I can. I press the clothes against my naked chest and return to the bathroom to get dressed, though already I feel as if I've violated her, walking around in front of her in nothing but a towel.

'Hi,' I say, coming back into the room fully dressed.

I see now why she's in here. She's sitting on the floor beside my bed stroking Frasier. He endures the affection at best, eyes closing milliseconds before each rough thump-pat, but his tail wiggles a little.

'Do you like doggies?' I say, but she ignores the question. Perhaps she doesn't know any English yet. She follows me out of the room and I feel this absurd pressure to make her like me. What do you say to a child? I've never been good at it. Even with my brother Hilton's kids, Simon and Lily, I find the whole thing so awkward. Baby talk, peekaboo, I cringe before I can start. And if I fail to entertain, which I will, what's to stop them saying the cruellest things to me? Children have no filter, no manners, no conception of how much words can hurt. I give Buhle the biggest smile on my way out – exaggerated, wide-eyed, the way you're supposed to with kids. I wave at her. She stares at me with her large, solemn eyes. She wraps a hand around her mother's leg, and pulls herself close.

*Bad with kids*

*Cruelty of children*

# 3.

*Psych.*

Emma watches me from her wingback chair. Decades of practice have made her a master at waiting; her body language is perfect for the task. Respectful but informal. Her eyes are soft and kind, but alert. I don't feel judged, or rushed, or hated – any of the things I usually feel when I try to speak to people. But I also don't feel molly-coddled or infantilised, like the clichés of therapeutic relationships in pop culture. She doesn't ask irritating, predictable things like "How does that make you feel?" This isn't a routine with set moves. She's paying attention, and it's unlike anything I've ever experienced before.

'I've tried cognitive behavioural therapy,' I say, 'and normal talk therapy. Lots of that over the years. And hypnosis. And medication.'

'Meditation?'

'That too, but I said medication. I've been on SSRIs for five years. I keep trying to come off them, but it never works. I feel like I'm losing my mind when I come off them, I get so angry I don't even recognise myself, which I don't understand, I wasn't an angry person when I went on to them. I was nice. I went on to them against my will because I was having panic attacks. At least that's what the doctors told me and eventually, after my third time in the emergency room, I had to believe them that it was anxiety even though I didn't think I was anxious. I didn't feel anxious. I even came home to tell Adrian what the doctor had said as if it were a joke, I thought he'd laugh along with me about what a quack the doctor was but he just

*Panic attacks + anxiety*

looked sad and said, "Ya, I think he's right, you do have an anxiety disorder." I didn't feel anything then, really, except physical pain in my chest, which was very scary because how was I so disconnected from my feelings that I didn't even know I had them until they showed up in my body? Since then I've been getting more and more unstable, even with the meds. I have to keep upping the dosage and I don't want to. I don't want to spend my life on drugs. What are they doing to my brain?'

Emma is a psychoanalyst. A psychologist friend recommended her to me when I told him, surprising myself with tears, that nothing was working. He said analysis is the thing to try. It's intense. Multiple sessions per week, so you can't build up your defences between sessions. You can't hide behind pleasantries or catching up on the events of the past week. Analysis is relentless. It breaks you down. And it gets to the root cause. I love the idea of a root cause, an original trauma, even though it seems too good to be true, an implausibly neat narrative structure, good for novels but nothing like how life works. I'm a mess in countless ways, for countless reasons. But I have to try it.

'This is my last resort,' I tell her. 'If this doesn't work, I'll go mad. I'll end up living under bushes in the park. Talking to myself and the pigeons.'

I don't tell her, this first time, how the scariest thing about this fantasy is that it's quite appealing. Letting go of the pretence. Allowing everyone to see what a failure of a human being I am, weak and pathetic. It would be a relief to stop trying to prove that I'm okay, that I can cope with the things other people can cope with.

'You probably don't even believe me,' I say. 'You probably think I'm fine, I'm wasting your time. I know I look fine. I don't know how to stop looking fine. It's like I'm trying to appease everyone with smiles and friendly questions and good manners, but even now my chest hurts. I know there are people outside with real problems. They can't afford food or they get beaten by their husbands or whatever. I think about the poor people who sift through my rubbish every Tuesday morning on collection days, desperate for something to eat or sell. I know this is self-indulgent.'

Emma's expression is impossible to read. I tell myself she has kind eyes. She isn't thinking any of the things I always think about me.

'I promise I'm not as okay as I look. You have to believe me.'

'I believe you,' she says.

'This might be a weird thing to say, but I heard once that when the ancestors choose you to become a sangoma, or an igqira, I'm not sure which, you have no choice but to agree. If you try to resist them, they just make you more and more sick until you acquiesce. They want to get through to the world of the living. They want you as a medium, and you don't have a choice. I'm not superstitious, or religious – sometimes I wish I was, I wish I had some kind of reassuring belief system – but that feeling is real, that something or someone is trying to get through to me, and it's terrifying. Like I might be possessed by this dark, powerful force.

'I'm afraid of everything. It used to just be flying that scared me, now I'm afraid to walk to the shops. I can only go running if I've chosen a circular route around the hospital, in case I collapse. I get dizzy. I think about cancer eating me up from inside. I used to be quite adventurous. I went backpacking on my own through Asia in my twenties. I was the first person in my high school to take a same-sex partner to his matric dance. It all just sort of . . . I don't know. I suppose I had a mental breakdown in New York, if that's even what they're called any more. That's probably not the woke term. But my life's shrinking around me and I don't know how to stop it. I don't know how to push the walls out again. I'm always thinking about

28

death and I know that worrying about it won't stop it coming, it's coming for all of us, but I don't know how to be less scared of it. How do people think about anything else? And yet I know I'm wasting the years I have left obsessing about when my time is up.' I take a shuddering, jerky breath. 'I think this is why I need to have a kid. So that there is life again, you know? Someone to live on after I'm gone, something beautiful in the world that can survive, even if I go down in a plane crash. Although I'm also worried I will be so anxious as a parent, about their safety and everything else, that I won't be able to function and I'll lose my job again.'

'What happened five years ago?' Emma says.

'What do you mean?'

'You said you've been on anxiety medication for five years.'

Emma doesn't take notes and it's a relief, I think, not to be imprisoned by the things I've said.

'It was a rough year,' I say. 'My flat got broken into, and I lost my grandmother. And I crashed my car. But I suppose the main obvious thing that happened was that my dad died, but there's no point talking about that.'

'Okay.'

'I don't want to talk about that. Talking doesn't bring anyone back. It doesn't change the fact that he died and we're all going to die, so what's the point of talking about it? Anyway, I can't blame this on him. We weren't close. We had a very difficult relationship.'

I'm a fraud for even mentioning it because I know this isn't grief. Grief doesn't make you afraid all the time. It doesn't make your chest sore. And how can you grieve someone to whom you were so cold? Someone you could never forgive?

'I crashed my car the day he told me,' I say. 'He was just going for tests, he didn't know anything yet, but I knew. I knew. I got into my car and I tried to reverse out of my usual parking space in front of my flat in Sea Point and somehow I ramped the pavement instead and burst two tyres and hit a tree and then I just sat there in the driver's seat until it got dark. Do you mind if I try the couch?'

At the start of the session Emma had told me I could try lying on the couch if I wanted. It seemed embarrassing to me, like a spoof from *Frasier*. People don't lie on couches any more, not since Freud's time. I have seen many therapists in my life and not once had they even owned a couch like this. We sat and we faced each other, like a chat between friends. Nothing theatrical or institutional about it. But those therapy sessions hadn't worked. I went round and round in circles, retelling the same stories, never letting the pain go. I spent so much of my energy trying to decipher the therapists' body language, and to modulate my opinions and thoughts to what was acceptable to them. To prove I was making progress, or having epiphanies, or whatever I was supposed to be doing. It was the same as every other conversation in my life, an act of reading the room and moulding myself to it. I never said what I really meant; I didn't even know what I really meant because I couldn't spare any mental energy to find out. My energy went into interpreting every glance, every twitch of the mouth, every tiny gesture of disapproval. They were bored or disgusted or disdainful. They thought I was laughably neurotic. There was nothing wrong with my life. It was all in my head.

Emma smiles and hands me a pillow. She tells me not to worry about my shoes on the fabric. That's what the little folded blanket is for. Easy to wash.

The couch is an immediate relief. Freedom from eye contact and her inscrutable scrutiny. I get comfortable on my back, watch the autumn leaves out of the window. They are brown and dry, nothing like the beautiful colours of Vermont or New York in the fall, the red maples and the yellow ginkgoes and the gold; these are the muted, quietly sad colours of the autumns I grew up with in Johannesburg.

It was a day just like this when my father called. 'My doctor thinks the thing with my lip is neurological. He's sending me for tests.'

'Where are you?' I said.

'I'm in the car.' I could hear the white noise in the background. A woman with a British accent giving a traffic report over the radio.

'Is Cheryl with you?'

Silence for a second, and then: 'No.'

It seemed cruel to ask why. How could his wife not go with him for tests like this?

'What do you mean "neurological"?' I said, as if the term were open to interpretation. I should have said, Dad, I love you, Dad, it's going to be okay, but I knew it wouldn't be okay and he hated platitudes. It didn't occur to me at the time that he was calling because he was scared. I assumed I was the last person he called, an afterthought, a duty he must perform so he could tell himself he hadn't forgotten about me. I think now that maybe I was the first.

'The tests might take a while, so I'll let you know tomorrow.'

'No, Dad,' I said, 'call me as soon as you know.'

'What's the time there?' he said. He lived in London, by then, with his British wife and his British kids – the two perfect daughters he'd always wanted. He'd emigrated when I was fourteen. Become more British than the British, immaculate in a pinstripe suit.

'It doesn't matter. Call me even if it's the middle of the night. Promise me you'll call.'

Every line I could think of was a cliché, a script from some TV tragedy we've all seen a hundred times before. And so I don't think I said anything after that. Maybe 'Good luck!' My father was the strongest person I knew. A titan. He was invincible, indestructible, immovable as the earth. Except he wasn't. He withered away in months. His body shut down one function at a time by a tumour that could not be stopped, not with anything our fumbling science could throw at it. First came the sleep. Hours and hours of it. He was always tired, always fighting to stay awake, to keep the conversation going, to tell jokes. He was awake for eight hours a day, then five hours, then three. A dark room with a little fire going in the hearth. He lost the ability to walk, to clean himself, but he would not surrender his mind. My father, who loved poetry as much as economics, who devoured *New Scientist*, *National Geographic*, *The Economist*, held on to his intellect and his wit until the very last day. The tumour could not take that from him.

'He was so strong,' I say, 'so fucking strong. I don't know how he did it.' I watch the leaves and don't care what Emma's face is doing. I don't have to look at it. 'You know, I remember the day we went for his last round of tests. I'd joined him by then in the UK and we were at the hospital and the doctor came back with the scan results that showed the tumour was still growing, it hadn't even slowed down, and he said that there was nothing more they could do. I caught a glimpse of my dad's eyes for a second. I don't think he knew I was watching him, he thought we were all looking at the doctor, and there was this moment of raw, naked terror in my father's eyes. He was tearing up, those deep brown eyes of his sparkling in the hospital light. But he blinked it away and smiled and thanked the doctor and we never mentioned it. We never mentioned he was dying. We couldn't talk about it. It was this bizarre act we all went along with, surreal, sitting beside his bed and shooting the breeze and acting as if nothing was wrong. But I'll never forget that look in his eyes, that one moment in the hospital. He knew what was coming. And he had nothing to comfort himself. He didn't believe in comforting yourself with false hope. He was a hardcore atheist. Thought religion was a sign of stupidity, a kind of unforgivable intellectual laziness. I can't even imagine what he would have done if someone dared to say, "You're going to a better place." He would have been so irritated and disdainful. He knew he wasn't going anywhere. Lights out. Annihilation. So we talked about some bullshit, I don't know, the cricket or something. He didn't even watch cricket.'

'Could you talk about what was happening with each other?' Emma says. 'You and your brother, I mean. Or your half-sisters. When you weren't with your dad, if he didn't want to talk about it.'

'Not really. What's there to say? Death is death. You can't talk yourself out of it.'

'Yes,' Emma says. 'But perhaps it doesn't need to be so lonely.'

# 4.

'It didn't take us long to have a braai,' Adrian says through the kitchen window. He's chopping vegetables for an oven bake and I'm in the courtyard, removing the canvas cover from the Weber.

Pale sunlight falls diagonally across the back wall, which is half-bare now, the Virginia Creeper a mass of brown twigs and the last few jewel-red leaves of autumn. It's a warm, late Sunday morning, the sun too low in the north to reach the courtyard floor tiles.

I lay out paraffin firelighters at the bottom of the black metal drum. 'We'll go see a play this week,' I say. 'Deal?'

We made a promise to each other when we moved back that we wouldn't become the kind of suburban South Africans who braai every weekend. The idea makes us both claustrophobic, even though we love having friends over and we love cooking. Braaiing has become fetishised in South Africa as the great cultural unifier – the one thing that holds this troubled multiracial, multilingual society together; you love it whether you're Afrikaans or Zulu, black or white – but Adrian's vegetarian and I just can't think of grilling meat as culture. What I loved about New York, more than anything, was the culture. High and low, everywhere you looked, from hip-hop and jazz in the subway to opera at the Met and readings at the Y. Being laid back is a good thing, sure, and South African culture is laid back, unpretentious, and maybe it's worth celebrating that, but wrapped up in this casual ideal of South African identity is the belief that anything more than meat and friends – anything more than the bare minimum – is affected or pretentious. Fussy. Maybe a bit gay. Why would you go see a play instead of just going to a braai?

Also, braais are gendered affairs. Women in the kitchen, making salads that go unremarked upon. Men at the fire, drinking beer and congratulating themselves for having turned the meat before it burns. I've long considered it my duty as a gay man to split and mix these groups, to tell male friends to bring interesting salads and ask female friends to tend the fire, but it's always a fight against inertia, a quirk that needs to be humoured. I'm making a point, resisting the inevitable. Will my attempts to recreate New York cultural life be met with the same amused inertia? Will friends agree to join me for a play or two, even a chamber music concert, but then see it as having humoured me enough? It's all a bit much. We just did something cultural last month. How about a braai instead?

I light the firelighters and empty a five-kilogram bag of charcoal briquettes into the drum. I join Adrian in the kitchen and pour us each a gin and tonic. My phone rings twice then cuts out.

'Hello!' comes the hollering from the gate. 'We're here!'

The previous owner had the buzzer removed to spare himself harassment by homeless people but it hasn't worked. They call like this, too, loud and hopeful through the gate. They tap stones against the metal and shout over and over until we come to the door. 'Please, sir, can I have some food, an old pair of shoes? Do you have any money to spare?' They know we're home. They know when everyone in the lane is home.

Jess and Johan arrive first with their two-year-old son, Nick, followed by Erica and Luke with their eighteen-month-old daughter. We were supposed to have had our kids together. We made a pact a decade ago, in our mid-twenties, to have children at the same time.

They would grow up visiting each other's homes multiple times a week. They'd get married, we joked, or be lifelong friends at least. It was appealing, that sense of certainty and community, the mutual support we'd offer one another as we navigated the complicated world of parenting. I reneged on my side of the bargain. Applied for a job in New York instead.

Steve and Loyiso arrive with their recently adopted daughter, Gugu. Two pregnant friends arrive. The single friends come last. Phumeza. Morné. Tshego greets us all with a kiss on the cheek and heads straight for the island in the kitchen where I've laid out the booze. She pours herself an enormous gin – halfway up a tall glass – and tops it off with ice and a splash of tonic. 'Cape Town in your thirties,' she says, eyes wide with mock desperation, 'everyone's either gay or pregnant.'

'Sorry,' Steve says, as he moves in for a hug. 'Guilty on both counts!' Gugu claws at his face. Sticks her tiny brown hand into Steve's mouth and pinches his lip and squeals.

Tshego laughs and waves away her comment with her free hand. 'No, man, I'm happy for you guys.'

'It's crazy how many gay couples are having their own kids, now,' Pieter says, pouring himself a glass of sparkling wine. 'Vonkel', he always calls it, even in English, a name I love because it's vernacular – Afrikaans, not the ridiculous French acronym 'MCC' that South African wineries have used since 'champagne' was reserved for the French – and because it's magical. From the Afrikaans for 'glittering'. It makes me think of the legend of Dom Perignon inventing champagne by mistake and saying, 'Come quick, I'm tasting the stars.'

'I know three couples who've used surrogates so they can have their own,' Pieter says, 'rather than adopting.' He turns to Loyiso and narrows his eyes in theatrical suspicion. 'Gugu's not secretly your real daughter, is she?'

He bursts out laughing, but Loyiso doesn't find it funny. 'We're both black? Is that the joke?'

An excruciating second. The whole room on a knife-edge.

Then Pieter laughs uproariously again and rubs Loyiso's shoulder. 'I'm only joking.'

'It's all about ego,' Pieter's partner Daniel redirects. 'People want to see a little carbon copy of themselves. They want to recognise their own features. It's conceited.'

'Exactly,' Pieter says. 'Look how gorgeous Gugu is. She's a little cherub.' I just wish he'd drop it. I know this is a kind of apology but it's unbearable. 'She's got much better genes than I do!'

'It's like those gays have something to prove,' Morné says. 'We can impregnate women too, just like the straights.'

'Our sperm is virile!' Pieter shrieks.

I think about all those hyper-masculine gay men on Instagram – bearded, muscled, the peak of virility and reclaimed power. John Updike once called Alan Hollinghurst's novels boring for being 'relentlessly gay', saying nothing is at stake if relationships don't lead to children. It's an insidious strain of the homophobic poison we grew up drinking, to believe our lives are superficial, our love is not equally worthy of art unless we are husbands and fathers, patriarchs and fountainheads.

'Come on, guys,' Steve says, always the peacekeeper, 'I don't think we should be judging anyone for having their own kids. Straight people do it all the time and we don't judge them for it.'

'Speak for yourself!' Pieter says, but he strokes Steve's arm and laughs as if to say, I know you're right.

I glance around to see if any straight couples are in the kitchen, but it's gays and single women only. The straight men are at the fire. The mothers are in the living room playing with their kids. I have failed

37

in my quest to subvert the braai gender roles, but at least Pieter's not offending any new parents. One anxiety at a time. Tshego seems to love Pieter and Daniel.

'We just figured we have an opportunity to be intentional about it,' Steve says. 'It's not like Loyiso and I can have kids by mistake.'

'Is that what it is?' Morné says. 'I keep trying and trying but nothing happens.'

I top up my drink. This is all quite stressful.

'For us,' Steve continues, 'the decision was clear. There are so many more kids who need homes and love than there are parents who can provide that. We see it like that. We're here to give Gugu a leg up. To love her and help give her the best chance she can have in life.'

I catch Adrian's eye and feel a flood of warmth. Gugu squawks and smacks Steve in the face with her tiny, open palm. She kicks her legs against his hip and I decide that now is the time to practise. I open my arms towards her and Steve passes her to me without hesitation.

She's heavier than I was expecting. Wild, frizzy hair, dimples in her smile. She looks just like the child I always imagined having.

'Plus, there are far too many people on the planet,' Daniel says. 'Seven billion people, and the earth can—'

'Only support two billion,' Adrian and Tshego both finish his sentence.

Daniel flushes and pouts, places a hand on his hip and says, 'Well, it's true.'

'Gays could save the planet,' Pieter says, 'if we'd only stop turkey-basting our girlfriends!'

I take Gugu into the living room where Jess is sitting on the floor with her toddler and Erica's, supervising their wooden block construction. I don't know where the toys came from, but I already know this about mothers, that they manage to produce distractions for their children out of nowhere. Secret treats. Pacifiers. Toys. I seat myself on the grey linen couch and position Gugu on my knee. Now what? I jiggle my knee up and down a bit. I hide behind my hand and reveal myself. I feel a bit stupid doing all of this. She's not my daughter. This probably isn't how Steve or Loyiso do it. I must look like a fool and I wish I didn't care so much. I wish I could just block everyone out. But Gugu thinks I'm a fool, too, and so my heart's not in it, and she can tell my heart's not in it. The spiral of disappointment begins. She's going to get bored and cry. I'm already telling myself not to take it personally, and already I know that I will.

'I feel like I might break her,' I say to Jess.

'She's more robust than she looks.'

'Are you kidding? She's tiny.'

Gugu's looking all around the room. I'm losing her attention. She doesn't want to be here, with me. Is it always going to be this hard?

'I can't believe you're having another one,' I say to Jess.

'Well, Nick's already two.'

'I know. I just can't believe how fast the time's gone.' It feels like only a few months ago that we were both single, both living in that grotty little flat in Sea Point. I remember getting so drunk at lunch with Jess that we passed out on my bed before the sun had even set, wrapped in scarves. I remember her mother coming to stay with us and all of us having to pretend we couldn't hear the screaming, butt-slapping sex coming from the flat beneath ours or the terrible acoustic guitar that followed. I remember breaking up with a boyfriend and walking for forty minutes in the dark and rain to get home and I couldn't find my key, and she let me in and made me tea and we stayed up talking until three a.m. I remember secret underground parties at abandoned factories in Philippi, and music festivals in the fields near Darling, and the blog she ran for a while, in the early days

39

of blogging, where she and her boyfriend and I cooked for one another and ranked one another's meals. I accused them of nepotism, of sleeping with the contestants. I remember road trips and sunset yacht cruises along the Atlantic Seaboard and hikes in Newlands Forest and clubbing and drugging and walking head-first into a filthy pink dildo that was poking out of a hedge at two a.m. and drinking sparkling wine, vonkel, to celebrate her engagement on a rooftop in the city with views over the Atlantic Ocean and the mountains behind us. How did all of it go by so fast? Is ten years all we get? Ten years of adulthood and meaningful friendship before there are children on our laps, wooden blocks on the floor, milk bottles drying on the rack. Before our conversations are all about kids. Jess can't even have a drink. I guess ten years is longer than our parents got.

My friend Brett warned me after he emigrated. *Don't invest too much in your straight friends,* he said, *because they abandon you. Your lives diverge. You can't compete with husbands and jobs and children. You visit, you can be a part of their life, but it's never the same. You're just not as important to them as you once were.*

'Are you guys still thinking about kids?' Jess says.

'Absolutely,' I say. 'It can't happen soon enough. Imagine, my own little Gugu. Maybe I can time it to line up with your second.'

'Yes! That would be amazing.'

'I'm going to need all the help I can get. You'll need to hold my hand.'

'You'll be fine; it comes naturally. But I'm here.'

'I've already called an adoption agency actually,' and I have to pause here for Jess to mime an excited scream, 'but I hung up! It's also so scary, you know. I don't know if I'm ready. Hilton keeps telling me not to rush it, to enjoy my time without kids – that it changes everything and if you don't have a biological clock to worry about, squeeze as much as you can from the time you have.'

'No, man, don't listen to your brother. It's never the perfect time. You just have to take the leap.'

'I agree,' Steve says. He's come into the living room now. He moves to sit beside me on the couch. Gugu immediately wants to be on his lap. 'I don't think you're ever ready. You become ready when your baby arrives because you have to. But it's a big decision. I'm happy to talk you guys through the process if you like. We did a lot of research into the different agencies. The whole thing's stressful.'

'How long did it take you guys?'

'It was quick for us because we didn't have any requirements. It's really sad actually – you get a form and you tick what kind of child you're happy to accept, and it's uncomfortable stuff, that you wouldn't have thought about before, like would you be willing to accept a baby with a genetic disorder, or HIV, or the child of incest or rape. And if you want a particular sex or race. We said we'd be happy with any sex or race, and so the social worker said we'd probably get a black boy because no one wants black boys.'

'Jesus,' I say.

The feeling is something between nausea and despair. I'm completely unprepared for it, the strength of my reaction. There's a whole universe of trauma and prejudice and pain presented in that checklist. It makes me think, immediately, that I want a little black boy, that I can put aside my fears about raising a boy. I can learn to play soccer, if he wants that. I can develop better coping mechanisms for the toxic environments he'll find himself in. The ones I couldn't survive. I'll teach him to be both thoughtful and strong, kind without cowering. It makes me sick to think there are little boys out there, desperate for love and acceptance, unprepared for the cruelty of the world,

41

whose whole existence is summed up in a checkbox that prospective parents can deign not to check.

'Why?' I ask.

'I don't know,' Steve says. 'Maybe they're worried they'll grow up to be violent or something, but it's rough. I'll give you the details of the agency we used. They were great.'

Maybe Gugu feels bad about abandoning me for her father. She leans off Steve's lap to grab my index finger with her tiny hand. She squeezes. I move onto the floor and position her between my legs, and together we start to build a tower with the little wooden blocks. Nick waddles over and tries to help. With a very poor conception of balance, he places a block carefully, but off-centre, onto the top of the tower, and the structure comes tumbling down. Gugu starts to cry. I start building a new tower as quickly as I can, but Nick simply looks at her.

'Sad baby,' he says, and comes to give us both a hug.

# 5.

The adoption agency occupies a converted cottage on what was once a quiet residential road in Newlands and is now lined with boutique shops, cafes, and a fine art framer – all of which are housed in converted cottages. The building is white and gabled, but it's not quite Cape Dutch. Some revivalist architectural movement from the nineteenth or early twentieth century, perhaps.

Adrian is giddy. He widens his big, beautiful hazel eyes at me from the passenger seat of my car and drums on his thighs with his palms. 'I can't believe this is happening! We're going to be dads.'

'Easy, tiger. I don't think we walk out of here with a kid.'

'Still, this is exciting. Aren't you excited?'

I turn off the ignition. 'We're going to make amazing dads.'

Nadia, the social worker who interviews us, is not at all what I was expecting. She isn't a large, matronly woman with a gruffly affectionate manner. She's too young to have placed hundreds of children into happy families, and she can't reassure me with her infinite wisdom and experience. She's my age, max, maybe even younger. Quite pretty. Nervous (I can tell from the earnest way she nods; the way her hair is pulled back in a severe bun that's all wrong for this laidback office). Her nervousness confirms for me that: I don't get to be reassured any more. No one is looking out for us. Our generation's supposed to be the one in charge.

'The way it works,' she says, 'is that I run you through the process now, then I interview you, to find out a bit more about your relationship—'

I glance at Adrian and he squeezes my hand. He doesn't take his eyes off Nadia.

'Then I'll do a home visit, but don't worry, it's nothing like in the movies!' She lets out a short bark of a laugh. 'It's very relaxed. We just want to make sure the place is safe, that the baby will have a nice environment. You did say you'd only want a baby, hey?' She checks her notes, presumably the query form we submitted online. I get that hollow feeling, like when you realise you've said something unkind without meaning to.

'Yes,' I say.

'No children over twelve months?'

'We just want to maximise our chances of bonding.'

Nadia pauses. Does she want to argue with me? I shouldn't have said anything about chances or likelihoods. It should be guaranteed that we'll love the child. But she only nods. 'Of course. And then there's a workshop where you'll meet other couples who are looking to adopt, where we'll discuss things like how you introduce the concept of adoption to your child, how to deal with teenage anger—'

'A little early for that, isn't it?' I say, interrupting Nadia's flow.

'Well, sometimes adopted children act out during their teenage years. We just want to help you prepare for that.'

'Why?'

Nadia shifts in her seat. She doesn't want to have this discussion now. 'There can be feelings of abandonment,' she says, looking down and shuffling her papers. 'You know what being a teenager is like. Struggling with identity and belonging and how you fit into the world, and sometimes being adopted makes these feelings more intense. They might feel that their birth mothers didn't love them, maybe they get teased for being adopted – you know how it is. But we will get to all of that in the workshop.'

'Wow,' Adrian says.

Nadia looks grave. She nods.

'Amazing that you guys cover that so early on, so we're prepared,' he says.

I almost say, I'm still struggling with identity and belonging and how I fit into the world, but I don't trust it will come out as the joke I intend it to be, and so I say instead, 'Straight couples should have to do these workshops before they fall pregnant. I bet half of them don't even think about this stuff and we have to jump through so many hoops.'

Nadia smiles at me, but it's a dead smile, all professionalism. She doesn't like me. She would prefer to be dealing with Adrian.

'The hoops are good,' I say, quickly. 'It's good to think about this stuff. I'm just saying – maybe everyone should do it.'

'About that. It is one of the advantages of going through us,' she says. 'We are a progressive agency, and we don't have any trouble placing children with same-sex couples. Our mothers just want to know that their child is going to be loved.'

My cheeks burn, and it's only partially embarrassment about my comment. Is Nadia trying to tell me I should be grateful not to be discriminated against? Is it progressive to see us as human beings? Why is our sexuality even a consideration?

'You know, some of the other agencies are more faith-based,' she says, as if reading my mind, and I know what she means; I know all about 'faith' being used to justify malice. I have an ex-boyfriend who grew up religious, and he's told me before he doesn't think gay men should be allowed to have children together. 'Kids need a mother and a father,' he said, even though he would have loved to have a child himself. I couldn't speak to him for a few days after he said that.

'What comes after the workshop?' I say.

'That's it. After the workshop you'll get a certificate to say you're paper pregnant – that's what it's called – and from that point on you can receive your child any time, sometimes within two weeks, depending on what babies are available.'

Adrian is grinning from ear to ear. He lets out a high-pitched squealing sound. I lean over and give him a kiss on the cheek. When he looks at me, his pupils are dilated, as if he's already in love; as if our baby is cooing and giggling on the desk that separates us from Nadia.

'Oh, hang on,' Nadia says, glancing at her notebook, 'there's also the criminal check, which I didn't mention, but I assume you two will be fine. And you'll have to make a profile together.'

'A profile?'

'Like a dating profile but for the mothers. You say a bit about who you are, what kind of work you do, what you enjoy for hobbies, that kind of thing, so the moms can choose a couple that they like the sound of. It all goes through us, don't worry. They won't have your contact details, and you won't have theirs.'

'Where do we sign?' Adrian says.

'I must just mention,' Nadia says, suddenly very serious, 'that our waitlist for white babies is currently closed due to limited availability. We're only accepting applications for black, coloured and mixed-race babies.'

'I've always wanted a black baby girl,' I say. 'Although our friends who adopted with you guys told us that black boys are always the last to get picked, and I'd be happy to have a boy, too.'

Nadia's smile is impossible to read. Again, I feel as if I've said something wrong. Am I supposed to sound disappointed? Am I supposed to want a white baby? Is that more appropriate, for my first choice to be to 'stay in my lane'? I feel as if both Nadia and Adrian have accused me of fetishism, and I don't think that's what this is, really I don't, but it's hard to argue with them when they haven't accused me of anything out loud.

Adrian squeezes my hand. He can see I'm spinning.

'Right,' Nadia says, 'shall we go through your criteria then?'

Afterwards, in the car, I feel a little dizzy. Adrian is elated and can't stop talking.

'I think our profile's going to be quite good, actually, don't you?' he says. 'I think it might count in our favour that I work in EdTech. Anything education-related probably appeals to mothers. And we have international experience – that always impresses people.'

'I'll leave out that I got fired, then?' I say.

'What?'

'Had a little nervous breakdown and got fired.'

'That was . . . What's wrong with you?'

'I don't know. I think I forgot to take my pills this morning.'

'Do you want me to drive?' he says, which irritates me because I've already pulled out and we're already moving, and yes, I would have liked him to drive.

'I just think it's so messed up that people worship international experience like that. So what if I worked for an advertising agency in New York? I'm prouder of some of the campaigns we ran here. We produce incredible stuff here; we have a lot of talent and creativity. Amazing artists that never get any recognition. Everyone just assumes America is better. Why?'

'Okay,' he says.

'Because they're richer? They have bigger budgets? It's just economics, not inherent artistic superiority.'

'Forget I said anything about our international experience.'

47

'And it was so easy to get a job when we came home. I got the first position I applied for. At a top agency. Isn't that fucked up? How many people were overlooked because they haven't had the opportunities we've had?'

'You were talented enough to get the job in New York in the first place.'

'But it's not just about talent!'

'Can we drop it?'

'It's just sick. We have something stupid like forty per cent un-employment in this country and you and I just waltz in and get whatever job we want because we've already had amazing jobs over-seas. It's not normal.'

'Is this all moving too fast for you?' he says. 'Just tell me if we're moving too fast.'

I grip the steering wheel with both hands, trying to steady myself against the rage that is coming, again, for no reason. I want to scream at him.

'It's not moving too fast,' I hiss.

He takes out his phone and starts scrolling. I can tell he's not really looking at whatever's on his screen. It's just to get away from me. We drive the rest of the way home in silence.

Not this again. The anger possessing me, frightening me. I'm not an angry person. I don't lose control or give in to base, violent emotions. I remember those days towards the end of our time in New York when I came off my meds and became so inexplicably angry, unprovoked, that I had to take myself on walks through Brooklyn just to try to get a hold of myself. I wandered the streets for hours, like a madman, except I didn't shout at passers-by the way madmen do. I wanted to, but I pushed the impulse down inside myself with all the strength

I could muster. I punched that lamppost and broke my thumb. I wanted to hurt something. Crush a little bird in my hand, maybe, until all of its bones snapped and blood came out of its throat. Now the fever rises out of nothing, turns my skin hot and my thoughts delirious. It's contagious. The rules of virology apply: unventilated car space. Close proximity. The rage swirls from my nostrils in a hundred thousand microscopic particles and pours into Adrian's lungs, even as we try to ignore each other. By the time we get home from the adoption agency, he's infected.

By then, my fever has broken. I can't make sense of the person who picked a fight with him.

'Sorry I snapped at you,' I say as I pull up the handbrake.

'It's fine.' He's a terrible liar. It's one of the things I love about him. Inherent trustworthiness. He won't look at me. He slips his phone into his pocket and exits the car. I catch up with him in the living room. 'I'm going into work,' he says.

'You took a half-day.'

'I may as well.'

'I'm really sorry,' I say. 'That was supposed to be one of the happiest moments of our lives.' He's moving quickly through the living room, collecting the things he needs for the office. The research report he was reading on the couch last night. His laptop. He slides them into his work bag without looking up at me.

'Ya, well. It is what it is.'

I can't let him storm out like this. But I won't beg. I know him. I know the more I apologise, the angrier he gets.

'You're going to be a dad,' I say.

'Aren't we both?' He searches under the couch cushions for his car keys.

I make my voice all husky. 'But I mean, like, a daddy,' I say.

He looks up at me. 'Don't be gross,' he says.

I feel gross. I don't feel sexy. I don't want to be making jokes. I want to hide in the bedroom and shut the world out. I want to cry. But most of all, I want everything to be okay between the two of us.

I lower my eyelids and lick my lips at him. 'Is Daddy mad?' I say.

He's frowning, but I can tell he wants to laugh. His eyes have softened at the edges.

'Stop that,' he says, 'this is serious.' But he's losing his resolve. 'Have you seen my keys?'

I let out a breathy moan. I bat my eyelids at him. I pout my lips. I'm hamming it up. The kind of overacted eroticism you see in sex workers in Green Point, or strippers in comedy skits.

And it works. He starts to laugh. I push him down onto the couch and I straddle him. I take his work bag off his shoulder and place it behind me on the coffee table. Then I press the back of his hand to my face, and I bite it.

'You're ridiculous,' he says.

'Am I a bad girl?' I say.

His cheeks flush. There's still amusement in his eyes, but there's something else, too.

'Yes, you are,' he says, and his voice is deeper than his natural voice, and slower, and he's trying to play along, to be ironic and playful, but that word has done something to him. 'Girl'. I felt it through his jeans. The name that had the power to destroy us when we were tweens and teens. Little queers. We would do anything not to be called that. He sits up and kisses me. A forceful, passionate kiss. 'You're very bad,' he whispers in my ear. He's hard beneath me.

I no longer know if I'm joking, either. I'm straining in my underpants.

He laughs, then, and pulls away. 'Sorry,' he says. 'This is weird.'

'Keep going,' I say. I reach between my legs and start to unbutton his jeans.

'No, it's weird,' he says. 'Let's just be normal.'

'Don't you want to feel my pussy around you?' I say.

His cheeks are blotchy red. His neck. I pull off his T-shirt and kiss him beneath his ear. He says nothing, and won't look at me. Jagged exhales.

I get up off him so I can remove my jeans and underpants.

'Do you want to go to the bedroom?' he says, and I tell him, 'No, stay here.' I run to the bathroom to fetch the lube – that most irritating, disruptive of rituals for gay sex – and when I return he's leaning back on the couch with his legs spread, touching himself. He bites his lip as he watches me but it's not a joke bite this time. 'Kiss me,' he says.

I kiss him and he grabs me by the hair on the back of my head. He forces me down onto my knees, and even though I wanted him to be like this, I hate it.

I enclose his cock within my mouth and he rams my head down onto it.

'Are you a little faggot?' he asks as I'm choking on his cock. I mumble assent as best I can. 'What's that?' he says, and I try to say YES, but it just comes out a gargling, choking sound. He presses my head down until the head of his cock is all the way down my throat and he holds me there, struggling to breathe. 'That's a good girl,' he says, and I hate so much that this arouses me.

'You want me to get you pregnant?'

My whole body comes alive. It tingles, everywhere, as if the nerve endings in my skin have been dipped in poison. Everything is amplified. I groan, imagining his seed inside me, taking root, starting a life in my belly. I swell with it.

'That's a good girl,' he says again. He begins ramming his cock in and out of my mouth with violence. He holds my head in place.

'I'm gonna come,' he says, and I don't want to swallow his come. I want to pull away but I love that he won't let me. He isn't asking. He's telling me. 'You gonna swallow Daddy's come?' he says. He's breathless, approaching his orgasm. I make garbled noises. 'That's right, you are,' he says. 'Little cocksucker.' He holds my head in place as he explodes down my throat. His rhythm slows, a languorous pulsing until he's squeezed every last drop into my mouth.

'Good girl,' he says again, and he smirks at me. 'Now get dressed.'

I haven't been allowed to touch myself. I haven't orgasmed, but this is part of the fantasy, too, this detail, the one-sidedness. He knows how much it turns me on. I'm angry. I feel dirty and disgusted in myself. But I pull on my clothes. I take the unused lube back to the bathroom and alone, behind the closed door, I touch myself. I imagine what just happened, replaying the whole degrading scene in my mind. Shame burns my neck. It splashes red across my chest. I wish I hadn't done this, again. It could have been different. He said at the beginning, let's not, let's just be normal.

I shoot so far up my stomach that a splash hits my chin. I wipe it up with toilet paper and flush it away.

I'm feeling worse after every one of these sessions. More ashamed, as if I'm in analysis, reliving the boarding school tormentors rather than having fun with my husband. 'There's nothing wrong with this,' Adrian said to me the last time I freaked out after sex. 'So many people have this kind of fantasy. Ask Emma.'

When I emerge from the bathroom, Adrian is gone. There's a message on my phone from him. *Gone into the office. See you later.* Two kissing emojis and a bright red heart.

# 6.

The rains return in June. Gunmetal-grey skies and torrential down-pours that last for days at a time. I position large plastic rubbish bins and buckets in the courtyard to catch overflow from the gutters. I line old towels along the base of the courtyard doors to keep the flood-ing away from the floorboards. It's the kind of Cape Town winter I have always loved – cold, soft, and wet. Evenings spent curled up on the couch with Adrian and Frasier, beneath a faux-fur blanket with red wine and a wood fire dancing in the hearth. Days like water-colour paintings. The mountains drift in and out of low clouds and mist. On the days when the clouds lift, the mountains are striped with waterfalls. Streams gurgle to life in the dry riverbeds.

Friends tell me there hasn't been a winter like this since we left for New York. In the three years we were away, the winters were warm and dry. I joke with them that I'm a rain queen, a Modjadji from the Balobedu who somehow got lost in the realm between death and birth and reincarnated as a white gay guy who grew up going to see superhero movies in the lame malls of Joburg suburbia, having for-gotten his own secret superpower to control the weather. *You need me for good rains, baby!*

But at night, none of it is funny. I lie in bed in the dark, thinking about the long-term precipitation trends. This rain is not enough. It's a blip on an otherwise downward trajectory. This fragile ecosys-tem at the tip of Africa, the smallest and most diverse floral kingdom in the world, is drying out. The Sahara wasn't always a desert. Its desertification might even have been what drove early man out of Africa, in search of rain and food. Now, again, the deserts are spreading, no matter how seductive it is to take comfort from this downpour.

Adrian and I can't bring ourselves to stop collecting the run-off when we shower, even after it rains. The buckets start lining up in the bathroom, full of soap-scummed grey water with nowhere to go. The courtyard plants don't need it any more. We keep our showers shorter than a minute. There's always the faint smell of unflushed piss in the bathroom, and on bad days, the muted but unmistakable smell of sewage throughout the house. Stale and sweet. Sibs tells me it's because the council decreased the water pressure throughout the city to save water, and so the drains back up. The waste rises out of the earth and into the pipes. We're the lucky ones, I know. Sibs also tells me about the communal toilets in the townships. They overflow when it rains like this. The sewage mixes with stormwater, and floods between the shacks. The Cape Flats is a floodplain. One of the excuses the recalcitrant housing department gives for refusing to upgrade the informal settlements and build decent homes for the poor is that where these people live, where they were forcibly removed to by the apartheid town planners, is not fit for human habitation.

Sibs shows me a video on her phone. Lots of shouting in isiXhosa. The sound of heavy rain and splashing as people try to cross the channels. The foul muck is knee-deep in places.

'Is this where you live?' I ask, but she doesn't answer me.

'You see,' she says, 'it's very bad.'

'Is this your place?'

'This is Philippi. This is where I'm staying.'

I don't know which of the shacks is hers, or if she's in one of the brick buildings, but even if she's in a brick building, there's little comfort in that. The sewage-stormwater is everywhere. It looks like the videos you see on the news of Louisiana after a hurricane. Or Haiti. I think about the notion of dystopian fiction, about how some of the most nightmarish fantasy is already true in parts of the world. What makes it nightmarish is imagining these things happening to *us* rather than *them*.

'Sibs, this is terrible,' I say. 'How can I help?'

She shrugs and makes a clicking noise with her tongue. The classic South African click that I missed so much in my years in New York. It can mean anything from disgust to frustration to resignation. Like our use of the word 'shame' as an interjection. The meaning is entirely dependent on context and tone. I'm not sure what her meaning is, but it might be irritation. Why do I say such obviously empty things? To make myself feel better? Clearly, I can't help. Or maybe it's that the help required would change my life, and we both know I'm not willing to do that.

'There's nothing,' she says.

'Do you have buckets?'

'I have buckets.'

'I'm going to call one of the city councillors,' I say. 'They have to do something.'

She smiles at me, then. A tired smile. Puts her phone back in her pocket. 'They won't do anything. But it won't rain forever.'

I check the dam levels on my phone every day. I watch videos of Theewaterskloof, the largest of the dams that feed Cape Town, and it's a barren, sandy valley with ghost trees, but then water starts to rush into the bottom. Over a few weeks, the dam levels inch upwards. Six per cent. Eleven. Fourteen. There's a website that lets you spy on your neighbour's water usage, and I check it every day. I'm surprised at how angry it makes me – even though I know that's the point of the site – when I see a neighbour who uses more than their allotted fifty litres per day. I notice which properties near mine show up as red dots on the map instead of green. Selfish, entitled pricks, I think. When I see the people who live in these properties out and about, in the lane or in the park, I wish them genuine harm. Maybe we'll survive one more year with this rainfall, but it's no thanks to *you*.

Maybe it's easier than I like to believe, being manipulated by government programmes. A water-use map and my own climate fear was all it took to whip me up into outrage and resentment against my neighbours. How far from here to mob justice and vigilantism? Witch hunts and pogroms.

I take Frasier for a walk in the park above our house, the park that borders Table Mountain, and I watch, relieved, as he drinks from the seasonal streams. Green shoots emerge from the bare, dead earth. Stormwater rushes down through the riverbeds, past the homeless settlements in the park and into the city, where it pours into concrete-lined underground channels that divert it out to sea. None of this water is collected. Millions of litres of fresh water pour into the ocean every day, where no one can use it.

# 7.

'I don't know what I'm doing,' I tell Emma. 'Why are Adrian and I even thinking about this? How can anyone bring a child into this world? You're just signing them up for a lifetime of collapse and violence.'

The sky's almost black out of the window and the rain lashes against the glass in loud spurts. I try to imagine the water seeping into the parched earth, the roots of the plants drinking as much as they can before the heat returns. They fill their cells, repair their damage. I try to imagine that they are resilient. Strong enough to survive another hot, dry summer when it comes.

'It all just feels so hopeless,' I say. 'Like we're at the start of the roller-coaster of climate collapse and nothing we can do will stop it. It's too late. Droughts will get worse. And floods and crop failures and starvation. Wars over dwindling resources. Unbearable heat. It's already starting to happen; it's not even in the future, and yet everyone's in denial. No one's doing anything. We're all just pretending everything's fine. Trump's rolling back environmental protections. We're building new coal-fired power stations. Even if we changed the whole global economy, if we did everything in our power to cut emissions and deforestation, it may still not be enough, and we're not even doing the bare minimum. We've had a few good days of rain this winter, and all of a sudden people are taking baths, washing their clothes and hosing down their cars. Everyone's acting as if we're through it, it's over, we can go back to normal, but that drought was just the beginning. We're on the cliff edge, and we're losing our footing. I don't understand how people can just go around acting as if everything's going to be okay when it's so obviously not going to be okay.'

'This reminds me of your fear of flying,' Emma says, and I'm irritated, maybe for the first time with her, because what the hell has my fear of flying got to do with any of this? 'You use very similar imagery to talk about it. You said you can't stop imagining the plane falling from the sky, while on fire, and you're trapped inside.'

Even hearing her say it makes my heart race. Remembering the intensity of that fear, that complete helplessness and terror.

'Falling off a cliff, falling from the sky,' she continues, and I wish she wouldn't. I wish she would shut the hell up and let me hold on to something that isn't falling. 'The planet is burning, the plane is burning.'

'Yes, everything's falling apart.'

'What do you mean by everything?'

'The world is falling apart around us.'

'You were dropped.'

'What?' I say.

'And you're afraid of what's already happened.'

'Bullshit,' I say, and then, catching myself: 'Sorry.'

Emma holds out on me. Silence from where she's sitting. Patient, endless silence. I wish she'd tell me it's okay that I swore at her, that she doesn't hold it against me, that she isn't retreating into herself and writing me off as a patient. Maybe she'll never be as kind to me again. A little of her warmth extinguished.

I try to explain. 'It's dread that I feel. Constant dread. It's an expectation, not a memory. Like a premonition. I know terrible things are going to happen to me. I can feel it. I'm just waiting for them.'

'And why do you think you have that expectation?'

'Because the world is falling apart! I just said. Look around you.'

'You know,' Emma says, 'one of the key differences between people who experienced trauma early in their lives and those who did not is that people who experienced no major traumas as children tend to believe that things will work out in the end. Even if they see terrible things happen around them, they think "it won't happen to me".'

'That's so irrational,' I say.

'It might be.'

'It's delusional.'

'Is it?'

'Those things happen to someone. Who's to say you won't be that someone? Even if planes are ninety-nine per cent safe, someone has to be in the one per cent of people who die in plane crashes. Do those people not matter? Aren't they real people? How can you just assume it'll be someone else? There's no reason to believe that.'

'Maybe there isn't, and maybe it's not logical. But maybe it's also necessary. A kind of faith that allows us to get up every morning and go about our lives. We need a level of hope. That's what gets taken away by childhood trauma.'

I watch the rain on the windowpane. What a relief it would be to believe all this fear relates to something that has already happened. Something that is over, finished. Not a disaster lurking in the shadows, waiting for me to drop my guard for a second so that it can destroy me. 'You can't make yourself believe something you don't believe,' I say. Suddenly, there are hot tears on my cheeks. It's a strange kind of crying that happens in analysis at first. Mechanical almost, unemotional. Like water escaping from a leak in a pipe. It comes out only because the water pressure is too great, but there's no feeling behind it. 'God,' I say, 'sorry.' I reach for the tissues I thought I would never use and I wipe my eyes. 'I was just thinking how amazing it must feel to believe everything's going to be okay.'

'It's a parent's job to instil that feeling in their children.'

'Even if it isn't true?' I say.

I'm half-joking, trying to make light of this conversation so I can claw my way out of this feeling, this realisation that I've never felt safe, and I don't want to have to say out loud that I've always known life is meaningless and empty and then we die, and the only relief we can hope for is a bit of distraction from the truth. Maybe drugs or sex or travel. It's so maudlin and self-pitying, so earnest to state the obvious like that. So humourless. Everyone already knows it; that's why they make light of it all. Although I don't think my attempt at flippancy is working. I don't think Emma is smiling. The best I can hope for, and I can't see her sitting behind me so I'll never be sure, is that her silence is gentle.

'What a joke,' I say, 'to think parents make their children feel safe.'

'Why do you say that?'

'No reason,' I say.

Emma waits. She's so good at this – this velvety pressure. I want to run away from this feeling and talk about something else. I want to ask her about her life, her weekend plans, the bloody climate crisis for fuck's sake – it was what I was trying to talk about – but she's cast some kind of spell in this room. Here, I can't avoid myself.

I'm sitting alone, except my dad is at the other end of the table, having breakfast. We're on the terrace of his first house after my parents' divorce, a little cottage in Parkhurst. He's reading the newspaper and I try to start a conversation. The first time, he ignores me, and I fall silent. I stare at the tessellations of sunlight in the pool and wait for him to finish reading. When I try again, he sighs, places a finger where his eye had been in the text, and looks up at me over his sunglasses.

'What?' he snaps.

'Never mind,' I say.

I'm eight years old and I have two theories as to why he makes me come to his house every second weekend. The first theory is that he wants everyone to think he's a good father, so he must go through the motions of seeing his son. The second theory is that he wants to rub my nose in how much he despises me. It's not enough for him to leave me with Mom, who loves me. No, I must be forced to endure whole weekends where he ignores me, shouts at me, tells me I'm too emotional. Most recently because I'd asked for a night light because I was scared of the dark.

'Rachel's coming over for lunch,' he says, folding the paper at last, and placing it beside his breakfast, 'and I need you to look after her son.'

'No,' I say. I can't believe I'm saying it. Even now, more than twenty years later, I'm terrified. 'I hate her son.'

'What did you say to me?' He's doing that shapeshifting thing, re-aligning his skin and his features to reveal his skull beneath his face.

'I'm sick of looking after her stupid son.' What I don't say, because I don't have the words for it yet, because I don't even know why I'm so hurt yet, is that I'm sick of being treated like the help whenever my dad wants to get laid. He's a different person with these women, not cold and aloof and angry. He doesn't make them sit in silence while he reads the paper or listens to opera at full volume in the living room with the curtains drawn. With me, the rage is always right there beneath the surface, glinting in his eyes.

But for the women: charm, wit. He comes alive for Rachel, for Cheryl, for Nicolette. He tells stories and listens to theirs; he laughs;

he squeezes their shoulders. What I would do for him to hold me in his attention like that, again, the way he did before he moved out.

I get up from the table. 'I'm going to go draw in my room.'

'Fine. But when they get here, you must play with Ed.'

'I'm not playing with Ed. He's three! He's so annoying.'

'I'm not asking you.'

I don't even know what I did next – maybe it's an expression on my face that he doesn't like – but suddenly I'm running towards my bedroom and he's following me, steady as the shadows coming at you at sunset. He pushes the door open as I try to close it behind me and he corners me against the bed.

'Leave me alone,' I shout, and I try to reach for my coloured pens on the desk because drawing calms me down, drawing helps me lose myself and forget where I am, but he knocks the pens out of my hand and he grabs my wrist and he squeezes it so hard I think he'll break my hand clean off the bone. He seizes the other wrist, too, and it's bubbling over now, whatever it is that glistens in his eyes. He's wanted to do this to me for so long; I've felt it. He twists my arms behind my back and it hurts, and I shout but he can't repress this urge any more. He pushes me over, onto the bed, face first, and he climbs on top of me. Both my arms are twisted behind my back, pinned beneath his weight, his knees which dig into the back of my ribs, my crushed hands. I try to writhe to release some of the pressure on my shoulders, to turn my head so I can breathe, but he's so much stronger than I am. He's holding both my wrists in one hand now, and he's pushing my face into the mattress and I can't breathe. He's heavy and he's pushing, too, forcing me down. I can't hear his words, or I can't remember them, just the volume of this uncontrollable wrath, the knowledge that if I continue to fight him, he'll kill me. That if I scream and scream, no one will hear me. We are alone in this house of his. And it's separated from any neighbouring houses by lawns and walls and trees, the thrumming of automatic pool cleaners and the hum of Saturday morning traffic in summer. What if he never lets me breathe?

My chest is tight again, now, in the room with Emma. I press my fingers between my ribs, try to massage the sharp pain that flares in the muscles around my lungs.

'I called my mom after that, and begged her to come pick me up,' I say.

'And did she?'

'I guess she didn't want to make things worse. She wanted me and him to have a good relationship.'

Emma does it again. She says nothing, and so my words just hang in the air, and the longer I let them hang there, the more they sound like an excuse.

'No,' I say at last, 'she didn't come to pick me up.'

# 8.

Sibs calls in sick with a fever. The next week, when she doesn't show up to work again, I call both numbers I have for her. (She's always changing phone numbers for some reason. I once asked her if they were burner phones, but she'd never heard the expression so the joke fell flat.) The first number does not connect. The second is answered by a gruff, phlegmy older woman who shouts a string of incomprehensible words into the receiver – it sounds like isiXhosa but she speaks so fast I can't parse one word from the next – and then hangs up.

Sibs calls me at four p.m. from a number I don't recognise.

'Who was that I spoke to earlier?' I say.

'What?'

'Who answered your phone?'

'No it's some lady.' And that's the end of that.

Sibs tells me that her daughter is sick. She must have caught what Sibs had last week but it's worse for Buhle. She keeps throwing up. She's shaking and sweating. She took her to the clinic and they gave her pills but the pills haven't helped at all. When I ask her what pills they gave her, she takes a few seconds to find the little sachet and then she reads to me over the phone, aspirin.

'Come in tomorrow, Sibs, and bring Buhle. I'll make an appointment with my doctor.'

It's a weird dynamic, arriving at my GP and telling the receptionist that the appointment is really for Buhle, but that I'll take care of the payment. I feel uncomfortable, paternalistic, like I've turned into a tone-deaf and meddlesome mother hen, protective and fussing over her charge. It's a kind of white saviour complex, and I hate it, but then Sibs tells me a story, while we wait on the beautiful mid-century furniture in the waiting room, about how she tried once to go to the clinic in Claremont and they wouldn't see her.

'They said to me I must go to the clinic where I live. I said to them my employer sent me, because I was working for a lady in Claremont at the time, but they said to me no you can't just go wherever you like. Who do you think you are? You must go where you live.'

'The clinic where you live is the one that gave Buhle aspirin?'

'There, in Philippi. They don't care.'

'So what did you do?'

'When I told my employer she got very angry and then she came with me and all of a sudden the people at the clinic were very nice. They said no of course they could see me. It was no problem. I was welcome anytime.'

Buhle is very quiet on Sibs's lap. She doesn't writhe or whine, like I imagined a sick child would, but stares straight ahead, eyes unfocused. Beads of sweat on her forehead and her upper lip. On impulse, I touch my fingers to her forehead and I'm alarmed by how hot she feels.

'Do you want me to go in with you?' I say to Sibs.

'It's fine,' she says – a response she often gives to my questions which I find impossible to decipher.

'Is that a yes or a no, Sibs?' I say, trying to keep my voice light. 'I'm happy either way.'

She shrugs and smiles and sighs, and I suppose that means she'd like me to come in with her but she doesn't want to impose, but I'm not at all certain, it might mean the opposite – that she'd prefer to do it alone but doesn't want to seem ungrateful – and so in the end I decide not to go in with her when the doctor calls my name. Paying for the appointment is more than enough. Anything more is infantilising. She is capable of describing her daughter's symptoms to the doctor, even if her English isn't perfect.

I wave at James when he comes through to collect me, and I indicate Buhle and Sibs with my eyes. He knows me well, this doctor. In the few months I've been back from New York, I've already been to see him at least a dozen times. For tightness in my chest, and spasms, which I believed to be heart trouble, and he believed to be anxiety. For difficulty breathing, which I believed to be lung trouble, and he believed to be anxiety. He's kind to me, and gentle, but I know he thinks I'm a hypochondriac, and I swear I detect a hint of relief when he realises it's not me he's seeing, but a sick child, someone who needs medical attention rather than reassurance.

I wait for them in the waiting room. I browse through the ancient magazines – *National Geographic*, mostly, but also some gossip rags like *YOU* and *Huisgenoot* – in the way I imagine everyone does in waiting rooms, not reading the words, not even really absorbing the pictures, just holding my gaze over pages for a few seconds and then flipping to the next image-heavy spread. I scroll through social media on my phone, double-tapping every image on my Instagram feed without reading the captions.

When they come out, Buhle is sucking on a lollipop. I didn't know doctors still did that – keep lollipops in their drawer for children; I thought that kind of thing fell out of favour decades ago, and it lifts my spirits to see it. She's still sick, still hurting, something in the way she walks and the shape of her eyes, but the lollipop has cheered her up.

'It's nothing to worry about,' James says to me. 'A nasty bug. Keep an eye on her, but I think she'll be fine. I've written her a script and told Sibongile which foods to avoid for a while.' He hands the script to me, and I want to pass it over to Sibs because it seems so disrespectful to give it to me, but I know that my duty in this matter extends to the pharmacy as well, that I must finish what I have started, and that giving Sibs the script only to take it from her again and hand it to the pharmacist and pay for the drugs makes the whole exchange even more awkward.

'Thank you, neh,' Sibs says to me after I've paid for the appointment.

'You're so welcome,' I say and I feel, for a second, simply good, before the tentacles of our history reach up and drag me back down into the muck.

I try to play with Buhle while we wait for the pharmacist to fill the script. I'm worried I've treated her like a problem to be solved rather than a toddler, and so I do my best to engage with her in the limited time I have left before I drop them both off at the taxi rank to go home. I start off with peekaboo behind my hands, but it gets no response, so I upgrade to hiding one aisle over and poking my head around the vitamins and supplements display. My cheeks burn throughout this ordeal, but half-arsing it isn't going to get a smile from Buhle. There's no way to get a reaction from children without making a fool of yourself.

On my third wide-eyed, over-acted, jazz-hand-accompanied emergence from behind the Berocca shelf, Buhle finally giggles at me. The lollipop stick is still in her mouth, but she scrunches up her eyes and lets out an angelic, high-pitched squeal. She does it again on my fourth attempt, but on my fifth, she turns away from me and clutches her mother's leg.

'Your medication is ready,' the pharmacist says to me, unimpressed with my breakthrough.

I buy Buhle some crayons and a pack of vitamin C sweets before we go.

When I drop them at the taxi rank, Buhle waves at me over her mother's shoulder.

# 9.

Every day I walk Frasier to one of the two parks near our house. They're both beautiful. The closest park, De Waal, is small, with a fountain in the centre and tree-lined walkways radiating outwards to the edges. Swamp cypresses, Monterey cypresses, European oaks. Gum trees and London planes and yellowwoods. If you look south through the gaps in the trees you see Table Mountain rising above you, and if you look north, down below, the squat high-rises of the city centre. Frasier loves it here, and would be happy if we did the same thing every day. He swims in the fountain. He chases after any ball that comes hurtling past for another dog. He runs up to the old lady who always has treats and he sits, nicely, like a good boy, in front of her with a lifted paw.

I am still surprised, five years after Adrian brought him home as a tiny puppy that fit into one hand, by how much I love him, and how much I rely on him. I disliked dogs growing up – their neediness, their smell, their unpredictability, their lack of personal space. When Adrian and I first met, and he found out about my distaste for dogs, he teased me. 'Maybe you can't accept unconditional love,' he said. For months after we first got Frasier, hugging him would make me cry. Something about his helplessness, his unrestrained love for me. He was happy to see me, no matter how miserable I felt. I didn't have to pretend to be okay. I didn't have to be funny or interesting or strong.

Walking him every day, the most basic act as a caregiver, forced me to get some sunshine and exercise and fresh air, even on the days when getting dressed and getting out of bed seemed futile and daunting. He let me witness pure, uncomplicated joy. Just the smell of a tree stump or a path through an unremarkable park fills Frasier with such joy that he runs in wide, wild circles to let it out. He loves being alive, the sounds and smells and freedom of it, and it's impossible to witness this without catching some of it myself. To feel that perhaps I enabled some of this joy with the small act of bringing him to the park. And then I feel the sunshine on my cheeks, too. I can smell the freshly cut grass and notice the dappled, dancing light in the trees.

In the northeast corner of the park, beside the small, white building that houses the public toilets, there's an informal sculpture garden, built by the homeless people who live here. They have filled car tyres with soil and planted spekbooms. They have dug channels from the stormwater drains into a network of flowerbeds full of birds of paradise, arum lilies. They have arranged fallen tree branches into elaborate shapes and covered them in tinsel and coloured paper. A disco ball hangs from an outstretched branch. They have painted tyres and stones. They have erected large papier mâché animal heads and suspended bicycle parts from the branches of the trees. None of it serves any purpose beyond imagination and beauty and this delights me every time I pass it, this unexpected celebration of beauty from those who have almost nothing. We expect poverty to be squalid. We pity and fear the dispossessed. We imagine they think about nothing but survival, the next meal, and yet here: creativity, generosity. The sharing of their dreams. I wave and greet the homeless people when I see them come out of their tents in the morning. I bring them sandwiches when I remember.

After sticking to the parks for many weeks, I start venturing beyond them with Frasier, into the residential areas nearby. Gardens, Tamboerskloof, Higgovale, Vredehoek. I take longer routes. There are enough pedestrians on the street that I start to feel safe walking on my own. It's something I miss from New York, the culture of walking. It's exhilarating to enmesh myself in the neighbourhood, to greet passers-by, to notice small details – the seventeenth-century Dutch water well, the old slave cottages behind the hospital – that I'd miss in a car. I grew up in a city built for cars. I hated that about Johannesburg. The way middle-class people moved around in bubbles, only ever seeing what they wanted to see, protected by metal and glass, expats in their own country. I tried often, as a teenager, to walk to the nearest shopping centre. Five or six blocks to Rosebank Mall, and I was terrified every step of the way. I accelerated until I was almost running, but I forced myself not to run. I was walking. I was walking to the shops. But what if someone was following me, watching me? It's one of my clearest, earliest memories, sitting in the back of my mother's car as we circled the block before coming home at night. 'Why do you always circle the block?' I asked.

'In case we're being followed.'

We might have been. She wasn't mad. Johannesburg was dangerous in those days, the time of the transition, though I wasn't aware of the transition at the time, or the war raging in the townships and hostels, only the stories of people being hijacked, pulled out of their cars in driveways or at red traffic lights, shot in the head, execution-style. It's difficult to know now whether the fear I felt sitting in that back seat, that my mother felt in the front seat, was proportional to the actual violence taking place all around us or if it was the anxiety of a newly single mother, a woman who felt overwhelmed by living alone and caring for me, or if it was fuelled by propaganda. The fears of the white middle class losing political power. Die swart gevaar.

'What do we do if you think we're being followed?' I asked from the back seat, and she told me not to stop at red lights, to take a zig-zag route home and head straight to the nearest police station.

I think about that still, when I drive anywhere alone at night. Even all these years later, in a country that is so completely different and yet the same, I still remember the tension in that car. Waiting in the dark with her, trapped in the driveway, sitting ducks, waiting the un-bearable seconds as the electric gate ambled open, hoping and pray-ing that there were no attackers in the bushes. I imagined them racing towards us in balaclavas with AK-47s. They had always been racing towards us in balaclavas with AK-47s.

She double-checked the lock on her door then, while we waited for the gate, as if that would provide any kind of protection when the moment came.

I think about the theory that only men can be flâneurs, that women can't write about walking in the city because they don't feel safe enough to observe the world around them with detachment. Perhaps gay men can't be flâneurs either, nor South Africans in general. It requires a kind of confident ease that's hard to imagine, at least now that I'm back home. I could wander the streets of New York almost safe in my own skin. I could blend into the crowd. I remember Sibs telling me once that she likes to be home by sunset and that she never goes out at night. Not ever. It's one of the many ironies of this coun-try that the middle class is so vocal about crime but the victims of the crime are so seldom middle class. It's the poor who get murdered by the thousands in the townships, while shrill conservative Facebook groups invent their own persecution, their 'white genocide'. Sibs has no electric fencing, no armed response. Nothing but flimsy sheet-metal walls on her shack, a padlock on the front door, and police who won't even look up from their phones when she tries to report a crime.

I walk a little further from home every week. I love the architecture of this city, the layers of influence and creolisation over the centuries, Dutch and British and Southeast Asian. The Victorian terrace houses with their broekielaced front stoeps, the remnants of old Dutch farmhouses and churches, the Art Deco and Mediterranean-style and ugly 1970s face-brick blocks of flats. The mosques. The tiny, brightly coloured mosques. They corroborate my side of an argument I'm always having in my mind. And they subvert the dominant narrative about Islam in the West – that it's an ascendant, violent force. There have been Muslims in this city for as long as there have been white people, and there is none of the tension America or Europe teaches us to expect. I think of the old man with the white skullcap who runs the corner shop near my home, his voice so warm and kind it makes my skin tingle. I think of my colleague at the advertising agency who wears sparkly black tops and loves Ed Sheeran so much she cried when she heard he was coming to South Africa. I think of all the families on the Sea Point promenade during Eid, the kids laughing and running around, the grannies and aunts offering biscuits to strangers.

As my walks get longer over the weeks, I start venturing into the city centre proper. And then I start walking to and from work. Frasier still gets his walks twice a day, before and after work; Adrian and I alternate, but I don't need him as my training wheels for the city any more. My job is on Loop Street, at an ad agency down towards the harbour, and I vary the routes to get there. I walk along Bree Street first, with its cafes and bistros and yoga studios and art galleries. Then

I try Long Street, to see what it's like during the day. It's nothing like the chaos I remember from my twenties, the road clogged with taxis, and bars bursting out into the street and onto the first-floor balconies, and the bass from the clubs ricocheting in my chest, and the drunk pedestrians shouting and singing and stumbling into stationary traffic, and drug dealers falling in step as you walk, whispering 'cocaine, ecstasy, dagga, you like pretty girls? Or maybe boys?' During the day, Long Street is a different beast. There are shops I'd never noticed in the gaps between the bars. Vintage clothing and designer footwear and African artefacts for the tourists – wooden masks and beaded sculptures and large handmade baskets. There are banks and restaurants, backpackers and European tourists. Only two blocks from Bree Street but a world apart.

If it's raining, or I'm tired or I work late, I take the bus home. Another crusade of mine, embracing public transport, as if refusing to give in to the class and race barriers of this country will inspire others to do the same. The buses on this route are often empty, but I feel a jolt of excitement when I board one that isn't. I get in and I don't sit anywhere near the other person. We don't talk or even lock eyes. But I know I'm sharing the city, this ordinary commute, with another human being.

# 10.

They interview us separately, first. They tell us they are going to do this long before it happens, when we are making the appointment, and yet I still don't want to let go of Adrian's hand when they call my name in the waiting room.

'Good luck', he mouths at me, in the way of supportive husbands to those being summoned into an oncologist's office or going on stage. Nadia also tries to put me at ease.

'You can't study for something like this,' she tells me. 'Just be yourself.'

Myself is a work in progress, I want to tell her, and analysis feels like one big project of deconstructing and unlearning whatever sense of self I might have started off with. Emma wants me to befriend my shadow, which would mean becoming a very different person from the one I've tried to be all my life. I don't tell Nadia I'm lost in the shadows, with only the tiniest oil lamp to guide my way.

Nadia and I talk for a while about nothing. Where did I grow up? What did I study at university? Did I play any sport or musical instruments? She wants to know about my brother, Hilton, and my sister-in-law, Mia. I tell her they live in Joburg and have two kids. I don't tell Nadia that Mia looks a bit like her because she might think I'm only saying that as a way of telling her that Mia is coloured. And while I might be annoyed that Hilton gets to live that perfect post-apartheid ideal of the rainbow-nation family and I squandered the

75

symbolism of my life by falling in love with a white guy, now is not the time to go into it. I tell Nadia about my niece and nephew, Lily and Simon, and refrain from using the word 'caramel' to describe them. She wants to know about my mother. My father. She wants to know why I want to have a child.

'I don't know,' I say, 'it's just something I've always wanted.'

She waits for a while before making a note on her pad.

'Sorry,' I say, 'that was very vague. Does it answer your question?'

'Whatever you want to tell me.'

I think about growing old without children, the emptiness I'm afraid of. A life where meaning is so hard won, where nothing lasts. I think about being alone in retirement, staring out of a window at the mountain day in and day out, no visitors, no family. But we might have destroyed the planet by then. Maybe none of us will make it to old age. Instead, I tell Nadia the fantasy I've always had about my daughter – pushing her in the swings in that little park near where I grew up in Joburg, her giggle, which is so clear to me, as if I've heard it in the real world. I know I'm probably making a million mistakes, revealing something I don't want to reveal about myself – some terrible motivation I'm not aware of.

'I feel like I'm in therapy,' I say when I'm finished.

'Are you in therapy?'

Sweat prickles in my armpits. I don't want to fuck this up for Adrian.

'It's okay if you are,' Nadia says, paging ahead in her notepad until she finds what she's looking for. 'Aaah, there it is, mental health.'

I notice that I'm squeezing my fists in my lap and I try to relax them. 'I am,' I say.

'That's good.'

Why does this whole process make me so angry? I picked a fight with

Adrian after we left these offices the first time. Something about the way this process is designed makes me feel insufficient. Straight couples have children all the time without anyone questioning their ability to love. They don't have to answer to anyone, don't have to prove their worth. They can be as incompetent, selfish, or unhappy as they like.

'You know, I think it's quite unfair to ask me this. It's healthy to seek help. It doesn't mean I'd be a bad parent. It's the parents who repress everything and don't even try to understand themselves who make bad parents. They're the ones who cause harm.'

It's Nadia's turn to look uncomfortable. There's some colour in her cheeks. She folds her hands over each other. 'I completely agree.'

'Good.'

I'm breathing heavily. I force myself to reduce the volume of my inhalations.

'People only think about violent parents,' Nadia says, 'when they talk about abuse, but unhappy parents can also damage a child. Numb or emotionally distant parents.'

I can't look at her any more. I focus on her hands on the notepad. Her fingernails are painted a deep burgundy red.

'So, um, well done on working on it,' she says. She's still blushing. 'Do you go every week?' she says.

She doesn't need to know that it's multiple times a week; that no matter how much therapy and medication I throw at myself I still don't have my emotions under control. If anything, Emma wants me to un-control my emotions, to let them rise out of me like some unstoppable tide, clearing the dead flesh, breaking the rigidity. I'm starting to want to go along with it. Let go of the handrail. Let the swirling, broiling storm take me where it needs to go.

I nod at her and make myself smile.

'And why did you start seeing a therapist?'

Another trap. Do I mention only this most recent iteration, or document the whole history of psychologists stretching all the way back to when I was eight?

'I struggle with anxiety,' I say.

'And depression?'

I'm not sure how she knows that but just hearing the word seems to conjure the feeling. I blink quickly to redistribute any moisture in my eyes, and I smile, again. 'Yes.'

I want to say, Aren't we all? I want to say, Isn't there just so much more sorrow in the world than anything else? But no one wants to acknowledge that. And in spite of everything, I don't think Nadia wants to fail me. She wants Adrian and me to get this. Well, she wants it for Adrian, but he and I are a package deal.

'It's good that you're working through it,' she says again, as if she knows anything about any of this. She's out of her depth, a nervous thirty-something as clueless as I am but without the constant torment, clinging to her questionnaire to make sense of the world, and it's unbearable that I have to flagellate myself in front of her like this.

When I come back to the waiting room, I mouth 'I'm sorry' to Adrian. His eyes widen as he stands up to take my place and I think, fuck, why did I do that, it'll only throw him off his game too, but he's more resilient than I expect. The fear falls from his eyes as fast as it collected there and his face crinkles into a smile. He rubs my shoulder and says, 'I'll see you soon.'

I scan the waiting room for something to read. There's a book on 'transracial adoption' on the side table next to where Adrian had been sitting. It's what we'll have, the agency has told us, so I may as well get a head start on the reading.

The author sounds very angry about having had white adoptive parents. I should put the book down, but her fury makes me read even faster. I want to know why she feels this way; I want there to be a reason I can understand and accept, not just that white people are fundamentally flawed and have no right to adopt. There are loads of reasons. Her parents didn't tell her she was adopted, even when she told them everyone at school said she was Latinx. I'd obviously never do that to our daughter. It wouldn't be possible, anyway, a black baby can't pass as white the way a Latinx baby might, but also Adrian and I are sensitive to these things. We'll include her birth culture in any way we can. I've read enough books and spoken to enough black girlfriends to know that we'll need to learn about black hair and find a salon that makes her feel like a queen. Adrian and I will learn isiXhosa, properly this time, and make sure she feels loved. We'll listen when she tells us how she feels, not impose how we think she should feel on her. I scan ahead in the book. The next chapter is on white saviour complex. I put the book down.

'How was it?' I say when I'm invited to join Adrian in Nadia's office.

'Great,' he says, and his smile isn't tense or false; he's been having a good time.

The next part of the interview is a couples interview, conducted with both of us at the same time. To better understand our relationship, Nadia says, and our home life. How we might integrate a child into our lives; how we might meet the child's emotional and physical needs. What kind of family we'd make.

It's a loaded word: 'family'. The cool queer kids of pop culture love to talk about chosen family. Friends as family. Family as an ideal of unconditional love. It's impossible to hear the word 'family' and feel nothing.

Nadia asks Adrian how we met. He tells her about that birthday brunch many years ago, for a mutual friend. It's only partially true, and I'm enjoying this: the retention of some privacy against the on-slaught of Nadia's questions. With me, she can see through my half-truths and evasion – she's an oracle of bullshit. But with Adrian, she hangs on his every word. She likes him, and I'm enjoying this too – seeing Adrian through her eyes. Adrian tells her about the brunch in detail. The mimosa I spilled on myself (which I had forgotten), the incredibly awkward way that we had to all go around the table say-ing what we loved about the birthday boy (which I will never forget; and which is probably the reason neither Adrian nor I see that friend very much any more). He doesn't tell her that we'd actually met the night before, at three a.m. in his hotel room. That we'd matched on a hook-up app. That he was travelling from Joburg for work and in a phase of saying yes to everything, including letting random strangers come to his hotel room at three a.m. That when we were introduced, at brunch, it was only six hours since I had left his hotel room, but we did need to hear each other's names because we hadn't bothered to exchange them the night before. Everyone around us could see immediately that there was something between the two of us, some inside joke.

Adrian is natural and confident as he talks to Nadia. He's quite funny, and he knows exactly which anecdotes to tell to make us sound cute, and like we're very much in love, and I think maybe I had forgotten that, too, or it was buried beneath the detritus of everyday life, with-in me but inaccessible. He's right. We did know very early on that this was something special, and it's still here, that flush of warmth when I watch him talk to her, that tingling gratitude that he exists. But I can't tell Nadia this. Far too soppy.

I must not have noticed it before, not consciously, anyway, how charming and confident he's become. And yet I have come to rely on him for this. I experience a pang of sadness that he seems to have blossomed as I have fallen apart, as if there is only room in a relationship for one person to occupy each role. Has the strength ebbed from me to him? When I met him, there was sadness in those rich, hazel eyes of his. It was one of the things that attracted me to him most strongly – this deep, unspoken hurt. I wanted to heal it. I wanted to drive out the darkness. Instead, I've caught it.

But no, he hasn't taken anything from me. His strength is not stolen; if anything, he has stepped up to help as the cracks in my imposed self-reliance started to show. We are both so different from the people we were when we met. This isn't even the same relationship. Photographs would prove we are the modern versions of those people – that we transformed slowly, imperceptibly, that there is some continuity in character – but is it true? I read a beautiful line, once, a meme on social media I think, that all we are is consciousness moving through space and time.

All of this change and yet we haven't drifted apart. We haven't drifted at all. It's a different kind of change – not movement in any direction, but beneath the skin. Or no, like moss growing on a boulder. Soil builds up in the crevices over the years, and plants with roots begin to grow in these pockets of soil, and their rotting leaves create even more soil, and more plants. Look again in ten years and the boulder is still there; there is just more life in the scene. It strikes me that I have never believed in long-term relationships. Even on our wedding day, I thought, This is great, let's enjoy it while it lasts. You can extend the duration of any relationship with duty and obligation and guilt, but any genuine affection withers and dies. What I didn't know could happen was reinvention. We're in, maybe, our third or fourth relationship together, and I think this one's going to be the closest and deepest one yet.

'I moved to Cape Town and we moved in together within a year,' Adrian says. 'Like a bunch of lesbians.' Nadia laughs.

Was the sadness I saw in him in the early years the grief that all gay men carry?

Everyone who is alive?

Did I project it onto him?

'Lovely,' Nadia says. 'And how would you describe your relationship?'

Adrian lifts his eyebrows at me, but this warmth I'm feeling has made me passive. I don't want to take this question. I don't want to upset this feeling.

Adrian tells Nadia a joke. 'One of my friends,' he says, 'on his parents' thirtieth wedding anniversary, asked his mom what the secret to their marriage was, and she said to him, "We never wanted to get divorced at the same time."'

It's a risky joke, and the silence stretches out for the longest split-second before Nadia laughs. But the laugh is throaty. She likes Adrian. It's all over her body language. *He* can tell a joke like that.

'We also have bad timing,' he says, and he winks at me.

And because he's made these jokes, and it's gone well and Nadia seems to accept, finally, that people are imperfect and relationships are messy and difficult and they can be nourishing even if they aren't exemplary in every way, that even if you irritate each other sometimes, it doesn't mean you're all wrong, or that you'll make bad parents or bad people, I feel the pressure loosen. I can breathe. And I can talk. I tell Nadia about the time Adrian lost his passport in Mozambique and we spent the whole day retracing our steps through Maputo and what started as irritation evolved into an adventure, and he tells her about the first time my mother met him and how she thought he looked like an old boyfriend of hers, and how that nearly made it impossible for me to continue seeing him, and we segue effortlessly into how we resolve conflict and how we might deal with a child who feels traumatised and abandoned by having been given up for adoption, and how we communicate when we're under pressure and what we've learnt about each other since doing Myers–Briggs and Enneagram and listening to James Hollis audiobooks together on road trips, and by the end I'm thinking hey, maybe we're quite healthy.

Except, the end isn't the end, because the couples interview is followed by an actual personality test. Standardised, multiple choice. We separate again and spend the next hour filling in a questionnaire that is designed to pick up psychopathy.

But even the hostility of the test is not enough to ruin the closeness I'm feeling with Adrian. We stop off at the promenade on our way home. We buy gelato. He lets me taste his multiple times even though he doesn't want any of mine. It's coffee flavoured and he hates coffee ice cream. We walk hand in hand down the promenade like embarrassing teenagers in a world where gay teenagers can do the things that straight teenagers have always been able to do.

'Why didn't you just tell her we met on an app?' I say to him when we reach the giant sculpture of sunglasses looking out to sea. 'Even straight people do that now; it's ordinary. She wasn't going to think it's sordid.'

'Depends how many gay men she knows,' he says. He grins at me. He's still on a high from this whole experience and the future that it promises. 'If she's good friends with any gay men, she'll think it's sordid.'

'Why?'

'Because she'll know we have the order reversed. When men and women hook up on an app, they have their date first.'

I lift Adrian's hand in mine, and I kiss it. His smile is relaxed. He winks at me. 'They're looking for wholesomeness at these adoption agencies,' he says.

'Anyway,' I say, 'Nadia doesn't have any gay friends.'

'How do you know?'

'She has that starstruck quality when she's looking at you, like she can't believe how cool you are.'

'Psssh,' Adrian says. 'That doesn't mean anything. That's just because I'm adorable.'

# 11.

'I think I've told you a screen memory,' I tell Emma in our next session. I've been reading about them online, and the whole concept freaks me out. False memories that our brain conjures up to replace what actually happened. 'What if I've made up half of the stuff I remember?'

Emma remembers everything I tell her. Sometimes she reminds me of my own memories: scenes I could access in a moment of vulnerability in this room that I lost again once my composure returned. 'I would be surprised if you didn't have a few,' Emma says. 'They are a way of protecting yourself.'

*Protecting myself from what?* I don't ask. The last thing I need is to scramble my mind any more. How am I supposed to better understand myself if my memory plays tricks on me? Stories have the power to change everything. They organise the chaos. They make meaning from the flashes of experience, the upswells of emotion. I'm realising that half the stories I've believed about myself and my life aren't true, but if I'm replacing them with similarly unreliable stories, I'll never find what's broken.

I don't say anything for a very long time, and eventually Emma shows some mercy. 'You know, memory is subjective. If it feels true, then the effect it had on your psyche is true. It's not lying if you remember things a certain way.'

A line from a Damon Galgut interview comes to mind: *All memory is fiction.*

'Apparently, I didn't call my mom after my dad attacked me. I asked her about it this weekend. She says I only told her when I was already back home after school on the Monday.' As soon as I've said it, I hear how it sounds. 'She wouldn't lie,' I add.

'Why do you think you invented the call?' Emma says, and I don't know; obviously, I'm not the expert on the subconscious mind. Maybe I didn't believe I deserved to be rescued, or maybe I thought Mom wouldn't have come even if I'd asked her to. The thought I'm really trying to avoid is that I'm making all of it up retroactively to make sense of how I felt. There's the feeling, and it needs a story to anchor it.

'You know, my previous therapist thought I was sexually abused as a child.'

I wait for a reaction, but none comes.

'It really pissed me off, because she became convinced of it, and that seems so convenient, you know, like, oh, this guy's a mess, he must've been a victim of sexual violence as a kid. Easy fix. Done and dusted. But I have no recollection of anything like that, and I know people can suppress memories, but wouldn't I have an inkling that it had happened?'

'If it took place when you were young enough, you might not have had the words to process what was happening. It lives on in a kind of wordless, amorphous feeling.'

That sets my heart racing. 'That's exactly what it feels like,' I say. A deep, black hole at the centre of my life, a fear hiding behind everything and gnawing at me from the shadows. I can't explain it and I can't attach any specific memories to it, but when I try to go there in my mind, my whole body shakes and my ribs tighten.

'I used to think maybe I was evil,' I say. 'Deep down beneath all my politeness and attempts to be kind and thoughtful and good.'

There is another long silence. And in it, I feel myself shift.

'I was so sure of it, actually. And I know the church says gay people are evil, but I wasn't raised in a religious home, so it's strange. My parents weren't religious at all. I guess homophobia was in the zeitgeist.'

I was fourteen when I first met a gay person. I'd had my first sexual experience by then. I'd given a blow job the year before to a boy a few years ahead of me at school, but he was straight. He'd told me over and over, just in case I got any ideas, that what we were doing didn't make us faggots. He would be with a girl if there were any around, but there weren't any around, so I would have to do. We were in his bedroom in the boarding house – the older grades got their own rooms; they didn't sleep in the dorms – and he wouldn't look at me. He closed his eyes and I suppose he imagined my mouth was a pussy. Or Rebecca's mouth. I think that was the girl he liked. He came, and he warned me before he came, because he didn't think I would swallow, he didn't think any boy would stoop so low as that, but I did. I didn't know it was possible to feel such powerful desire.

He pushed me off him when he was done. There was no mention of reciprocation and I didn't want it. That would ruin everything. I didn't want to have blown some queer. 'If you ever fucking tell any-one, I'll kill you,' he said.

'I won't. I promise.'

'Good. And don't fucking look at me in the showers again.'

So that's how he'd known. I couldn't believe I'd slipped up. I tried so hard not to look at anyone in the showers. 'Or anywhere else,' he said.

But I was no better than he was. I deliberately tried to distance myself from the obviously gay guy in my year. We sat together in History and I hated it. He wanted to be friends and I could barely bring myself to respond to him when he spoke. His nasal, effeminate voice. The way he crossed his legs. It was bad enough that people saw us together. Could he not at least try to rein it in?

But I was excited to meet Evan at my grandmother's eightieth in Durban. He was related to me somehow, a distant cousin, but he was an adult and he was openly gay. He'd come with his boyfriend to the party and I was terrified for him, for both of them, to be risking so much. My grandmother adored them. She rested her hand on Evan's arm while he told her some story out by the giant pin oak tree, I don't know, I couldn't hear or I was too awed for his words to make sense. She laughed at his jokes. Evan came over to me afterwards – maybe he'd seen me watching him from the marquee – and he introduced himself. I blurted out that I knew who he was because I'd heard so many stories about him, and he tilted his head and laughed. It didn't bother him. 'Don't believe all of them,' he said. He winked at me and I went bright red. He was so lovely. So confident and normal.

I had never known that his kind of life was open to me.

Later on, when the adults had settled into the soft golden glow of late afternoon and booze, he ran around with some of the children in the garden. He chased them around my grandmother's lawn and he put one of the little girls on his shoulders. He allowed himself to be led around the bushes and shown all the various hideouts the kids had made. The pillow forts that would land them in trouble for getting mud on the upholstery. He was patient and good-natured and he was taking some of the pressure off their parents for a bit, letting the parents relax and have a drink and not worry about their kids.

'It's absolutely disgusting,' one of my mom's cousins said to me. 'To let Evan run around with the children like that.'

I looked over at Evan. I didn't dare say anything in case my voice betrayed me. My cheeks were burning. I smiled as blandly as I could.

'How can their mothers leave their children with him?' another relation said.

'Now now,' said a third relation, 'it isn't catching. He won't contaminate them.'

The others looked at this third woman with such naked contempt and suspicion that she quickly tried to show she wasn't soft. 'I just feel sorry for his mother,' she said. 'Can you imagine?'

And I thought of my mother, and that book she'd given me to get me through puberty. *What's Happening To Me?* it was called, and it explained the changes I could expect in my body and my thoughts. The hair in my groin and underarms. The breaking voice. The fact that I was going to start feeling attracted to girls. I read that part over and over. What about boys? I searched all over the book for that. I became frantic paging through that book, desperate to find the section that spoke about me, about what was happening to me, but there was no mention of people like me. Was I, like Evan, a sexual predator? Was I broken in some way? Rotten in my genes.

I distanced myself from my best friend Asher in primary school because I started to feel things for him. Things you're not supposed to feel for a boy. Butterflies in my stomach. A warm glow whenever he was near me.

'I think I was in love with Asher,' I say to Emma, only realising it as the words come out of my mouth, 'but I knew he'd hate me if he knew that. He'd think I was disgusting, and that our whole friendship was a lie. So I pushed him away. Avoided him at break. Said I was busy when he invited me over after school. Eventually he stopped asking.'

Silence. I lift my head off the pillow and check to see if Emma's fallen asleep, but she's watching me, alert. She doesn't smile, and it's unnerving.

It feels good to remember Asher, after all these years. There's the shame of my secret, but underneath it, the warmth of something pure. I could have been so much less lonely in the years to come if we had remained friends. But then the real memories of those years come back, summoned by this imagined alternative future and quick to smother it.

I'm back in that dormitory, the first year of high school. I must be thirteen, and I feel like a caged animal. Trapped in a hot, dusty town a thousand kilometres from home, forgotten by everyone who ever knew me, who could tolerate me. The dormitory is long and thin, with bunk beds on either side of a central passageway – a mattress on top, a desk and closet beneath each – and my 'cubicle' is right at the end, furthest from the only exit. The windows offer no escape, either. We're four storeys up here, raised into the sweltering rafters of this old colonial stone building, and all I can see through the glass is a church spire and the outskirts of town, where shanties give way to dry, brown veld. Each morning I run the gauntlet to the showers, hoping to get through the dorm without eliciting an attack. I think, if I can just make myself small enough, quiet enough, invisible enough, they will eventually tire of tormenting me. In the showers I keep my eyes glued to the floor, terrified of giving myself away. Hormones flood my body and I'm blushing, trying to control my raging imagination, aware that the smallest glance at their naked bodies might make me swell and expose the pervert in their midst. My body betraying me. I focus only on their feet, but there is even something in their feet that excites me, an erotic quality of masculinity in the more developed boys, those who have started growing hair on their legs, the tops of their feet. I focus on the grouting on the floor, the drain, even if one of them tries to talk to me. I can't even go into the showers if Carl is there. I'll turn around, pretend I forgot my

90

soap dish or shampoo, dawdle back in the dormitory until he comes back from the showers. Beautiful, gentle Carl, with his wavy, almost-black hair, his Roman nose and soft eyes. He hadn't yet realised how beautiful he was, then. His water polo physique was only just coming in. But he'd learn. By Grade 11 he was arrogant, smug, and indifferent to me. But in Grade 8 we could have almost been friends. He was kind to me, if no one else was around to see it. Even made me a mix tape, once. I have to listen to him, every night, in the bed right next to mine, masturbating as quietly as he can under the covers. An almost inaudible thumping against fabric, and then a quiet sigh. It's an almost physical pain, that longing.

I make it back to my cubicle without any jeers. I dress, head to the dining hall for breakfast, and then on to class. Lessons are the only time I can relax. It's safe, here, in class. There is an adult in charge and there is a predictable structure to the conversation. I am smart. I know this about myself, now. The history of the Frontier Wars. The geography of mountain ranges. The metaphors of Shakespeare and J.M. Coetzee. I am good at this and it becomes a place to hide; a way to prove that I am not despicable, a way to shore up approval. Or maybe it's just a simpler way of understanding the world. These subjects have all been worked out beforehand; I only need to learn the rules. Life as mathematics, as science. It is not chaos. It's predictable.

If I make it back to my cubicle unscathed at the end of the day, it's a good day. But evenings are often the most dangerous time. It's usually David who saunters into my space during prep, or afterwards, when there is no scheduled structure to hide in; those terrible gaps between dinner and prep, after prep and before lights out. He'll come into my space slick with friendliness. That's how it starts. 'How was your day? How's it going? I didn't see you at rugby. Oh that's right, you're a fag, you play hockey.'

I laugh, casual as I can fake it. If I don't resist, maybe he'll lose interest.

'Come on, show me how you hit the ball.'

More nervous laughter. I want to slap myself. Why must my laugh sound so frightened and small?

'Ah David, leave it man. You know I'm not like that.'

'Go on, just take a swing. Let me see how you hit the ball.'

He rummages between my closet and the wall, extracts my hockey stick. The rest of the dorm is silent, now. No background noise. No chatter.

I ignore him, desperate, not sure what else I can do.

'Anyone else want to see her moves?' he calls.

A few of the boys come in. Among them, Carl. 'Come on, David,' he says, 'let him be.' I think Carl wishes I would stand up for myself, fight back. He looks so disappointed in me.

'No, I just want to see,' David says. 'I'm sure you're very good,' he says to me, drawing out the words like you would to a child.

I get up from my desk and seize the hockey stick from him. I'm about to shove it back where it belongs, between my closet and the wall, and I'm feeling proud of myself, this is decisive action, it's masculine, but at the last minute I change my mind. I don't know what it is. The last vestiges of pride, maybe, the naive belief that I can prove myself to this person who does things like this to me every day. Maybe it's even cool-headed rationalism; there's nothing effeminate about hockey. It's brutal. The puck can do damage. And I'm not bad at it. Maybe David will admire me.

I swing the hockey stick through the space between us and the movement is firm and quick, but David has won. He shrieks with laughter. 'That's it, Princess, show us how it's done!' He swishes from my cubicle across the passageway, into the opposite cubicle and back, sure to attract a larger crowd with this foray into the public space. And gather they do. Teenage boys can't resist this. They smell blood.

David minces back and forth, hips popping, wrist limp.

I don't move like that, do I? I thought I had mastered their movements. I study them so closely. The weight distribution, the gait. Even standing in that way they all do on Sundays, in tracksuit pants, shoulders back with their hands in their pants, holding their dicks like kings. I've modified everything about how I present to the world so that I don't attract attention, and yet there must be something that gives me away. They can smell it on me. Is it my quietness?

I hold myself rigid but it's not enough to end this. I've been through it enough times to know that I need to be broken to satisfy him.

'Leave me alone,' I say, but my voice is trembling and even I want to hit me for the way I sound. What is this impulse to crush the weak?

'Don't tell me what to do,' David says. He steps closer and slaps my cheek. 'How's that,' he says. I'm frozen. I can't get a single word to form in my mouth.

'What about this?' he says, and he slaps my face again. The other cheek this time.

One last time, Carl tries to save me. He tells David they should finish their homework but he's half-hearted about it. He doesn't want to attract David's wrath either. No one wants to be in my position. When David ignores him, Carl simply leaves, so he doesn't have to see what comes next.

I try to take my seat, again, to pretend none of this is happening so I can get back to my homework, but David topples my chair as I'm sitting down and I fall onto the floor, the chair shooting off to the side.

'Since you're down there, Princess,' he says, and he pushes his crotch into my face. He lets out another shrill laugh, amazed at how easy it is to overpower me, to humiliate me.

'You'd like that, wouldn't you?'

I don't think I cry. I think I manage to hold it in, but my cheeks are so hot it feels as if my skin's on fire. There's laughter from a few of the boys. One or two grunts of disapproval, but no one intervenes. And the thing that makes me the most ashamed, and the most disgusted in myself, is that maybe I would like that.

'Do you know what it does to you?' I say to Emma. 'To be scared of someone, but desperate for their approval. I couldn't make their abuse stop no matter how nice I was to them. I had fantasies about these same people who hated me so much. I was ready to love them and they hated me for it. It made me believe everything they were saying – that I was twisted and perverse. I deserved their contempt.'

I almost say to Emma that I'm aroused, even now, recounting this, but I'm not ready to go into that, not yet, not with her. Down this path there is nothing but darkness and shame. Humiliation. Degradation. Fantasies about being tied up, drugged, surgery forced on me while I'm unconscious so that I wake up with a vagina that perfectly fits what these men want to do with me. So that I have what they really want.

And yet, I don't think that thirteen-year-old boy had these fantasies. I think he wanted to be tender with Carl, to love him and not for that love to be something worthy of disgust.

Back in the dorm, I pull myself under my desk. I wrap my arms around my knees. David prods me a few times with his foot, tries to topple me over again, but he's got what he came for. He laughs. 'I'm just kidding, you big baby,' he says. And the crowd disperses. That's one night down. Only fifty-eight to go until the end of the term, when I can go home.

I have to shake myself because my body is heavy and it feels like it might be dying. All the light is going out. 'Anyway, I don't want to talk about this. I'm just punishing myself and it's not going to help the issue at hand. I thought I was evil even before I realised I was gay. I was already afraid of myself by then.'

'You might have always known you were gay.'

'No, I mean when I was seven or eight. I started having night-mares then already, where I was possessed by an evil spirit. Before I was sexual.'

'We're sexual from birth.'

I roll my eyes, safe in the knowledge that she can't see my face. 'I know you're a Freudian, but that's a bit much, sorry. I wasn't sexual when I was seven.'

She waits.

'Although I do remember thinking that I wasn't supposed to play with the toys I played with. My favourites were My Little Pony. I don't know why boys weren't supposed to play with them, maybe because they're so beautiful and had perfumed tails? But I had the sense that it was wrong, even though my mom let me. She never dis-couraged me, but I knew. There were subtle clues everywhere. Dis-approving looks. I was doing something I shouldn't be doing.'

'You've told me how cold your father was with you after he'd left,' Emma says. 'How was he with you before he moved out?'

I have an early memory, surprisingly clear, of Dad coming home from work. I hear the front door open and I'm so excited I run down the stairs and jump, before I've even reached the bottom step, into his arms. The force of my leap knocks us both back against the door and he's laughing. He squeezes me tight and kisses me on the top of my head. I think about curling up in his arms in bed that night, or it might not have been that night, safe and happy while he reads me stories from a picture book he liked to read. I think about being tucked under his arm and then, because Emma has put Freud into my head, I think about how attractive I find that part of the male physique. The curvature of the muscles around the armpit. The hair where the muscles meet. It's so masculine. So powerful and beautiful. So safe.

I think I'm going to be sick. I swallow hard.

'No, you're right,' I say. 'He was very different. He was nice to me.'

'You loved him.'

That really makes me want to be sick. I take a deep, steadying breath.

Like those embarrassing, needy exes who never got the hint, who pine after someone who's left them, who never felt anything for them. 'I suppose so,' I say. I'm struggling to breathe, and so I shove my fingers into my ribs, trying to force some space between them.

'I don't know,' I say. 'It's all so murky the further back I go. Just shadows and dread. Maybe something did happen to me, but I don't know what it is.'

'That's okay,' Emma says.

'Maybe I was afraid of my own feelings?'

'I think we all are.'

I'm surprised to hear her voice, even though she's been speaking on and off throughout the session. It is surreal to be in a room, to be grounded in time and space. I shake my head and blink. The room holds its shape around me, solid in the swirling shadows.

'Please don't just assume it was sexual abuse,' I say.

'You may never know what it was. You may never be able to explain it, but you need to be able to feel it.'

'I've built my whole life around avoiding this feeling,' I say.

'I know,' she says, 'but the only way out is through.'

96

# 12.

'Don't forget, it's Buhle's birthday next week,' Sibs says to me on my way out to the car.

'Okay.'

'Don't forget. It's on Friday.'

'You already told me last month,' I snap. 'I saved it in the calendar on my phone.'

I can hear the chorus of old white people in my head. The Ones I Will Never Be Like. *This is what happens when there are no boundaries,* they say. *This is what you get for letting your maid think she is your friend. You're her employer and she's bossing you around. Demanding a present for her daughter. Who does she think she is?*

Whose voice *is* that? Where did I even hear these things? Perhaps it is not a chorus of other voices, but the ugly part of my own mind. I think of my niece, Lily, saying to me once that 'someone' had weed in her pants. She was outraged. Who could have done such a thing?

'I haven't forgotten,' I say to Sibs, gently this time.

I try out a new voice in my head: Emma's. *There's no point denying uncharitable feelings,* she says. *There's no point pretending they don't happen. We have little control over our subconscious mind, and denial and repression only give those negative feelings more power. Thoughts are not the same as actions. If you have bad thoughts, you are not a bad person. You can have bad thoughts. Everyone does. What makes you a bad person is whether you act on them or not.*

So there's no point trying to pretend to myself that the reason I'm annoyed is that I already knew the date and I don't like being told something I already know. That's not it, even if I'd prefer that interpretation. I am annoyed because I wanted Sibs to be grateful, and maybe surprised, when I gave her a gift for Buhle. I wanted her to think I'm a generous person, an unusually kind person. Maybe I even wanted grovelling and effusiveness in her thanks. Not for all of this to be expected, assumed, taken for granted. I decide to let the ugliness rise up, my mean-spiritedness, like the sewage that I can still smell in the pipes on bad days. I won't look away. I'll look right at it, into its festering centre, and I will try to trust that it won't possess me. It will pass. Isn't that what happens in psychology literature? The all-powerful shadow that chases us turns out to be a small, hurt, afraid little boy when we finally face him. He can't turn me into a monster if I hear him. If I let him speak and I listen and I hold him and I understand why he feels like he does. It makes no sense to be possessed by myself.

Why does he feel so aggrieved when his kindness is taken for granted?

I buy Buhle a doll for her birthday, and I have fun shopping for it. In my fantasies about my daughter, I'm not only changing the world by raising a happy, loved and well-adjusted human being, breaking the chains of intergenerational trauma by working my stuff out in therapy and demonstrating a path of interracial understanding and love in this country where that is still so rare; I'm changing the retail and cultural landscape too – supporting black-owned, local small businesses, buying isiXhosa picture books and stories that centre strong black female leads, and insisting on black-is-beautiful toys. It bothered me as a kid, long before I thought of having a child of my own, that so many childhood references are white. White dolls. White

Disney princesses. Even here, in Southern Africa, shops paint snow-flakes in their windows for Christmas. Christmas, which falls slap bang in the middle of summer. Over the years I've been building up a collection of African Christmas ornaments. Felt angels with Afros and dark skin. Shweshwe wraps. Beaded stars. Woven raffia stars. The tree each year is local. Driftwood from the beach, or acacia branches or *Widdringtonia cedarbergensis*.

I know where to go to find Buhle the perfect doll. There's a woman who sells them on Greenmarket Square. She sews them together from cuts of cloth and felt. They are soft toys, not hard plastic dolls. The one I choose is about thirty centimetres tall, with braids for hair, skin the colour of espresso, an indigo skirt and a white T-shirt with a wink-ing, kissing emoji in the centre.

'What is it?' Sibs says when I hand her the parcel, lovingly wrapped in expensive paper with a local artist's illustration of Camps Bay beach printed on it.

'It's a doll,' I say. Sibs wrinkles her nose as if she's trying to work out if the milk in her tea has soured.

'Okay.'

The thanks that I give myself in my head, at least, is bright and enthusiastic.


The next time I see Sibs she tells me that Buhle loves the doll. She has been playing with it all morning.

'That's good,' I say. 'It looked like you didn't think she would.'

We're standing in the street. Again, I'm on my way out to work. Sibs is on her way in. A big, dramatic wig today. Black ringlets, fading to light brown at the tips.

'I was scared,' she says, 'when you gave it to me that it was a white doll.'

'You know, Sibs, some people might be offended to hear that.'

She laughs, loudly, and winks at me. 'Ya, but not you.'

'I wouldn't have bought her that,' I say.

Sibs narrows her eyes. A conspiratorial grin on her face. 'You know,' she says, 'Buhle doesn't know any white people.'

'She's met me!' I say, but Sibs isn't finished.

'I have a white doll at home that I bought her when she was younger, and she's so scared of it. I use it to scare her when I need her to do something. As soon as I bring it out, she starts crying. I chase her with it, it's too much.' She's really laughing now, tears forming in the corners of her eyes. She waves the phantom white doll in my face and widens her eyes. Wiggles her arms and galumphs her whole body in a kind of comedic, menacing dance. A big bad creature coming to get me.

'Shame, that's not nice,' I say, laughing in spite of myself.

'What?'

And I'm not even sure what I mean. The cruelty of using your own daughter's fears against her, or the fact that it's a white doll that's a monster?

I don't want to have this conversation, but I can't just walk away.

'Does she really not know any white people?' I say. I feel embarrassed whenever international friends visit Cape Town for the first time – friends from America, or Europe – because of how disproportionately white the city seems. The restaurants we visit. The beaches. I can see them thinking, isn't this supposed to be Africa?

It's one of the few things I miss about Joburg. The normality of being a minority. The relief from this cognitive dissonance.

'Sorry, neh,' Sibs says. 'Are you offended?'

'No, I'm fine.'

'She likes the one you bought her. It's very nice.'

'Great.'

'Come to her birthday party this weekend.'

'Sibs, you really don't need to invite me to that. It's fine.'

'No, I want you to come.'

We watch each other for a moment. I think we're about to do something neither of us wants to do.

'I'd love to,' I say. 'Thanks.'

# 13.

Buhle's party is to be at the Company's Garden. Sibs has told me before how much she loves it there. The greenery. The dappled shade. Buhle loves to watch the ducks, apparently. I couldn't think of anywhere less like the townships – hot, dry, sandy and overcrowded – and it makes me feel heavy. I suppose at least the Gardens are free to enter. A genuine public space, unlike the rest of the country where safe public spaces are private, sterile shopping malls. Fluorescent lighting. Right of Admission Reserved.

I persuade Adrian to join me even though he thinks it will be awkward, and we walk down to the Company's Garden with Frasier. Buhle liked Frasier, I remember. And he loves any outing. He's making friends before we even reach the party. Three different groups of people stop us on our walk down Government Avenue so they can say hello to him. He jumps up as soon as the attention is turned on him. He wiggles his tightly curled donut tail.

We find Sibs up towards the top of the park, the less beautiful end near the National Gallery and the Iziko Museum. It's not as lush and overgrown here. There are none of the ancient trees that she told me she loves, so it's a strange choice, and she looks irritable when we arrive. She has three friends with her, all women, and there are two extra children beside Buhle in the group, all of them just sitting on the grass, and the adults are talking loudly. I can't understand a word because my isiXhosa isn't good enough for complex sentences and certainly not for sentences being spoken at this speed, but Sibs's body language and tone seem angry. She doesn't wave when we arrive, or smile at me. She looks up at me like she's waiting to hear what I have to say for myself, a deep frown fixed on her forehead.

'We brought a cake!' I say, and Adrian presents the box he's been carrying with a theatricality that is unlike him. It's unconvincing and self-conscious, and I have to look away.

Frasier runs at the children and all of them but Buhle scream. I pull on his leash and he whiplashes backwards. I pick him up and hold him under my arm. We brought a picnic blanket with us, but no one else is sitting on a picnic blanket, so it feels like a wealthy, out-of-touch thing to do. I drop the blanket, still folded in its carrier, on the grass and I sit down beside it. I put Frasier on my lap. Adrian sits beside me. His eyes move from the picnic blanket to me and back to the picnic blanket, and he smiles at me, but he says nothing.

Adrian and I introduce ourselves to everyone. I forget their names as soon as I hear them.

'It's beautiful here,' I say, and two of the women nod and mumble something that sounds like assent.

There is a long silence. I take Adrian's hand. I don't know if these women know that we're gay. I think they'll probably disapprove. But I need the contact to get through this. I want to ask Sibs what's wrong, but Adrian's always telling me there's nothing wrong when I feel like this. Nobody hates me. It's my anxiety. I read too much into everything.

'Happy Birthday, Buhle!' he says, turning to the kids. 'Do you want some cake?'

I'm so relieved to have something to do. I help him slice the cake and distribute the slices on little paper plates that we brought with us. I squeeze Frasier, and try to keep him from eating the cake as I pass it along.

103

'Are you having a nice day?' I ask Buhle, but she doesn't respond. She shovels cake into her mouth like it's very serious business. Gone, our little breakthrough in the pharmacy aisle a few weeks ago.

'No,' Sibs says. 'There was a man in the bushes down there.' She waves her hand towards the lower part of the park, where I thought we would find them. 'He was watching us.'

'What do you mean?'

'No, he was watching and watching. And then I want to say to him he mustn't watch us because he's making us feel uncomfortable and when I go to the bushes to talk to him, he has his penis in his hand and he is shaking it and touching it and he won't stop even when I'm there. He goes even faster when I get close to him.'

Sibs's friends click their tongues and shake their heads.

'Oh my god,' I say, 'did you call the police?'

Sibs watches me through narrow eyes.

'Do you think this is normal?' she says.

'What do you mean, do I think it's normal? Of course it's not normal.'

'Ya, I think maybe he is a crazy person.'

'Definitely.'

She laughs, suddenly, and it's almost as jarring as the story she's just told me. 'No,' she says, 'because you know white people are too polite. How can he do that and everyone thinks it's fine? There were lots of people there, but no one stopped him. They just look away. If he was doing that in the location we would beat him. He wouldn't do that.'

'We would beat him!' reiterates one of the others.

I try to laugh. I think that's the reaction I'm supposed to have. I'm trapped by this declaration about white people. If I said what I really think about vigilante justice, Sibs would think that's 'too polite' and maybe she's right. Maybe it relies on the assumption that there are other kinds of justice available; that the police will protect you. And I think that if I lived in a shack, in a dark, ignored part of the city, terrified all the time, I would also want my neighbours to help me feel safe.

'Was Buhle okay?' I say. 'Did she see it?'

Sibs stops laughing. I feel as whiplashed as Frasier, trying to make sense of her emotions. 'I don't think she knew what was happening, so it's fine, but it made me very angry. I shouted at him.'

'Did you hit him?' I say, trying to get in on the joke, I suppose, and she clicks her tongue in irritation. Shakes her head. I've clearly missed the point.

'Do you want us to report him to the police?' Adrian says.

'You would do that?'

'He can't be allowed to expose himself. Especially in front of children.'

Sibs thinks about this for a second. She confers with her friends. 'No,' she says. 'It's fine. We must just have a nice day now. We are far away from where he was.'

Two of Sibs's friends start talking to each other in isiXhosa and one of them laughs and claps her hands and it seems the moment of tension has passed, that they have processed whatever anger needed to be felt, but now it feels like it's me, somehow, who has done something wrong. I am from the same foreign place as the man in the bushes. I am alien to these women, bizarre and incomprehensible, and the only reason they tolerate me is that I pay their friend's salary.

'Do you want to go see the ducks?' Adrian says to Buhle, and I wish I had said it – I know she likes ducks; Sibs told me that – but Buhle stares at Adrian blankly, with white icing all over her lips. Sibs, taking pity on us at last, translates his words and Buhle smiles at him. She so seldom smiles, this solemn child, and it's never the smile I expect. It's compact, narrow for her face, dazzling. Adrian stands up and Buhle sticks her hand out, ready to be led to the pond. 'Awww,' he squeals, grinning at me like he did the first time Frasier fell asleep in his lap.

'Can I come?'

'Of course, man. Grab a vetkoek.'

I look at the small spread of snacks that Sibs and her friends have brought. A clear plastic bag with vetkoeks in it. Two small, empty packets of chips. Five or six sweets – Fizzers, hard candy, fruit gums. The kind of food you get from those vendors on the side of the road at the train station, or on Adderley Street. Maybe there was more before we got here. The kids could have eaten some of it? But I don't see any wrappers. I try to communicate to Adrian, with only my eyes, that we can't raid their snacks. I hope I am conveying to him that this meagre selection of snacks is all Sibs can afford as celebratory birthday food, that she would have paid for this because she loves her daughter and wants her to have a happy day, but it was a sacrifice, and it's insensitive to waste this food on ducks. My eyes are not able to communicate any of this, unsurprisingly, and so Adrian repeats himself and points at the vetkoek. It would be even more insulting to drag out this reticence, to draw attention to the fact that I think of Sibs as poor, and so I reach into the plastic bag, avoiding eye contact with any of the adults, and I retract a vetkoek to take with us to the pond.

I try to match Adrian and Buhle's glacial, dawdling pace. It's a struggle, with Frasier pulling as hard as he can to get wherever we're going. I distract him a few times by dropping onto my haunches, so that he turns back and comes to get showered in affection. He turns on Buhle then, licking her and rubbing against her, and she giggles and puts out her free hand for balance, or to pat him, maybe, but he's too fast for her developing motor coordination, so if she is trying to pat him, she misses, but she is delighted by his attention. Her usually serious face is squished into the brightest smile, and she giggles and squawks and tries to chase after him when he loses interest and sets off again towards the pond.

At the pond, Adrian is amazing with Buhle. No surprises there. He's the same with Lily and Simon. Throwing them in the air when they're in the pool together. Playing dress-up and making potions from leaves and soil. Even with the language barrier, he and Buhle have fun together. He walks Buhle to the edge of the water nearest the ducks. They dip their hands in the water together. He breaks off a bit of vetkoek and throws it into the water, then breaks off another bit and hands it to Buhle to do the same. He coaches her with another mimed demonstration and then she hurls. She's a poor shot. The piece of vetkoek flies off at a wide angle, but the ducks follow it, and so she screams with excitement and tries again.

'Do you want to try it with her?' Adrian says to me, and his eyes are warm and kind, but I can't bear it. I can't bear the pity. I can't bear feeling so inept at all of this. What if she doesn't want to do it with me? What if she cries as soon as I take over from him? She'll want her mother again. She'll want Adrian. Anyone but me. I don't know how to be this fun, easy-going, natural person who's great with kids. They can see through the act.

I shake my head, and even as I'm doing it, I'm hating myself for doing it.

I need to get home. Away from these people.

'Let's go,' I say.

Adrian sighs and nods. 'Sure,' he says.

I've dragged him here against his will and now I've let him down again, but he's endlessly patient. I know he won't say I've done anything wrong. He'll take his sadness and he'll wrap it up tight inside himself.

We deliver Buhle back to her mom. Sibs and her friends break their animated conversation to say goodbye. They must be so relieved we are going.

# 14.

It's time to learn isiXhosa. The adoption agency has all but guaranteed we will get a black baby, so we can't leave it too late. It's also ridiculous that I can't communicate with Buhle. When I'm with her, I feel like an alien. I need to try, again. Si-zo-zama. I still have a few of the grammar and exercise books from the first time I tried it. They're at the bottom of a box at the back of the closet in the guest room. They've been there since before we left for New York, undisturbed by the tenants who lived here while we were away.

I ask Sibs if she'd like to teach us. She can talk us through the books I already own. Explain any questions we may have. I'd rather the money go to her than to some night class at the university.

I invite my friend Tshego to join Adrian and me. She moved down to Cape Town from Joburg at about the time we returned from the US, and she's struggling to pick up isiXhosa, too. 'I've never felt so white,' she told me last week over a glass of wine on Bree Street. 'The last time I was here, a beggar asked me for money and I didn't have any, and nor did any of the people I was with, and they were all white, so the old man tried to backchannel with me separately – I think he was appealing to our shared experience and oppression – and I didn't even know what he was saying.'

She's already a polyglot. Speaks Setswana with her family, can understand Sesotho and Sepedi, and grasps the basics of isiZulu. Her English is perfect. But she doesn't get enough practice with isiXhosa.

roblem,' she tells me, 'is the black middle class of this city could fit in my living room.' She's made variations of this joke before: 'I can't get sick. If I don't come to your party, I'm setting Cape Town integration back a generation'; 'Babes, I'm already a quorum'; 'Oh, you think just because I'm black I'll know your other black friend? Well, I have news for you – of course I know them.'

There's a similar joke about gay men. Outrage and incredulity if straight people assume we'll know their other gay friend – it's homophobic, we're not all the same, we don't all know each other, we have nothing in common etc. etc. – until we see a picture. *Oh, that bitch.*

'Why are you laughing?' she says.

'No, it's nothing.'

Tshego knows much more than Adrian or I do. There are no desks and there aren't enough of us for rows, but if there were, she'd be at the front of the class. She grasps the basic principles of noun classes and how the prefix of every word in the sentence needs to change according to the noun class. She can count to twenty. Her vocabulary is better-than-basic, although Sibs does have to correct her a few times because she's using the isiZulu word and it's not quite the same. We meet in our living room every second Thursday after work. We set ourselves homework assignments and Sibs tells us if we've got them right. Sibs is nervous, though, and uncharacteristically shy. She can't explain why our sentences aren't right if they don't sound right to her ear, but instead of getting frustrated, we decide on a new approach. We'll leave the grammar to the professionals: textbooks and teach-yourself audio courses. Only every second class will be with Sibs – and for that, we start doing story hour.

I find a bunch of illustrated Xhosa-language children's books at a nearby indie bookstore. Ages 3+ and 5+. There's the one with a little girl, Mpumi, on the cover, and together we learn what kinds of things she likes to eat (it's watermelon on the cover; ujodo.) There's the little girl astronaut. There's the story of the little girl who keeps asking animals if she's small. It only takes us reading one of these books to realise we're at the same level as Buhle. And so I order duplicates of each book for Buhle.

I want to ask Sibs to bring Buhle into our lessons. We could read to her, and practise our pronunciation, but I remember Tshego's desperation at our braai ('Everyone's either gay or pregnant,' she cried, reaching for the gin.) She needs this to be a child-free space, so I don't invite Buhle to join us. I give a copy of each book to Sibs at the start of the lesson. I just have to hope she'll read the stories to Buhle when she gets home.

# 15.

I try to time my arrival at the bus stop to the minute, but this isn't Switzerland or Japan. The bus is never on time. It's either early and I've missed it, or it groans up from the harbour ten minutes late. I hate waiting for it when it's late, and I almost don't. I almost decide to walk home, but it's been a long day at work and I'm going to have to do some more work when I get home. A campaign we came up with for Volkswagen isn't getting the kind of user engagement we anticipated. The social media is a mess.

At the bus stop, I try not to make eye contact with the beggars lurking in my peripheral vision, but I can't help myself. It's a human impulse, I think, but what is it? The urge for connection, to show that I come in peace, I mean no harm, I wish they weren't so lonely in their suffering? Or is it a kind of permission I seek? I know if I ignore them they'll leave me alone, but what kind of person ignores this suffering? So I smile at them and they read my smile as an invitation to approach. The old man with a cane and a clouded-over eye is here, as he often is. He comes and stands right next to me. He stares at me and doesn't say a word. I fumble around in my wallet, which I hate doing among people, especially here on bloody Loop Street, and hand him a twenty. I withdraw cash especially for beggars and car-guards, since I don't use cash for anything else any more; I use my phone at restaurants, bars, even official city street parking attendants accept contactless payment. The old man doesn't thank me.

He just moves on to the next person. I have a sudden urge to snatch it back.

Is it his hopelessness that makes me so angry?

The young mother approaches next. She's also often here, appearing out of nowhere whenever passengers start to coalesce at the bus stop. I stare at the ground, at the neat rectangle of orange brickwork that delineates the bus stop from the grey, tarred pavement, but she taps me on the shoulder. 'Please,' she says, 'can you buy me something to eat.'

She's so thin, her body is almost that of a child, but her face is in its twenties. She has long black hair in a tangled ponytail, walnut-brown skin, exhausted, hooded eyes. Sometimes she has her daughter with her, a little girl of about five who gets dragged up and down the street by her hand without complaining but today, the mother is alone.

'Please,' she says again, and I want to yell at her, tell her to leave me alone, but her voice is soft and sad and it makes my eyes sting.

'Come,' I say to her and she follows me into the little corner shop. I buy her a chicken pie, an apple and a bottle of water. I want to buy sweets for her daughter, a chocolate bar or bag of Skittles, but my mind trips on itself as I think about how poor their nutrition must be and how I should buy her daughter something healthy like one of those little punnets of carrot and cucumber crudités with hummus in the centre, but the truth is I want the daughter to feel delighted by the treat, not just to eat something that's good for her health, and who am I to presume I can tell her what to give her daughter? So I end up not buying anything for the little girl. The mother is grateful all the same. She clasps her hands and offers a real, relieved smile.

She's already nibbling on the edges of the pastry, cautious to avoid burning her mouth on the hot gravy inside, when I step outside the shop and see the back of the bus.

'Fuck!' I say, and she startles. I lift my palm in apology.

I walk home via the Company's Garden. I turn right beneath the archway and walk up the tree-lined avenue, past the bust of the Great White Queen, Victoria, set between the roses, and Parliament to my left. The park itself is to my right, the National Library, the cathedral. It's a busy pedestrian thoroughfare, especially now, when businesses are closing for the day and workers are rushing through the park to catch trains and minibus taxis to take them back to the townships. A busker plays saxophone beneath an old oak tree. Squirrels dart across my path. There are homeless people on the benches along the avenue, sleeping, somehow, through all the commotion.

I head uphill until I reach the National Gallery, where I turn left down a side alley towards St Johns Street. It's here I realise I've made a mistake. The crowds disappear. There's no one in the alley but the vagrants asleep against the wall. I accelerate towards the next large road. St Johns Street is deserted, too. No pedestrians, only cars. The quality of light has changed. The sky is pallid. The shadows, colourless. Dread courses through me again, cold and black, but I tell myself it's only my anxiety. I'll never be free of it, but I can learn to live with it. I try to slow my breathing. I remember my mother's words from the front of the car. If you think you're being followed, don't stop. Take a zigzag route home. There are no AK-47s in Cape Town, at least not in this part of Cape Town. This is a different time, a different world. It's a memory, not a premonition.

I take the next left into Vrede Street.

'Hey buddy,' someone says, 'can you spare some money?'

He's right beside me, though I can't understand how that happened. There was no one there a second ago.

'Sorry,' I say, 'I'm in a rush.'

I keep walking and he falls in step beside me. 'Please,' he says, 'just five rand.'

114

'No,' I say. 'I don't have anything on me.'

I walk a little faster and he walks a little faster, too.

'Hey, man, do you live nearby? It's a nice neighbourhood,' he says. 'Come on, just a little something. Just so I can eat.'

Where is everyone? How can the streets be this quiet during rush hour? I get the sudden, absurd idea that he's a kind of sorcerer, an all-powerful underworld being. He's changed the light. He's emptied the city of people so that he can isolate me.

I look at him and I've seen his face before. This malicious smile, these dark, alert eyes. He's done this to me before. This exact thing, and the memory sends the hairs rippling upwards on my arms. He's good-looking, too; it's what makes the fear even more alarming. Olive brown skin, sharp jawline, thick black eyebrows. I would have tried to catch his eye if I'd seen him in a bar when I was single. I would have swiped right if I'd seen him on the apps, and waited, hopefully, too nervous to make the first move.

'Look,' he says, 'don't make me do something I'll regret.'

He stops in front of me, blocks my path. He's no longer smiling.

'I've been to prison before,' he says. 'You believe me? You think I've killed someone?'

It's the tear tattoo that means that, isn't it? That he's killed before. He moves his hand into his oversized blazer. It was navy once, I think, but it's hard to tell beneath the dust and grime. It's tattered, frayed on the cuffs and lapel. Metal glints in his hand. It's obscured by a dirty rag wrapped around the handle, but the blade is unmistakable.

He looks up and down the street before stepping so close to me that I think, for a second, he might kiss me.

# 16.

'I don't know how to feel about it,' I say to Emma. 'I know why he did it. I understand. It's not his fault. No one wants to beg or live on the street. He's not a bad person. He's desperate and I get it. What choice do people even have? I have somewhere to sleep at night, I have a home and food. It's pure random luck to be born into the families and situations we're born into. I don't understand people who get defensive about privilege, as if they somehow earned it before they were born.'

'You don't feel angry?'

'I never feel angry,' I say, but I realise while I'm saying it that it isn't true. I often feel angry, but I force it down. I've only noticed this since starting analysis. There's a split-second of fury before my instincts kick in and make it disappear. I remember the rage after coming off my meds in New York. The hot flush of anger, out of nowhere, that made me think I was losing my mind. It was so out of character. Like I'd been possessed by a vindictive spirit.

'I don't know what's wrong with me,' I say. 'I don't have the impulse to defend myself. I know there are people out there who respond to being mugged by wanting to beat the shit out of the person who's attacking them. And I've always thought that's so stupid – the guy could have a knife or a gun, and it's such a pathetic display of bravado – but actually I think I'm envious of that reaction. All I ever do is cower and hide. At school, the more the boys mocked me, the more obsequious I became, as if I could stop them hurting me by being extra nice.'

'I bet you were very nice to the mugger, too.'

I want to pull my skin right off when she says that.

'It's not even fight or flight for me. I just freeze.'

'That's the third option no one knows about. It's fight, flight, or freeze. The body's response to danger. You see it in animals, too. It's sort of like playing dead.'

'So it's normal? I'm not missing something?'

'It's a survival mechanism.'

'I wish I didn't have such a cowardly survival mechanism.'

'You know what this makes me think of?' Emma says, and I watch her as she says, 'Your parents' divorce.'

This is unlike her, this therapist trope, trying to make everything about my childhood. What does being mugged have to do with my parents' divorce?

'You don't allow yourself to own your pain.'

'What?'

'You're trying to only see the mugger's point of view. You're probably right about his life, but what about you? What about your truth, your feelings? They're there, even if you don't want them to be, even if they're in conflict with his. You won't let yourself get angry at your mother, either.'

'Are you kidding? What's there to get angry about?' I can hear the irritation in my voice but it doesn't matter any more. Maybe I'm irritated enough to let her know it. Maybe that's growth. I watch the bare branches out of the window and I listen to the oil heater click and hum. Emma's rooms are freezing in winter, dark and damp, but already they feel safe, a refuge from my life.

'I hate the way people always think divorce is bad for kids. It's better

117

to have happy, single parents than unhappy married ones who fight all the time.'

'And were they? Happy single parents?'

It's so ready to rise into my consciousness – the endless sleeping. The dark bedroom. The silence. 'When you first told me about it, you said your mother was "broken".'

'It took her years to recover,' I say, and then, because I can't trust these memories any more, they seem to come from another realm where time and causation are slippery and distorted, I add, 'or it felt like that, anyway.'

'That's your whole childhood.'

The last weeks of my father's life are right here, too, in this room. Him fighting to stay awake. The way he looked at me at the end, a week before he died, the light sparkling in his deep brown eyes, when he told me I was 'magnificent'. After he was gone, people I'd never met reached out to tell me how proud he was of me, and I thought they must have mistaken me for my brother, or for one of his newer children, the British family, maybe Grace, whom he adored. The daughters he had always wanted. But then they'd mention something specific about my life and I knew they weren't mixing me up with anyone. He was proud of me. He loved me. He'd told anyone who would listen. How could I have wasted our time together? How could I have misunderstood so much?

'Sorry,' I say.

'Why are you sorry?'

I don't even know. They're blurring into one experience now, one terrible loss, twenty years apart. 'I don't want to talk about my dad,' I say. I spent so much time talking about him with previous therapists and I never got anywhere. I just went round and round and I never felt any less angry with him. I still feel so angry with him, even now that I know that how he treated me in those years after the divorce wasn't because he hated me, and that I became complicit in our failed relationship, in the dance we got trapped in, aloof and defensive with each other even though it's what neither of us wanted. I never saw the ways he tried to make up for how he'd been when I was young, even though it should have been obvious, he tried so hard, and now it's too late to fix anything, he's gone, and maybe I put all the anger from my life into him. More anger than he deserved. He was the one person I could feel angry towards. I knew that he could take it.

'I thought we were talking about your mom,' Emma says.

'I don't want to talk about any of this,' I say, and I'm crying now, in spite of myself. 'It's ancient history and I want to talk about being mugged.'

But Emma is silent for a long time and it's too late, now; I can feel my mother's grief rippling towards me from the shadows. A black, suffocating smoke.

'She felt so humiliated, you know, on top of feeling betrayed. I think she thought everyone knew about the affair.'

'I'm sure it was very difficult for her. How was it for you?'

It's hard to separate her sadness from my own. Whose feelings are these?

I remember knocking on her bedroom door in the middle of the afternoon. Her soft voice calls 'Come in', and I open the door to darkness. Blackout curtains drawn. The smell of rose soap and endless sleep. She sits up in bed and forces a smile for me and clears a space on her bedside table for the mug of tea that I've made her.

'Thank you, my darling,' she says. Her face is gaunt. Sandy-blond hair pressed flat against the side of her head. Her blue irises look grey in this light, colourless against the dark circles beneath her eyes. 'You're very sweet.'

'I'll take care of you, Mom,' I say and she takes my hand over the covers and squeezes it, tries to smile. 'Thank you, my love, but that's not your job.' And maybe I do feel a brief flash of rage because what's the point of these empty words? What's the point of saying I don't have to take care of her when she's wasting away like this? I have to keep her alive, but nothing I can do is enough to bring back the light that was inside her. She tries to look happy to see me, but I'm not fooled. There's no joy when she looks at me.

'She loved me,' I say to Emma, 'and she tried so fucking hard to be okay. As hard as she could. You know sometimes you give it your all and your all is not enough. You still can't cope. You're still over-whelmed. I feel like that myself, often, so how can I hold it against her?'

Back in Mom's bedroom, I want to beg her not to die. To get up. *Please, please don't hurt yourself* . . . But I can't let on that I'm scared. I have to be okay. She can't worry about me on top of all of this. It would be too much for her.

I look at the big vase of bright spring flowers in the fireplace. They're plastic, here since we moved into this house, and they are coated in a thin grey film of sticky dust.

'I'm almost finished my homework,' I say.

'Clever boy.'

She hasn't touched the tea I brought her.

'I think we're having spaghetti tonight,' I say.

'You go ahead, I'm not hungry.'

'It's bolognaise, your favourite. I asked Patience to make it for you.'

'I think I'll just get some rest.'

'I can bring you a bowl in bed?'

'I'm really not hungry.'

'You must have felt so powerless,' Emma says.

'She loved me,' I say. Emma waits. I feel that gratitude all over again, the relief that at least one of my parents loved me. It makes my eyes sting, even now. 'She was just so unbelievably sad.'

'And what about you?'

'It wasn't about me!' Why is this so hard for Emma to see? This isn't my story. This was between the two of them. 'They told me many times that none of this had anything to do with me.'

'And did it feel like that?'

'That's what you're supposed to tell your child if you split up. What else could they have done? It's model behaviour. It stops the kid feeling responsible.'

'I think you felt responsible all the same.'

There's a great weight on my chest. I shift onto my side to ease it, and I watch the sky for a moment out of Emma's window. I'm tripped up by my own words, because even though I've always said that this was their stuff, their fallout, it only now feels like I could ever start to believe it: they behaved that way because they were both so unhappy, not because I'd done anything wrong.

'Where was your brother in all of this?'

'Oh, he was long gone. He's much older than me. He was at university in Cape Town by then.'

'So you were alone.'

It isn't a question and I don't need to answer it.

'Maybe here, in these sessions,' Emma says, 'let's not think about it from anyone's point of view but yours. You're right that she was trying her best, that she loved you – that's all true. Go ahead and hold on to that. But you were also scared by her depression. It was traumatic for you, just like your father's sudden anger towards you. They both completely changed. You're so worried about blame and finding fault and being fair, but this isn't about fault or blame, it's about acknowledging what you went through, because you can't heal if you're in denial. It wasn't her fault. Depression. Grief. They're nobody's fault. But that doesn't mean it didn't affect you. The mugger's life is probably hopeless, as you say, but you're allowed to be angry that he pulled a knife on you. You felt things even if you didn't think you had a right to feel them, even if you didn't want to feel them. You tell yourself you don't feel these things, but you do. And these feelings will never go away unless you allow yourself to feel them. Pushing them down doesn't work.'

I feel something stir in my chest. A flutter in the muscles, a swelling.

'That's so selfish,' I say.

'Is that so terrible?' There's a pause, and then she says, 'You say you never feel angry, but I think you were angry with your mother for falling apart.'

'What kind of monster would feel angry with someone in so much pain?'

'Children need their parents. It doesn't make them monsters.'

'I'm not angry,' I say.

'Okay, maybe we're not there yet.'

'I never wanted to grow up to be like my dad. He was angry, and his anger ruined our lives. I refused to let myself become a typical man like that.'

'What is a typical man?'

I don't even have to think. 'Selfish,' I say, 'cold, and quick to anger.'

'That's quite a thing to believe as a little boy. When you're destined to grow up to be a man.'

Yet again, it isn't a question and I don't have to say anything. I let the strangeness of the description settle on my skin. Man. I've never thought of myself as a man. A 'Man'. It's a foreign word. What does it even mean, aside from all the toxic traits I've spent my life running away from? Strength, maybe. Maybe a kind of strength that isn't the same as violence. I shake myself. It's all wrong. It's a label for other people.

'And so you crushed any negative feelings before they could emerge,' Emma says.

'I guess I must have.'

'You've said before you believed you were evil,' Emma says. 'I think you felt evil because your parents abandoned you. You thought your need for them is what drove them away.

'Children always think it's their fault,' Emma continues. 'Always.'

There's a strange, tingling sensation throughout my body, as if dead flesh is coming alive again. I start to laugh. I turn from my view out of the window and I face Emma. 'My anxiety can't be about their divorce,' I say. 'How embarrassing is that? Everyone gets divorced. Especially in the nineties! What an overreaction to have all these disorders because of something so ordinary, so long ago?'

Emma says nothing. I watch the clock. Five minutes until the end of the session and I can't face feeling any of the things I've just felt again.

'I've always thought I was fine about all of this. The divorce didn't affect me. I even got irritated when people pitied me for having divorced parents. So much for knowing myself.'

'I don't think you experienced a divorce,' Emma says. 'I think that little boy felt like he'd been orphaned.'

# 17.

Sibs is in a good mood on Tuesday. I hear her music long before she unlocks the front door – gqom blasting from her cellphone, tinny and reverberated, louder with every step she takes up the street. She removes her enormous, red-rimmed Jackie O sunglasses and squints into the darkness of the house. She has on a blonde wig today, a voluminous bob of tight golden ringlets.

I wave at her from the kitchen where I'm finishing my bowl of muesli and she smiles and offers all the standard greetings, as far as I can tell – How are you? How's Frasier? How's Adrian? I have to lip-read because I can't hear a word she's saying over the music which she leaves playing in her hand. It's an older, but less-severely cracked, model of cellphone than the one she had last week. A different brand, too.

'Another new number?' I shout over the music.

She laughs and picks up an unopened utility bill from the stack by the front door, writes a number on the back of it, and hands it to me. 'But you can keep the other one. I still use that one too,' she says. There must be at least five different phone numbers saved in my phone under 'Sibs'. It's a fun game guessing which ones are in use and which are defunct whenever I need to get hold of her.

'Did you have a nice weekend?' I ask and finally she turns off the music. She removes her wig and hangs it on a picture hook in the hallway. I love that she hangs her wigs there whenever she arrives in one. Adrian and I have thought about hanging some art on that lonely hook – we even tried out a small acrylic painting of the shipwreck near Llandudno – but it didn't spark joy the way the pixie cuts, the severe, angular bobs, and the mounds of ringlets do. It's Sibs's hook. An ever-changing exhibition of glamorous furry animals.

'Uh uh,' she says, shaking her head. 'Yhu, it was not a nice weekend, I can't lie.'

'I'm sorry. What happened?'

Sibs takes a seat at the dining table, very businesslike, and I brace myself for what I know is coming. She's going to ask to borrow money. I'm already annoyed. I pay her more than average to clean for us. I'm also paying her to teach us isiXhosa. And yet this won't be the first time she's asked to borrow money. She's asked many times in the last few months and she never pays it back, and I said to her the last time it was coming out of her salary but I couldn't bring myself to follow through and deduct it, because who could survive on her salary? She only works for us once a week, and I think she only has one other couple whom she cleans for, so she isn't earning five times what I pay her. She's probably not even earning twice what I pay her because I bet her other employers don't pay her the same. People are disappointing, and they're especially disappointing when they are given a bit of power over others. Nothing distributes power more unevenly than our unemployment rate.

'Listen, Sibs, it's not a good time—'

'I want to leave my husband,' she says.

I take a seat opposite her at the table. 'Oh god.'

'Is it bad?'

'No, not at all. Tell me.'

'He's not nice, you know. He doesn't work, he has no job, but then

125

he still expects me to make the food, to buy the groceries, to look after Buhle. Everything.'

'What does he do?'

'Nothing.' She clicks her tongue. 'That's what I'm saying. Even when he's at home all day and I have to come to work, he still thinks I must make food. And he's like this for a long time. He was a waiter before, but he lost his job a long time ago and he doesn't even look any more.'

As always, I don't know how to respond. It seems pretty mean-spirited to hold unemployment against him when half the working-age population of the country is unemployed, but then I'd probably also be annoyed if I were married to him. Get off your ass, guy, or at least help with the housework and raising your kid.

'Everyone says it's normal,' Sibs says. 'I'm the wife so I must do it and not ask questions.'

I remember before I left for New York, when Sibs was going to marry him. She didn't seem excited. She felt pressured by her family. But it was none of my business.

'Who says that, Sibs?'

She looks as if I've scolded her, and I feel the chasm yawn between us, the genuine difference in experience that is so difficult to bridge, especially when the thoughts that flare in my mind – this is about culture, traditional values and gender roles in Xhosa society, things I have no business commenting on – are so tainted. The whole idea of traditional African culture in the Western mind is poisoned, if a Western mind is even what I have, which I don't suppose it is. I have some sort of hybrid mind, a Frankenstein's monster of Western and African parts, alien to both. I don't believe Sibs should have to put up with anything because of 'tradition', but this is not a friend I'm talking to. This is not my brother, when he wanted Mia to stay home to look after Lily. A friend who works in the non-profit sector told Adrian and me once that when he was working on a development project in rural KwaZulu-Natal he was served his meal by a woman on her knees. She entered the room on her knees, did a strange, stunted shuffle along the floor, still on her knees, and offered the food to our friend and her husband, our friend's host, on her knees. Our friend hated every minute of it, this grotesque display of sexism and subservience, but he said nothing. Only thanked her. It would be rude to kick up a fuss about it, he said to me. It would only alienate his host and the guy's wife, make him look disrespectful of their culture, another Joseph Conrad or Cecil Rhodes. 'Culture' doesn't give people a free pass to be sexist, I said to him at the time, and yet here I am, choking on my tongue when I want to tell Sibs she mustn't put up with this, that everything should be equal, that her husband must pull his weight, gender roles are bullshit. Adrian and I divide our chores down the middle, I'm fanatical about it – but Sibs grew up in the rural Eastern Cape, and that's another world. If her friends tell her to put up with her husband, and she feels scolded by the outrage I feel on her behalf, what does that achieve?

I try to soften my voice: 'You deserve better than that, Sibs.'

'You think so?' The tears come quite suddenly. I get up to find her a tissue and when I return, she says, 'A month ago he brought this child to my place. He says no, this is his child that he made with another woman, but that other woman she has no money and can't raise it, so I must look after it.'

'You've got to be kidding. Did you know he had another child?'

She shakes her head.

'And that he had a girlfriend?'

'This child is the same age as Buhle, so he's had this girlfriend for a long time.'

'Sibs, this isn't normal.' To hell with cultural sensitivity.

She smiles at me, though she's still crying. 'Ya, you see. I don't want this.'

'Do you need anything from me?'

She wipes her eyes and shakes her head, and I hate to admit it, but I'm relieved that it's not about money, and then quite moved. Sibs is talking to me because she's lonely, because her friends don't get it, because she needs someone to hear her. It's my father calling from the car on the way to the neurologist again. Why am I always so blind-sided by vulnerability? Why do I never think people want to talk to me just so we can connect?

'It's good that you're leaving him,' I say, hoping to make her feel better about her decision, but her crying intensifies. She sniffs, wipes her nose, hacks. 'But I'm worried about Buhle, you know. She loves him. He's her dad. Do you think it's okay for her?'

'I wish you'd asked me that a month ago!' I say, and I laugh, but she doesn't get it. 'I had a whole speech lined up that I gave about divorce. That it's fine for the kids.'

Sibs looks at me confused, blank. She crinkles her nose. I'm grate-ful for another chance to handle this better, for her faltering English.

'Do you love Buhle?' I say.

'Of course.'

'Just make sure she knows that. No matter what. You love her and this isn't her fault and she must feel what she needs to feel. She might get angry and you must let her get angry. You must let her be sad if she needs to be sad. Let her have tantrums and hold her afterwards. And then she'll be fine. It might take a while, but she'll be fine.'

I don't know if I believe it, but it's what Sibs needs to hear. She wipes her eyes again. The tears have dried on her cheeks. She smiles awk-wardly at me, and stands up. 'Thank you, neh.'

128

'Are you sure you don't need anything?'

'No, I'm fine. I just wanted your advice.'

'What are you going to do?' I ask.

She's composing herself, closing up. She's embarrassed by her out-burst, but I don't want this moment to end.

'I'm going to tell him he must change or he has to go.'

'An ultimatum.'

'A what?'

'Nothing.'

'Ya,' she says, looking through me. 'I will give him three months to decide. It's me and Buhle, or this other woman and her child.'

She starts to walk towards the guest bedroom.

'Sibs,' I say, and she turns to face me again, 'does he hit you?'

The headshake is difficult to read. Quick, small. Either *No* or *I'm done talking about this now.* She swats the air by her face and continues into the guest room.

When she returns a few minutes later, she's a different woman. Cotton dress, threadbare pumps, lighter spirit. 'Tell me,' she says, 'when are you having your baby?'

'I don't know. We haven't heard back from the agency.'

'You must hurry up. We're getting old.'

'We're not old! When we're fifty you can say that to me.'

Sibs laughs. She's not wrong. The days feel like they're accelerating. Close friends on to their second children already and I'm still trying to figure out when someone came in and swapped all the people in my life out for character actors. The mother. The doting aunt. The overworked, absent father. Who are these middle-management peo-ple, these parents who look like tired versions of my friends? Changing nappies and baking cupcakes and exchanging stories about teething? Men playing golf on weekends to escape their lives and wives. Is ъrybody kidding? I'm anxious about being left behind, and maybe forgotten, but I'm also starting to feel more and more resistant to the inevitability of all of this. Why must children be the next step? Why must we trade in our hobbies and interests and travels and friendships, our whole personality, so that we can have what – a legacy? The continuation of the species? It's a cop-out. A lazy solution to the problem of existential dread. Don't think too much about what it all means – just have a baby and *voilà!*, life has meaning.

One of the many things I loved about *A Little Life*, Hanya Yanagihara's novel, was this glimpse at another kind of life, another way to grow older – friendships that remain central, childless friends who find intimacy and community and meaning in one another and their own passions. Why is it frightening to imagine a life like that when it's also so lovely? Am I brainwashed by the heteronormative patriarchy (down with all that), or is it that I don't know anyone like the people in *A Little Life*? My friends fall into two camps: those who want families and suburbia, and those who want open relationships and sex parties and polyamory. I think I want something in between.

'You must make it nice in that room,' Sibs says. 'To get it ready. Get some baby things.'

She's right. Part of the problem is that it's all so abstract. A generic future child, a placeholder baby. The guest room isn't helping. It's an adult room with an adult bed, desk and bookshelf. Ready for the friends who don't come to stay any more because they have families and need more than one bedroom. Ready for Adrian when he can't sleep and wants to read at three a.m. without waking me. But it's not yet ready for a baby.

'Her name's going to be Khanya, hey?'

'You remember everything, Sibs.'

'I remember.'

I named my future daughter years ago, back at university, after a singer I loved whose feel-good music seemed to bridge all of South Africa's ugly divides. A black singer whom white people loved, she could drag even the most resistant and reactionary folk into our shared bright future. She was decolonising by stealth, getting people to sing along in isiXhosa. Looking back at it now, it was blissfully naive, the kind of rainbowism that makes Black Twitter seethe these days, and I get it: it doesn't matter how palatable things are to white people, that shouldn't be the metric and we've lost so much time trying to appease those who will not compromise. But it was a beautiful moment nonetheless, when it felt as if we were moving towards one another instead of into laagers. Hearing the name now, after all these years, reminds me of that optimism and how good it felt. My generation was going to fix racism. We were going to show white people how to be a minority with humility and grace, instead of bitterness and entitlement. We were going to make this country the envy of the world. I can't help but smile.

'You think Buhle will still want to be friends with Khanya if she only comes next year?' I say. 'She'll be four years younger.'

'No, it's fine,' Sibs says, turning on the tap to wash her cup. 'We'll make them be friends. They won't have a choice.'

# 18.

We must have passed the interview phase of the adoption process, because we progress to the next round. A home visit. My friend Steve, who adopted his daughter, Gugu, about a year ago, tells me not to panic. They just want to make sure the house is safe and big enough for a child, and that the life we told them about is in fact the life we lead. I try to follow his advice, but it's impossible. Everything in the house suddenly looks like it was designed to lacerate or electrocute children.

I buy a bag of child-lock mechanisms and spend a Saturday morning installing them on all the kitchen cupboards. I move the knives from a lower drawer into a cupboard above the counter.

I agonise about our glass dining table for a week, aloud and repeatedly. Adrian thinks it's fine and tells me the agency will think it's fine, but after he catches me running my fingers along the sharp edge while we're having breakfast, over and over, he sighs so forcefully he expels a bit of cereal from his mouth. 'For fuck's sake, fine, let's get a wooden one.'

I sell the dining table online and that weekend we go to four different furniture shops before we find a wooden dining table that we don't hate. They're either old-fashioned or cheap-looking or too big and heavy. I loved our round glass dining table. It was just like the one we had in our apartment in New York. Sleek and modern and minimalist. But also dangerous and sharp. The wooden table isn't any of these things. 'Practical,' I say to Adrian at the checkout counter, trying to muster a smile.

'Like Crocs for our dining room,' he says, which is a low blow.

Sibs thinks we should get a cot too, but I worry the agency will think that's presumptuous. 'After we're paper pregnant,' I tell her, and I don't think I've explained to her what that means, but she gets the gist and loses interest.

The home visit is uneventful in the end – Steve was right – and it begins to dawn on me that there aren't too many hurdles left. This application process is exhausting and time-consuming and long, but it isn't infinite. We've been at sea for weeks, rowing as hard as we can, too fixated on the oars, and our blisters, and the sideways thrust of the waves to notice much else. Now there is a sense of land on the horizon. We could get the baby at any minute.

I'm not sure if I'm elated or terrified.

There must have been some mistake. Do they really think I'm fit to become a parent? Did they read the profile we wrote about ourselves?

'Don't worry,' Adrian says and winks at me, 'we could still be rejected by all of the mothers.'

It's a different social worker who comes to our house – not Nadia this time – but she is easily satisfied. She even tells us we have a beautiful home. 'I love your dining table,' she says, stroking the clunky, polished surface on her way out. I have to make sure I don't catch Adrian's eye.

Before we know it, we're at the workshop – the final step before we are either rejected or approved. If we pass this test, all that's left is to wait for one of the mothers to choose us.

Nadia tells us at the start of the workshop that all of us should become lifelong friends – all of the people in this room. There are four couples – half of them straight – seated cross-legged on the floor as if we are the children waiting for Assembly to start. We're all embarking on this journey together, Nadia says, and it will help us to be part of a community, to have friends who have children the same age. It's easier to arrange playgroups and plan weekend activities.

I'm waiting for her to tell us that it takes a village to raise a child. I'm bracing myself for it, intensely and pre-emptively annoyed by the overuse of that expression. There's a particular discomfort I feel at these 'African idioms' regurgitated by well-meaning white people in earnest conversation on talk shows or inspirational videos and in cheesy online memes, that I don't understand. The sentiment is sweet, and it's true, so why is it so irritating? Is it the laziness of Westerners even coming up with the phrase 'African proverb', as if African people and cultures are homogenous or interchangeable? I hope it's that. I hope it's not that I'm giving in to the new orthodoxy of believing no one can say anything that doesn't come from their own narrow social circle and life experience.

'You know what they say,' Nadia says, 'it takes a village.'

Adrian catches my eye and clearly I look pissed off because he gets the giggles. I look down quickly so we don't egg each other on. Nadia isn't even white, but in my defence, she isn't 'African' in the way these homestead-spun folk wisdoms mean, either.

Maybe the 'it takes a village' thing irritates me because I wasn't raised by one? My mother and I had no one else to lean on.

Where I resist Nadia's attempts to make us befriend these other couples, Adrian is a ray of sunshine in the room. They love him. He jokes with one of the straight couples about gender reveal parties (two of their friends have just had one, and they refused to attend). He jokes with the other gay couple, conspiratorially under his breath, about how weird it is that straight couples tell everyone they are 'trying for a kid', as if it's normal to declare to strangers that one of them keeps dropping loads in the other. 'Do they not hear it like that?' he says.

There are posters all over the room about various adoption and childhood topics. Maslow's hierarchy of needs. Milestones in early childhood development. Common trauma responses. How to help a child feel safe and loved. Nadia points to a photograph on the wall – full colour, laminated A4 – of a man reading to a child in bed, presumably a father and son. She is talking about the Romanian Orphan Study and the correlations between early childhood neglect and/or separation from primary caregivers, and the increased risk of mental health and developmental problems later in life. Their brains didn't develop in the way they should have developed. She goes on to talk about the importance of reading to a child every day, for language development and bonding, and the transformative power of attention. 'It's getting rarer,' Nadia says, 'full, devoted attention. You see it all the time. Go to a coffee shop and see how many parents are ignoring their children, because they are glued to their phones. It does lasting damage,' she says, 'never to be present.'

Adrian is taking notes. I see him write the word 'ATTENTION' in all caps in his notebook, and underline it three times. He catches me watching him and smiles at me. 'Don't make fun of me,' he says.

'I'm not.'

'This is important.'

'It is.'

I return my gaze to the father and son in bed together. Why do they use these detached, sterilised words? Separation. Neglect. Damage. Can no one, not even the people whose careers revolve around these children and placing them in loving homes, inhabit that state of loss and grief? They can't bear it. They can't allow themselves to feel what the children feel, even as they claim to understand and ameliorate it. They don't want to talk about how it feels, for a father to look at you and see nothing worthy of his attention.

# 19.

I had forgotten, in the years I was away, how windy Cape Town gets in spring. On Instagram and Twitter and Facebook, the country slides into summer in September, the dusty interior bakes, but in Cape Town, where the winter drags on for months, the only sign that the southern hemisphere is drifting towards the sun is the wind. The rain persists and each shower soothes my climate anxieties. It's been a gloriously wet winter, like they are supposed to be, like they were when I first moved here for university, and the dams are at sixty per cent – not enough to scrap the water restrictions, but enough to ease them, to flush the piss smell out of the toilets, to allow myself to think we might have survived the climate apocalypse for now. We're no longer front-page news around the world, the frontline of climate collapse, desertification, thirst.

But the wind grows so angry and powerful that it becomes diffi-cult to separate it from the drought in my mind. I find a dead baby bird on the sill outside of the living room window, ripped out of its nest before it could fly and smashed against the glass. Out on a walk with Frasier, I see an old woman pinned to a fence, unable to fight the force of the wind. I see viral videos of trucks being blown over on the freeway near the Huguenot Tunnel. Branches come down in our courtyard, in the lane. A three-hundred-year-old oak rips in half in the night, tears down the power lines on the street parallel to ours. I become too afraid to go for walks in all the falling detritus, the branches and street signs and brick dust.

'It's always been this bad,' Adrian says to me in bed, as I lie awake and crush his hand in mine. 'You've seen those milkwoods in Sea Point.' He's right. They grow at an absurd angle, comically bent and deformed from the wind.

This was the Cape of Storms once, before European sailors re-branded it the Cape of Good Hope, probably to encourage more sailors to brave the journey, but this howling outside is too much for me. It sounds demonic. Leaves and branches thrash against the windows, and burglar alarm sirens wail up and down the lane. The air screams into the room under the door, through the poorly sealed Victorian sash windows.

'It's just your anxiety,' he says with nothing but kindness in his voice, but it makes me want to cry when he says things like this; it makes me feel untethered from reality again because how am I alone in this? How are there people in the world who don't have anxiety disorders? Have they not been paying attention?

I am trying, again, to come off my medication but the chest pains are back. I've been to a pulmonologist in the past week, and a heart specialist the week before, and what I have, the pulmonologist said, is dysfunctional breathing, an interruption to the natural function of the chest muscles brought about by intense and prolonged anxiety. Another diagnosis, another dysfunction, another way in which I cannot cope with the world around me, but isn't the madness out there, outside of my mind and my chest? Isn't the madness that we tear down forests for profit and burn carbon in planes and cars and power plants when we know it's killing us, and bully the weak and the poor and fire live ammunition on protesting miners, and force terrified cattle into mechanised killing pits, and give tax breaks to billionaires and then say there's no money for healthcare, and avert our eyes from the suffering all around us? Close your window when the beggar approaches. Run when the homeless man gets too close.

138

'I hate that fucking label,' I say to Adrian, and it feels good to be angry; I must remember to tell Emma. 'It makes me feel like I have no agency against this fear and that's true – most of the time it turns me into a cowering animal – but I refuse to believe it's my fault. I had resilience once. It was beaten out of me. It was taken from me.'

'I'm just trying to give you some perspective,' he says, 'to remind you that there were storms before.'

And in one sense he's right, the wind is well documented, and I've lived through some pretty scary wildfires in this city, too, before we left for New York, when the sky was black with smoke and the mountains all around the city were ablaze and the helicopters droned above with their pitiful loads of water and whole neighbourhoods had to be evacuated. But it is also impossible not to see the pattern. Increasingly severe weather, droughts and storms and fires and floods. It's all happening so much faster than they predicted, and just when everyone should be freaking out, half the world elects climate change deniers who roll back environmental protections. It's hard to shake the feeling that it's the end of the world, even in this warm, safe bed.

How can we possibly think about children? Raising vulnerable little humans to go off and fight for the scraps of a collapsing economy, struggle to survive, suffer ever more miserable conditions, more tyrannical regimes? Aren't we supposed to be able to protect our children? I want to hold them in softness and compassion. I want to raise empathetic, compassionate, thoughtful kids – not for them to have to be tough. Resilient. Unbreakable.

'Thanks,' I say to Adrian, 'you're right.' I give his hand a squeeze and he squeezes it back, and then suddenly I'm kissing him. I'm up on my elbow, leaning over his body and pressing my lips against his. They are soft and warm and full and my body floods with arousal and he kisses me back but then he pulls away.

'What's going on?'

I'm as surprised as he is. I never want to have sex when I'm anxious, or when I'm depressed, or when I'm any kind of vulnerable, and I've realised it's because I think of sex as violent and shameful. I'm unravelling in analysis, discovering knots I never knew were there, defences that keep me rigid and safe and unreachable.

'I want to try something,' I say to him. 'No dirty talk. I want you to look at me and I want you to be tender.'

He's grinning when I climb on top of him. 'Yes, sir,' he says, but there is relief in his eyes, maybe even pride, like he's been waiting for years for me to get here.

I lie on top of him, and he places both of his hands on my face, holding me in his gaze while he kisses me. His eyes are nothing like the raging winds all around us; they are the warmth of a fire in the hearth in winter, the colour of damp earth. His tongue is warm as blood. It's not an invasion. He's not taking what's his. That whole mental structure shifts, and it's disorientating, a kind of madness, this tingling of my body, this desire without abasement.

I am here. I am in the room. I exist, and he knows that I exist. It's like nothing I have ever felt before.

# 20.

The analysis starts to shift things, even when I'm not in it. My dreams come back. I hadn't dreamed since I was nine years old. For more than two decades my sleep has been empty, dreamless. An oblivion. The only visions to visit me were the shadow presences at the end of my bed. The malevolent figure waiting for me when I woke. He was often there when I opened my eyes. He stood over me, or he sat at the end of my bed, watching me. The half-light bent around him. His gravitational field was that of a black hole and I knew, always, that he was going to possess me.

Now my mind is awake in sleep. I see my childhood garden. I fly through subterranean cities and catch school buses with friends I haven't seen since primary school.

The angle of the light shifts, sometimes, and I'm in a parallel universe where nothing is different except my sense of how it all fits together. I experience moments when I'm a person with resilience, where I can get a headache and know it's only a headache, it's not cancer. I can look car guards in the eye and smile. I feel what it's like to see ordinariness in other people. They are bored, maybe, or irritated and having a bad day, but they are not all grieving and hopeless, desperate for love and meaning and finding none of it. They are neither vicious nor despairing. For a moment in these universes, the colours are all different, though the colours are exactly the same.

And I start to see him. I can feel him, almost, take shape from nothing. Where there was no one at the centre of my memories – merely a lens on the world, a frightened eye observing from the safe distance of another planet – a small human being starts to lift out of two dimensions and expand into three. He has little arms. He has fingers and feet. He has a weight that leaves an imprint on couches. When people look towards the lens, they see someone. There is a person there. A little boy. He's trying to be invisible, but he isn't.

I see him, too.

I don't see him for long. It's too painful, how small he is, how overwhelmed. So frightened all the time. I'm used to feeling that way; I've grown accustomed to it and maybe I deserve it. But to see all of this happening to a child. I can't hate him for it. I can't despise his weakness and vulnerability, his neediness. Children are needy. It's okay. They need to feel loved. He's only nine years old. He's desperately trying to make his father love him again, to bring him home. He's trying to put his mother back together. He's doing the best he can.

And in these glimpses into parallel universes, I feel, briefly, freed from the one in which I grew up. The one where life is brutal and pointless and the only way to cope with it is to 'man up', 'grow up' and 'stop being so emotional'. I believed my father's reality, even as I raged against it in my conscious mind – that emotions are weak, that faith is unforgivably stupid, and that companionship is a delusion, a pretence, something people act out to keep busy. I can see now, for whole minutes at a time, that this paradigm was his, not the world's. *His* reality. As subjective as any other.

Not everyone would surprise their son with the news that his grandfather had died just as he was dropping him off at school, so the boy couldn't make a scene. Not everyone would tell a child who was developing a fear of flying that the safety cards in planes are just for show, that if anything goes wrong, we're all going to die and nothing will save us. It was a philosophy, I see now, not the state of existence. The Philosophy of Hardness. He believed it. He believed the world was capricious and violent. He was trying to toughen me up to survive it.

Was his own gentleness crushed out of him at boarding school? Was he bullied? In the army, when he was conscripted to 'defend' the apartheid state against the 'terrorists' who turned out to be on the right side of history – what was he made to do?

Maybe I can live in a universe with softer edges. One where we all die in the end, sure, but where the cold, hard facts are ameliorated with kindness, with moments of deep connection with others. We're not trapped in burning planes hurtling to the earth, rigid and unable to speak. Maybe we're on a slowly sinking ship, and the band is playing. There is space, and time, for intimacy and love. To listen to the music. To be vulnerable with each other and feel the tingling aliveness of recognising another's soul. There is a universe where joy is possible and it occupies the same time and space as our own.

# 21.

Hilton calls me when I'm on my way to a boutique baby shop in Green Point.

'You're on loudspeaker,' I say, 'and Adrian's next to me, so no skinnering.'

It's a joke I make whenever I take a call and Adrian's in the car with me. Adrian rolls his eyes, again, because he doesn't like being announced – he finds it awkward, and he doesn't see the point of it. He's quite happy to let me talk to my brother without getting involved, but I feel embarrassed if I learn halfway through a phone call that someone else has been listening. No matter how bland and impersonal the conversation might have been, how devoid of gossip or nastiness, I'm suddenly convinced I said something shameful.

I mouth *social anxiety* at him, and he shakes his head in mock exasperation.

'Hi, Adrian,' Hilton says.

'Hi, Hilton,' he replies. 'How's Joburg?'

'All good. Listen, it's that time of year again,' Hilton says, 'where I try to convince you guys that we don't need to buy each other Christmas presents.'

'I don't know why you bother,' I say. 'You know I'm never going to agree to it.'

'Come on,' Hilton says, 'Christmas shopping is so shit.'

'It's the worst,' I agree. 'It's stressful, the shops are packed, I can never think of what to get anyone.'

'So why can't we drop it?'

'Because it's all worth it on Christmas morning, when we open them.'

'Why don't you buy yourself something nice? It'll be better than anything I can get you.'

'It's not about the stuff.'

'Oh, of course. It's about the birth of little baby Jesus?'

'Don't be irritating,' I say. It may be a secular holiday in our family, but it's an important one all the same. Holy in the sense that it's the only time the family comes together. A mandatory gathering of the tribe.

'So if it's not about stuff, let's not have any stuff.'

'I want a present.'

'You're in your thirties!'

'What's that got to do with anything?'

'Christmas is for the kids.'

I stop at the red light on Buitengracht. One of the familiar beggars approaches the car. She's about my age but walks with a limp. Her face is the colour of walnuts, leathery and lined from booze or sunburn or both, and she pretends to have a missing arm. She's been here for years, always this intersection or the one on the next block, always the same macabre act. She raps on all the car windows with her right hand. Her left arm is pressed against her breasts, visible beneath her T-shirt. She twists her face into the most pained expressions. Today, she's Edvard Munch's *The Scream*. I open my window halfway, extract two five-rand coins from the partition between the seats, and drop them into her hand.

'It is *not* just for the kids,' I seethe. Hilton tried this argument with me a few years ago. It makes me as angry now as it did then. I imagine Emma in the back seat behind me, waiting for me to discover why I feel so outraged.

'I don't need a present from you,' Hilton says. 'You're off the hook.'

'And yet I presume you expect me to buy for your kids.'

Adrian has been staring out of the window until now. He snaps his head around and frowns at me. Hilton is stunned for a second, too.

'You don't have to get them anything,' Hilton says.

'Of course I will. I want to. I just don't know why you always try to ruin it for the rest of us.'

'Because we're adults! Actually, it doesn't sound like you are one,' he says.

'I have to go.'

We pull up at the baby boutique. I end the call and storm into the shop. Adrian gives me space. He doesn't follow me in just yet. He faffs outside by the car, pretending to do something on his phone. Then he busies himself in a different part of the store. It's a beautiful little shop. Clean and white. Smells of neroli candles. They sell none of the usual mass-produced, imported baby things. Everything here is hand-made, locally made, organic. When I first told Adrian about it, he said, 'Fine, but I draw the line at reusable nappies.'

We browse on opposite ends of the small space. I look at the shelves of soft toys; he studies the organic ointments and lotions. The first few toys I see make me want to punch something, because Lily and Simon would love them and now Hilton will think they're a grudge purchase. That I never wanted to give them anything.

I find Adrian and shove a soft toy in his face. 'What do you think about this for Lily?'

'It's beautiful,' he says.

I wander off. He comes to find me back in the soft toy section. 'Are you okay?' he says.

'I'm fine.'

He squeezes my shoulder. 'Let's get one for Lily and one for us.'

146

'For baby Khanya.'

'Or Khanyo,' he says, sticking out his tongue at me. He knows that's not how it works. The name's not Italian, not re-gendered by the substitution of an 'a' or an 'o', but the toy is good for a boy or a girl. It's a hand-knitted grey woollen monkey with a white face and white hands and feet. The limbs must have been knitted to completion before the body was assembled because each of them can turn three hundred and sixty degrees. The tail is long and malleable. I loop it around my wrist and the monkey dangles without falling.

'I don't know if I should get Simon the same thing, so that they don't fight. But maybe that looks like we couldn't be bothered thinking of something different for each of them?'

I buy a little outfit for my friend Nomi's upcoming baby shower in Joburg, three of the monkeys, a shweshwe-patterned giraffe and two framed illustrations for Khanya's room. An owl and a gecko in pastel shades of yellow and grey and green. The main purchase, the reason we came here in the first place, is the cot. I found it online and it's exactly the one I want. Hand-carved wood, white, with spindles along the sides like an antique chair.

'Are you sure we're not jumping the gun?' Adrian says when I hand the cashier my credit card. 'We haven't heard anything from the agency since the workshop. It's been nearly a month.'

'Steve and Loyiso told us to be prepared. We won't get much notice before our baby arrives.'

He smiles when he hears me say our baby. His shoulders relax. I return my gaze to the card machine and wait for the prompt to enter my PIN. I can't look at him.

'I'm glad we're sprucing up the room,' he says.

'Sibs was right. It'll help us feel ready.'

'You don't feel ready?'

'Is anyone ever ready?' I say, keeping my voice light. I try to catch the cashier's eye, but she wants no part of this knife-edge conversation. She focuses on wrapping the toys in tissue paper. Adrian tilts his head at me. He says nothing.

I hook the paper bag over my elbow, and the two of us carry the cot out to the car. It's too large for the boot in my hatchback. I collapse the back seats and slide the box right up against the back of the front seats.

We drive home in silence. Inane chatter on the radio. Howling wind and dust and leaves outside the car. The tension eases when we set up the cot in the guest room. It comes in pieces, like furniture from IKEA, and it takes us about an hour to assemble the whole thing, but once it's done, it transforms the room in exactly the way I had hoped.

I open a bottle of wine while Adrian hangs the new illustrations on the wall.

'I can just see little Khanya in here,' he says, taking a glass. 'Kicking her tiny little legs and watching us with her big, bewildered eyes.'

I don't tell him that those eyes make me feel panicked. I wrap my arm around Adrian's waist and kiss his shoulder. 'Or Khanyo.'

# 22.

Johannesburg has grown a new city since I left. The skyline of Sandton is unrecognisable. High-rises loom over the streets Mom used to drive us along to get to the mall when I was a kid. They're not as intimidatingly enormous, or as densely crammed together as the skyscrapers of New York or Hong Kong or the UAE, but they're from the same handbook. The architecture is global – shining glass obelisks that reflect the sky and announce the triumph of capitalist 'modernity' over any specifics of culture or climate.

I emerge from the underground train station in Sandton into a white-hot October afternoon. The metro is new since I lived here, constructed in the halcyon days of the early 2000s when the economy was booming and all of us were love-drunk on post-apartheid African optimism. It's clean and efficient and 'world class', though I hate the way that phrase was trumpeted at the time, as though hiding the poor is the mark of a great, modern society. Riding on the Gautrain makes it feel like the dream of '94 was realised. The service is good, and the stations are impressive, but what feels so much like progress to me is the sense of black upward mobility, black success, black excellence. It's a capitalist notion of progress, but what else have we been able to come up with? The trains are full of businessmen and -women, pencil skirts, expensive suits, Afros, AirPods. Black lawyers and investment bankers and executives. The energy is so different from Cape Town. The people hustle. It feels good to be surrounded by this energy, this pride. My white skin elicits neither hatred nor obsequiousness in Johannesburg, but blissful indifference.

Katlego picks me up from the Gautrain station and takes me straight to the party. It's our mutual friend Nomi's baby shower and it's my first ever baby shower because gender normativity is proving difficult to disrupt. Katlego thinks it's hilarious that I'm nervous. 'The only thing you've got to worry about,' she says, 'is being bored to death.'

She isn't wrong. Much like the kitchen teas I attended a few years ago when all my same girlfriends were getting married, the thrill of being allowed into this women-only space fades quickly. A large part of the party is taken up by watching the mother-to-be open her presents. There are nappies. There are ointments and creams. There are devices I've never heard of for problems I've never thought about – chafed nipples, what to do with dirty nappies if you're far from a bin, dummy-disinfecting machines – and all the guests look on with soft-eyed wonder. I feel the walls closing in on me. The idea of these helpless, tiny creatures, the endless responsibility. They take and take and take. I snap out of it when Nomi's mom announces we are to play a game, only to discover it's a quiz where all the questions relate to the prospective parents as babies: how much did Nomi weigh when she was born? How many hours did Hanlo's mom spend in labour? What was Nomi's favourite toy at her first birthday? I remember how desperate Tshego looked at our braai a few months ago when she saw all those babies and new parents arriving. I get up from the circle and take myself to the kitchen.

I rinse out the orange pulp from my mimosa and fill the glass with vonkel.

'It's heavy going, isn't it?'

'Liam! I didn't know you were here.'

'I've been out in the garden,' he says. 'Talking to Nomi's gran.'

I lift the bottle, and my eyebrows, towards him. He shakes his head and smiles, and I catch myself before I make a joke about it. I know Liam's been in rehab a few times. I've only known him at parties, drunk or rolling, but I've heard about these dry spells.

'It's so good to see you,' I say.

He's looking good. The same dimpled, mischievous smile I remember, and it's even more dangerous now that his dark eyes are clear and alert. He looks amused, as if the two of us are in on something together, and as the only two gay men at the party, I suppose we are. He's been working out, putting all that sober energy into growing his chest and his biceps. His upper arms are full and soft, bulging out of his T-shirt. It's not the kind of lean muscle we're supposed to fantasise about, the kind you see on models and actors and influencers, but it's real and weighty, and alarmingly attractive. His olive skin. The way his fine black chest hair rises above the V of his T-shirt. I feel myself flush.

'Where's Adrian?' he says.

'Back in Cape Town. I'm only up for the weekend.'

'Ah, okay. Well listen, I'm meeting some friends in Melville tonight. You should come out with us.'

'That would be great. I'm actually staying in Melville.'

'Meant to be.' He winks at me, but it's not a leering wink. It's fun and playful. We exchange numbers and he tells me he has to run. Another commitment, he says, though I don't know why he bothers. Neither of us believes he's leaving for any reason other than to escape the baby-themed games. I wish I could follow him.

I've always liked Melville. It's a Bohemian neighbourhood, laid back and unpretentious, lined with cute coffee shops and bars and art galleries and small indie bookstores. For as long as I can remember, it's been swinging between 'up and coming' and 'getting a bit dodgy again', never resting in either state for more than a few years, and I catch it this time in the apex of its pendulum swing, a period of calm. No unsolicited break-in stories from friends when they hear where I'm staying. My Airbnb hostess tells me it's safe to walk on the Koppies – the little nature reserve that covers a rocky ridge in Melville – as long as I'm out by dusk.

I go for a run towards Emmarentia, cut up to Zoo Lake, and across into Parkview. It's the part of the city I grew up in, quiet and tree-lined, a little corner of suburbia tucked between congested arteries and the scattered nodes of business and retail. The houses here are set far back from the road, hidden by high walls and electric fencing, but they're not as grand as you'd think. It's one of the oldest residential areas in the city and the houses are humble. Single-storey, modest, with pressed-tin ceilings and wooden floors, holding on to the charm of the 1920s and '30s. The gardens are what make this area feel so luxurious. They billow over the walls like abundance itself. Bougain-villea in giant cumulus clouds of pink and lipstick red. Birch forests and birds of paradise and ivy so dense and layered it protrudes a metre out from the property walls. And jacarandas. Everywhere, the jacarandas. They line the streets; they poke out over the walls. They transform these roads into tunnels of purple, above and below. The sweet scent of fallen flowers. A path of crushed blooms where jog-gers and pedestrians have walked, and a canopy of colour held up by thick, black branches. There are very few leaves yet, only the purple blooms. It's a surreal, disorientating world where the rules of nature, of photosynthesis, no longer apply.

I run past the childhood home of an old friend I haven't seen since university. I visited her here once, in the holidays, and met her Slovak parents who understood English perfectly but asked her to translate for them when they spoke to me because they were so ashamed of their accents. I run past Asher's house, my best friend from primary school, where I listened to Paul Simon and Ani DiFranco with him in his bedroom, and felt the first flutterings of love, where I dreamed about kissing him on a sleepover once and woke with an erection and blushed throughout breakfast as if he and his mom had both seen it, both knew what I had dreamed. There, another primary school friend's house. Anxious sleepovers, staying awake all night on a mattress on his bedroom floor, counting the hours until I knew I was being picked up, until I knew Mom was safe.

I run and I run and the air burns in my lungs because there's no oxygen in Joburg; it's raised too high into the sky for a city this size. I stop when I reach my father's old house, the one he lived in before he emigrated. I can't see the house from the street. The driveway snakes into the garden behind high stone walls.

I touch the ochre stone with my hot palm. I don't know the people who live here now. I know nothing about them. My chest shakes as I try to open my bronchi, try to get some air into my lungs. I have happy associations with this house, but they dissolve when I try to bring them to mind. They disintegrate into sad and lonely images – twelve-year-old me sitting on the granite countertops in the kitchen laughing with Gloria, my dad's domestic worker, while she cooked. Sitting with her on the couch while she watched *The Bold and the Beautiful*. My brother hosting a party for his friends while my dad was away, and me smelling marijuana for the first time, thinking how dark and unknowable the world was, how someone I loved could have been taking drugs right in front of me all along. My dad is absent from these memories. Glimpses in the passage. Flashes of imagery – his return from the gym, red and sweaty. Him sitting at the desk in his study, working. I can't hold these memories for longer than a second; I can't turn them back into scenes, into conversations. I was only ever with Gloria in this house. I remember following her from room to room, talking to her in the kitchen, accompanying her on her trips to the shops, showing her my drawings. She was so alive I never noticed the deathly quiet of the house. She was extra chatty if Dad was in one of his moods. While he ignored me, she made me snacks and made me promise not to tell him I'd already eaten when he and I sat down to our formal dinner, just the two of us. She roped me in to helping her cook and told me stories about her own son back in Mafikeng. He was my age, she said. I never asked her who was looking after him. When she laughed, her laughter shook her whole body, deep and rumbling in her throat.

I don't know where he's buried.

I press both hands against the warm stone wall. My eyes start to sting. How am I supposed to grieve if I don't know where he's buried? How am I supposed to heal? I don't even know if he was buried, or if he was cremated and scattered somewhere, if he's sitting in an urn in his second wife's home in England, ignored on a mantelpiece. Cheryl wanted nothing to do with Hilton and me after the funeral, told us never to contact her or the girls again. It broke my brother's heart, but I pushed it down with all the rest of the ugliness that I couldn't process because I was only angry. I wasn't hurt. I was fine never seeing those kids again.

I hated that my father had gone to their dance recitals and school plays, that he talked to them at breakfast. That he'd finally got the daughters he always wanted. I saw him read to them every night I was with them in their house in London, a girl tucked under each arm in bed.

I hated that in the early days after the divorce, when I still had tantrums, when I wasn't yet too frightened of him to say anything, and all I wanted was someone to acknowledge what had happened, to hear me when I told him how sad Mom was, how much I missed him, to hold me and tell me it was going to be okay, or that it was okay to be sad, he told me, instead, to grow up. Stop being so bloody emotional. Pull yourself together, for fuck's sake.

'Joke's on you, Dad,' I say to the stone, 'because I still don't have my shit together.'

The electric gate starts to open, startling me. I step away from the stone wall to see a sleek blue BMW waiting in the road behind me, about to turn into the driveway. The driver is a middle-aged black man, bald, in a white polo shirt. I wave at him, presumably the owner of this house, and he half-smiles in return, a little skeptical of this person loitering outside his property.

I walk the rest of the way back to my rented room in Melville. When I crest the hill of 7th Avenue, there's a group of three black women taking selfies in front of the Airbnb. They laugh when I approach, embarrassed at being caught. They have come to this particular spot to take photos. They are heavily made-up, faces caked with light-brown foundation, bright-pink lipstick, eyelash extensions. Their wigs are cheap and ill-suited to their faces, and their clothes are bright and formal. One of them is in a cocktail dress, one is in a floor-length pleated skirt and lacy top, and one wears a power suit in batik fabric. They must be taking photos for their social media. Profile pictures of elegance and success. I smile at them and unlock the front gate. They resume their poses, hands on hips, looking back alluringly over their shoulders. I glance down the street to see the view they have chosen for their backdrop and it is nothing special. You can't get a vista of the downtown skyline from this angle; we're too far down the street for that. All you see from here is a line of garage doors and front walls, pavement gardens and suburban homes. And that, I realise, is the point. They are in the suburbs. They are photographing themselves *being* in the suburbs. They have made it.

# 23.

I haven't packed any clothes for going out. I brought one nice shirt with me to Joburg – a midnight-blue button-up with faint white crosses on it – which I wore to the baby shower. Everything else in my luggage is casual, faded. A grey T-shirt with botanical drawings on it, one of my favourites, but old now and stretched around the neckline. A plain white T-shirt that doesn't fit as well as it used to. It hadn't bothered me until now. It's comfortable and I was planning on spending the night reading in the Airbnb, or streaming some canned-laughter show while doom-scrolling on my phone and eating take-away Asian food. I try on the plain white tee with my navy jeans – a classic combination – but it's loose and unflattering. Falls like a pillow-case would. I'm not fat – that's not the word for it – but my body has lost the sharp angles it had when I was single. This is a married-person body. Can men be frumpy?

I change back into my shirt I wore earlier at the baby shower. If Liam's in a different outfit from this morning, I'll say I haven't been back to the Airbnb all day.

He hasn't changed. The same charcoal V-neck T-shirt. The same chunky biceps curving out from its rolled-up sleeves. He's at the bar when I arrive, sitting on a stool with his chin on his fist, concentrating on whatever his friend is saying. There are four of them, all obviously gay, all beautiful. Liam cheers when he sees me. He introduces me to his friends. I hold in my stomach as I shake their hands. Thapelo is wearing green eyeshadow. He has a large gold hoop earring in one ear. A silk shirt that . . . There's no other word for it – it's a blouse. I straighten my posture and suck myself inwards. I laugh more than I should.

'We were just talking about the balls that have started up in Jozi,' Thapelo says. 'I'm entering next month.' His voice is sexy and deep.

'The balls?'

'You know, like *Paris Is Burning*, *Pose*. Ball culture is taking off in Jozi.' He clicks his fingers and raises a hand above his head.

'Oh right, drag balls,' I say, then quickly, because I sound like a straight guy who's been made to watch RuPaul by his girlfriend, I add: 'Amazing.'

I know the lingo. I've seen *RuPaul's Drag Race* and many of its spin-off shows. I've seen loads of this new generation of queer movies and I've attended drag performances at gay bars in Cape Town and New York. I've even stuffed dollar bills into the bra of a huge, beefy queen as she sashayed past me on her way back to the stage in a bar in the West Village, while semi-ironically shouting *Gurl!* There are thousands of campy catchphrases I could say to show I belong – I get the subculture – but they wither in my throat, paralysed by awkwardness. I used to think I was afraid of straight men, of their abuse and disdain, but I'm afraid of gay men, too. Of the cliques and the cutting wit, of saying the wrong thing and having them turn on me. I spent my childhood suppressing my femininity – 'He walks like a faggot!' they said, over and over again, until eventually I learnt how to walk not like a faggot – and now, when femininity is sexy, when gender fluidity is the new normal and people choose their own pronouns and their own families, when everything I ever wanted is coming true, I'm a bumbling, awkward loser who has no idea how to act.

I excuse myself. In the bathroom, I splash water on my face. I take one of the benzos that I've been fingering in my pocket since I arrived. I remove a piece of lint from my tongue.

When I emerge from the bathroom, Liam is sitting at the booth nearest the bathroom door, away from his friends. He hands me an olive-green drink in a coupe with a velvety white foam on top.

'This is delicious,' I say.

'Are you okay?'

'Sorry, yes. I'm fine.' I take a seat beside him and immediately start to relax. We're tucked into the corner of the room, my back to the wall. There's the reassuring, indistinct buzz of crowded spaces – laughter and voices and music. A neon sign on the far wall, above the bar, of a pink rat drinking a beer. It flashes between two positions: beer up, beer down.

'Didn't this place used to be a gay bar?' I say.

'Years ago,' Liam says. 'You remember that?'

'I had my first kiss here.'

The more time I spend in psychoanalysis, the more symbolic everything seems. I see patterns everywhere, coincidences and metaphors. It's probably part of the process. A shifting sense of self. The closing of the gap between my conscious and my shadowy subconscious mind. Our subconscious loves a metaphor, Emma says, picking up where Freud and Jung left off, it communicates in symbols and dreams – but I didn't think this was how real life worked. Symbols are a tool of literature and nothing else, imbuing the world with a narrative coherence it lacks, to appease our desperate search for pattern and meaning. But Sibs brought up her divorce so soon after I'd reopened that particular wound in therapy. I was followed and attacked so soon after telling Emma how afraid I am of being followed. It feels symbolic that I'm here, back in my hometown after so many years. I know I'm here for a friend's baby shower, but it feels as if I'm here for something cosmic, too. A circle is closing. I'm meant to be learning something, healing something, but what?

'You never kissed a girl before that?' Liam says.

'Oh, that doesn't count.'

Liam laughs.

'I was always a hundred per cent sure I was gay. I did kiss a girl once, when I was trying to fit in at school, but I was thinking about her brother the whole time.'

'You dirty boy.'

The drink is calming my nerves, the benzo is warm in my blood, and I'm laughing, remembering that tween crush, remembering how at a party, once, one of his friends pranked him by pulling down his pants while he danced with his girlfriend. The point was to embarrass him. The sudden exposure of his hairy legs and the tent of his erection inside his boxers made everyone laugh and it made him furious, but it did something very different to me. I was alone in that feeling. It makes me stop laughing.

'It was my first boy kiss that I had here,' I say. 'You remember the feeling. Stubble in your hands, the roughness and force. It was electrifying.'

'Ah man, I was so much older,' Liam says. 'I was twenty-five when I first kissed a guy. You're lucky.'

'What about your first blow job?'

Liam presses his hand against his collarbone in mock propriety. 'Excuse me. That was also when I was twenty-five.'

'I was thirteen,' I say.

Liam slaps his hand against the table and shakes his head. I don't know what I'm doing. Trying to reclaim my gay history, I suppose, against his friends with their eye make-up and their confidence, against my conventional life. I want him to know how much casual sex I used to have, how dirty and transactional and unapologetic it was, how easy I was before I met Adrian.

Liam's eyes are focused. They sparkle in the dim light of the bar. 'I needed you as my life coach when I was at varsity.'

I make a shrugging, upturned-hand gesture. A wise guru accepting his role. I'm Oprah. I'm finally having fun.

Liam slides up beside me on the bench, wraps his hand behind my head, and kisses me. His breath is warm on my lips. His tongue pushes into my mouth, slick and hot. I feel weak in his hand, held in place, set on fire. Without taking his lips away from mine, he grabs my hand and places it on his cheek. The stubble is rough, sandpaper against my palm, and he smirks while he kisses me. Electrifying, I'd said.

I move my free hand to the bulge in his jeans. He's hard and it's thick, and it's so easy to imagine the damp sweat in there.

'Do you want to get out of here?' he says, pulling back for air. He raises his arm above his head, strokes his neck in a way that makes his bicep bulge. He must know it has this dizzying effect. It's one of his moves. But the lights cut out. The bar is plunged into darkness. The background buzz loses its music.

'Fuck!' someone shouts.

'Is it just us?'

'The whole street's out.'

Liam's friends have found us. Hovering faces lit from beneath by the cool blue glare of their cellphones. 'We're going to get an Uber, babes,' Thapelo says. 'You guys want to split it?'

'Sure,' Liam says. His hands are back in his own space, as if I dreamed the whole thing.

'I'm going to take off,' I say.

'We'll drop you,' Liam says.

'It's fine. It's a short walk.'

'No, man, you definitely can't walk it. It isn't safe.'

'It's like three blocks.'

Thapelo's eyes dart between Liam and me. 'Okay,' he says, 'I'm going to go stand on the street. There's no signal in here.'

'Thanks for the drink,' I say. 'It was nice to see you.'

Liam tries to stop me, but I can't get out of here fast enough. I slip out between the crowds of people milling on the street trying to hail taxis, and I head down the darkened street towards my Airbnb. The streetlights are out, the restaurants and bars black caves sparkling with tiny stars of cellphone light, but there are enough car headlights to see where I'm going. I turn left onto 5th Avenue and all life disappears. No people. No cars on this residential stretch. Only the silhouettes of darkened homes. I'm trapped in a tunnel of high walls, shadows in the shapes of trees.

My chest tightens, remembering the last time a street emptied around me. My heart thunders in my ears and my hands prickle with sweat. This is stupid. I'm being stupid. What am I trying to prove to myself?

I run back towards the twinkling lights of phones and cars and people. I find Liam out on the street with his friends. I'm just in time. Their Uber has arrived and Thapelo is already in the car.

'Can I get a ride with you?' I say, and Liam smiles at me and it isn't the kind of smile I was expecting. He isn't smug that he won. He isn't trying to be seductive. It's just warm, and open, and it makes me want to cry.

'Of course,' he says, and he steps back for me to get into the vehicle. 'Where are we going?' he says when the car pulls away.

My heart is still racing. I can see that man again from a few months ago in Cape Town, stepping out of the shadows, appearing as if from nowhere. How was he so close, so quickly? I can see the metal glinting under his jacket. His charming smile, the thin veil over his violence.

I hate that I couldn't even walk the short distance to my room in the dark. I couldn't do it. And now I don't want to be alone in the dark, either. I rest my head on Liam's shoulder.

'Wherever you'd like.'

There's no light in Liam's street either. His apartment building is in darkness. I hold one of his hands as he uses the other one to fumble with his front door key, unable to see anything. He laughs, and takes his hand back to feel for the lock. I know I'm too close. I'm being too physically intimate, too needy. This is boyfriend behaviour. But the part of my mind that knows these things has shut down. Or rather – it is trapped behind glass. I am a passive observer of this terrible decision. I am somewhere else, watching my life unfold from far away, unable to intervene. My body waits out in the ink-black hallway with Liam. My body follows him into his apartment when he is finally able to open the door. My body will go through with this, as a kind of punishment. The passivity is frightening but familiar. The same feeling I get when I force myself to eat food I do not want.

Liam finds matches near the stove and begins to light candles. He removes a whole stack of white candles from a kitchen drawer, and I help him attach them to side plates and candlesticks, melting droplets of wax onto the surfaces and pressing the base of each candle into this wax so it stands upright. We light dozens of candles. The kitchen takes shape. The living room emerges from the darkness into a warm orange glow.

He takes off my shirt and kisses me.

It's beautiful. It is so absurdly beautiful to be surrounded by all of these candles, sparkling in clusters around the room. I'm not sure why it doesn't feel fake, contrived. It's too early for romance. We aren't partners. This wasn't a date. This is supposed to be a hook-up. Perfunctory and animal and unsentimental, and yet I'm not annoyed by the candles. I don't want to roll my eyes. I feel something when I look at Liam, and it isn't only lust.

The sex is strangely good. He is tender and attentive, which I wouldn't have thought I could bear without laughing or wanting to run away. We make out a lot. We take it slow. We even flip-flop. Because I know this can never happen again, will never happen again, I feel free to ask him if I can top him. I'm inexperienced in that role, and probably no good, and the urge is new, anyway, and unreliable, but I feel it tonight and I let it flow through me. Liam seems to enjoy himself. He seems to enjoy me. And when I get tired, when I am pulled back to familiarity, we swap places, and it isn't awkward. It isn't failure. He fucks me with slow, steady rhythm, kissing me often, smiling at me in the candlelight as if this is fun. Turns out: sex can be fun.

His eyes are gentle and kind. I close mine so that I don't have to look at them.

When we're done, he tries to hold me and it is this, at last, that brings me back into my body and ends my fugue state. I want to be held. I want to fall asleep in his arms, and this desire is so much more of a betrayal than what we have already done.

'Thanks,' I say, extricating myself from his arms, 'this was great.'

'You're not leaving? It's like two in the morning.'

'I can't stay.'

The warmth I had been avoiding in his eyes cools. 'Okay,' he says. He blows out a few candles nearest his head. Maybe to expel the urge to kick me.

I take an Uber back to the Airbnb through pitch-black streets. The menace is still there in the darkness, and I am relieved the driver does not try to make conversation with me, so I can keep guard.

I must have woken the owner of the house when I was fumbling with the keys because when I finally manage to get the front door unlocked, she's standing in the hallway with a candle and a carving knife. 'Jesus,' she says, 'you scared the hell out of me.'

'Sorry.'

She sighs and starts walking back to her room.

'Do you know what's going on with the power?' I say.

'The whole of Melville is out. I guess we'll find out tomorrow.'

'Okay. Goodnight.'

'Goodnight.'

I lock the door to my room and pour myself a glass of water from the en suite bathroom. I can smell Liam's cologne on my shirt and it makes me want to cry. I strip down and have a scalding-hot shower in the darkness. It feels good to burn my skin. I leave the water running over me for a long time. There's plenty of water in Johannesburg. Their droughts aren't in sync with the droughts in Cape Town. And in spite of the power having been off for hours now, the water in the geyser is still hot. I'm raw and clean when I step out and change into my sleeping shorts and T-shirt.

I call Adrian from bed. 'Hi, baby,' I say when he picks up. 'I'm sorry to call so late, but I miss—'

'What the hell is wrong with you?' he says, and my mouth goes dry. How does he know already? He must know Thapelo. Or one of the other guys. Or anyone could have seen us, really – the country's small when you don't want it to be. It doesn't matter. He's right. What the hell is wrong with me? I had a front-row seat when I was boy. I saw what infidelity does to a person. Is this why I'm here? Is this the symbolic circle closing? So that I can turn into the monster I've always been afraid hides within me? So I can destroy the tender shoots of love in my life? Or am I meant to better understand my father? To realise he never meant to hurt us?

'I'm sorry,' I say. And that's the other thing that's changed because of analysis. For so long, I didn't feel any of the things I said. I was going through the motions. But I feel this. My eyes sting and tears pour out before I even understand what's happening.

'How could you do that without checking with me?'

'Checking with you? What do you mean?'

'I called the adoption agency today to find out if everything's okay,' he says, 'because we haven't heard anything in a while. They told me you'd withdrawn our application.'

I'm so relieved I almost laugh. 'It's not withdrawn,' I say. 'Just on hold.'

'We'll talk about this when you get back,' he says, and then the line goes dead. In all our years together, he has never hung up on me before.

# 24.

'What I don't understand,' Adrian says, 'is why you'd make us buy a cot if you don't want to do this. It's really fucking sick to make me choose things for the baby's room when you've pulled our application.'

'I didn't pull it. I just needed more time.'

'I never pressured you into this. It was your fucking idea! I said all along if one of us was unsure, we didn't do it. What the fuck?'

I drop my duffel bag onto the living room floor, next to the coffee table that separates Adrian from me. I'm not going to make it to our bedroom to unpack before we have this out. He hasn't bothered to get up off the couch to greet me. I know better than to try to hug him or sit beside him. Frasier looks up at me from his bed in the corner of the room and it's impossible not to read despair into his face. The large eyes, the furrowed brow, the downturned mouth. He's pulled himself into the smallest ball and I think, for a second, of how I used to pull myself into a ball on my bedroom floor when I was six and my parents were screaming at each other through my wall. I would try to squeeze my head between my knees and I'd hum to myself, rocking back and forth, back and forth until it stopped. But this is not the same. I am not my father. It was a once-off mistake. I will never, ever, ever do what I did up in Joburg again. I know that about myself, at least.

'I'm sorry, baby. I'm really sorry.'

'I can't believe we passed the interviews at the adoption agency. They don't know what the hell they're doing.'

I have to keep reminding myself that this fight is about the child. It is a relief, every time I remember. This isn't something that will inevitably break us. It's not all over. It can be fixed with a phone call. A resumption of processing. This isn't unsalvageable.

'I should have spoken to you about it. It was all just happening so fast, and you seemed so excited about it, and I didn't want to ruin it. I thought I'd be fine in a month or two, my doubts would disappear, and I'd un-pause the application without your ever having to know.'

Adrian's nostrils flare. I know that feeling, when you want to fight but the other person apologises too soon. There's nowhere for the anger to go, but it takes a while to dissipate in the body. 'Fuck,' he says.

I avoid his eyes. I take a seat on the armchair opposite him.

'I should have spoken to you about it,' I say, again, and suddenly my cheeks are hot.

He sighs. 'Don't cry, man.' And I can't tell if he's irritated because he thinks now we have to divert the conversation to comforting me, or if he's relieved that I feel genuine remorse.

I'm not just saying the words. It was stupid, what I did. Unnecessarily destructive. We are not our parents. We are not straight people trapped in some tragic story of gender roles and unspoken expectations and societal norms. It is not inevitable that we become lonely in our marriage. Our marriage can be anything we want it to be. We get to make it up as we go along. And we've said before that if one of us wants to sleep with someone else, let's talk about it. We can find ways to make it work. We can try opening the relationship up; or a threesome or polyamory or 'free pass' nights. What hurts when someone cheats is the deception, we agreed, not the act of sleeping with someone else. Lying about it, hiding it. Nothing poisons intimacy more than being on the outside of a secret, feeling like a fool. Adrian is not some prison I need to break free from. He is not the institution of marriage. He gets me, and I get him, and he deserves better than this. He deserves not to be cast in this role.

'Okay,' he says after a long pause and a deep sigh, 'well, let's talk about it. Do you not want to do this?'

How can I explain that I feel less ready than I did a year ago? That parenthood demands more from a person than I can give. That when I see how exhausted our friends with children are, it frightens me. They never get a break. Never. And children are mean and impatient and demanding. They say whatever they're thinking, even if it's cruel. If you're boring them, they'll tell you. You can try to make them happy, to hold them and love them and sing to them, and still they cry. They don't want you. They want someone else. This whole process is going in the wrong direction.

'Imagine I'm Emma,' he says, which is lovely and compassionate, and a little absurd, but I don't dare laugh when he still looks so angry. 'What are you feeling?'

'I don't know . . .'

'I'm not kidding.'

I try to listen to my body. Feel the tension in my chest. The panic that I'm losing him. 'I'm worried that I want a kid for the wrong reasons. Like, what if it's just to prove I'm "normal"? It's what you're supposed to do when you reach a certain age, and I want to belong to that club of normal, respectable people. So I can be accepted or something.'

'We had a team-building exercise like this at work,' he says. 'The coach said to us, "How would you live your life if you had nothing to prove and nothing to lose?"'

'Fuck me. I think most of my life is trying to prove things. To myself and everyone else.'

'Okay . . .'

'Like, I don't even know what I want. My starting point is never What do I want? It's How do I survive this situation?'

'What does that mean?'

'I don't think I like children.'

'It's not the same when they're yours. You didn't like dogs until we got Frasier and now look at you. You're obsessed.'

'I don't know.'

'You have so much love to give. I've seen it.'

The tears are back, just when I thought I'd finally got them under control.

'I don't think I know how to love,' I say. 'I don't do it right at all.'

'Don't be stupid,' he says.

'Do you really want kids just for the sake of it?' I say. 'Like, do you feel like you're bursting with all this extra love that needs to pour into a little human being? Or is it just so we're not lonely when we're old?'

'You can't have a child so you're not lonely when you're old!' he says. 'That's a terrible reason.'

Isn't it everyone's reason, though?

'Why else would you sign up for years of sleep deprivation?' I say. I don't even mention the constant mess. The never having nice things. You can't go on holiday. You can't talk to your friends without having to get up every five seconds because the kid is eating something it shouldn't be eating, or crying, or you're worried because it's not eating or crying. Our friends with babies look like they're losing their minds. The only thing that could possibly make it worthwhile is knowing you're not going to be abandoned and alone in some depressing frail-care facility when you're eighty-five, with all your friends dead and no one coming to visit.

I wish we weren't talking about this. I don't care about any of this, right now. I want to be talking about Liam, and what happened in

170

Joburg. I want to confess and beg for forgiveness, but is that fair? I'm still not even sure why it happened. Was I trying to reclaim something? Or to run away? Is my impulse to tell Adrian healthy or selfish? Do I hurt him to get it off my chest, in the name of intimacy and authenticity and transparency, or is it some kind of test – to see if he can forgive me? Do I carry this betrayal with me, alone, because it's never going to happen again, and feeling alone in this is the punishment I deserve?

'Wow,' Adrian says. He rubs his hand over his mouth. He isn't angry any more, I don't think. We're somewhere else.

'I think it's probably worth it in the end!' I say.

'Babe, that's not a reason.'

'Hey, all feelings are valid, right?' I say, quoting a line from an inspirational Instagram post that Adrian sent me once, after a discussion about our fathers. It's become a bit of a mantra for us, quoted semi-ironically because it's so cringe to be earnest about this stuff, but also so liberating to find an antidote to the culture we were raised in, where no feelings are valid, especially if you're a boy. Emotion is weakness. The realm of animals and stupid people. Intelligent people make decisions based on their minds, not their feelings. Which isn't true, it turns out. I listened to a podcast about the neocortex, the rational part of the brain, and how it's the first part of the brain to go offline in situations of stress, but it's too late to win an argument against that voice in my head, my father's voice: if you can't say what you mean clearly and rationally, then I don't want to hear it.

'Of course,' Adrian says. 'Sure. But it doesn't work. It's an unreliable insurance plan. We don't live in the same city as our parents. You see your mom maybe two or three times a year? And you like her.'

'Low blow, Adrian.'

'No, I'm not saying that to make you feel guilty that you should see her more. I'm saying even kids who adore their parents struggle to find the time to see them, or they live in different cities to them. They get jobs somewhere else. Life happens.'

'Maybe it's capitalism,' I say.

He smiles at me. 'Maybe.'

'We'd be awesome dads. They'd love us.'

His smile is sad. 'We would be.'

'This is what I'm saying, Adrian. I don't know if any of my reasons are the right reasons. When I think about being old and childless, it makes me really sad, but when I think about giving up so much of my life and feeling bored and stressed for years, it also makes me feel . . . Well, it makes me angry, actually. Like, who are you, random kid, for demanding so much from me? No you can't have a second fucking ice-cream and can you shut the fuck up so I can read my book or hear my friend who I never have the time to see, it's been a long week.'

'Maybe the moral of the story is: life is sad – pick your sadness?'

'I'm not saying I don't want to do it.' It was easier when I'd made him angry. I can't bear to see how this conversation is breaking his heart. 'I just need more time to interrogate my motivations. I realised in therapy that part of what was driving me was not wanting to be a peripheral character. You know, the gay uncle at Christmas, the fun, eccentric relative or friend who makes a short appearance in the main storyline. They're never the most important person to anyone; they're just included for a bit of comic relief, before the main family gets back to being a family.'

Adrian's eyes fill with tears. 'You're the most important person to me. Doesn't that count?'

I move from the armchair to the couch and I wrap my arm around him. 'I love you so much,' I say. 'Of course it does. That's why I'm all over the place. Maybe we're already all the family we need. You, me, and this little guy.' I point my eyes over to Frasier in the corner. He's given up monitoring our fight and is snoring in his bed, his head draped over the edge like he's trying to asphyxiate himself. 'We're our own main characters, our own main storyline, so what difference does it make how we feature in others' stories?'

He rests his head on my shoulder for a second; then the anger finds him again. He sits up and moves away from me and rubs his eyes. 'Fuck,' he says. 'It wasn't even me who pushed this.' And he's right. I've been manoeuvring him into a role again, and one that he didn't choose. 'I was happy either way. You were the one who was so desperate for a kid. We moved home from New York for this!'

'It was one of the reasons.'

'It was *the* reason.'

'I mean, was it? I basically had a nervous breakdown.'

'Don't gaslight me. I remember your breakdown. You could have found another job there. You could have gone back on your meds there. We could have pulled through.'

The memory of that time makes my chest tight all over again. Trying to find work within the shrinking window of an expiring visa. Interviewing for jobs when I thought I was losing my mind.

'I didn't want to have an American baby,' I say.

'I know, I know,' he says, and the tenderness is gone. He parrots my reasons with air quotes and rolled eyes: 'We owe it to this country. If we're going to privilege a child, it needs to be a black South African baby. That's also bullshit, you know. Adoption isn't charity. You can't think of your child as a charity case. A way to atone for being white in this country.'

'I know,' I say.

'Do you know? Because it shouldn't matter whether the baby is

173

American or South African. The point is it would be ours. We would be a family.'

'But being black in America is terrifying.' I regret it as soon as I've said it. I was thinking of the police killings, the unarmed black teens pulled over for nothing more than broken tail lights, imagining what that must be like if it's your child, but Adrian is so angry his whole face has flushed.

'Who said the baby has to be black? Why? I have nothing against it, cool if we have a black kid, great, but you're obsessed with that idea.'

'I can't imagine loving a white child.'

'Jesus. Do you hear yourself? Emma has her work cut out for her.'

'I just mean, they don't need us. They have so much already.'

'Kids given up for adoption?'

It's a mic-drop moment. My cheeks burn. There's nothing I can say to that.

'You're right,' I say at last.

'Everyone needs love. When are you going to accept that? Literally everyone. Even white babies. Even you.'

I don't know what to say.

'And now we're here for no reason and the country's falling apart around us.'

'So is America,' I say. 'They've elected Trump.' I stick out my tongue at him but it's too soon for a joke. He glares at me.

'I give it a week before you're freaking out about the blackouts,' he says. 'About what they mean for the future of the country. About how much easier crime is going to be now the streetlights never work and we can't turn on the alarm.'

I tell him that I'm going to go unpack, and he lets me. When I return to the living room fifteen minutes later, he's about to take Frasier for a walk. Frasier's in his harness and clipped to his lead. Adrian's wearing his navy Yankees cap and earphones. I tap his shoulder as he reaches the front door and he removes one earphone to hear me.

'I'm really sorry,' I say again. 'I should have kept you in the loop with all of my doubts. I promise I'll communicate better from now on.'

'Cool,' he says, his face closed up, 'and I guess I'll just wait around for you to decide what you want.'

He replaces the earphone before I can say anything else. He steps out into the street and takes Frasier to the park without me.

# 25.

I try to be extra nice to Adrian. I cook for him almost every night, and when I get home from work too late, and I'm too tired to cook, if he hasn't started on something already, I order us salads or any of the light, healthy meals from that vegetarian place he loves that I never feel like eating. I do the dishes, too, and it upsets our regimented division of labour, our equal distribution of chores. The golden rule of student digs and gay marriages: he (or she or they) who cooks does not wash up. I feel like a '50s housewife and it doesn't work to placate him, anyway, but I can't stop doing it. He glares at me when I steal his used plate and fight him away from the sink. He doesn't need me to cook and clean. He needs me to include him in my decisions. To stop running away from my emotions, to be present and honest. What's so difficult to understand?

I don't even know if he wants, necessarily, to stick to the adoption plan so much as he wants time to process the fact that I threw it all out (his words) without consulting him.

The more time that passes, the more difficult it becomes to resolve the crisis. I know Adrian. I know that if I now call the adoption agency and tell them to reactivate our application, he'll resist it. He'll think I'm doing it to avoid conflict, and he'll refuse to go along with it.

I pull up the adoption agency's number on my phone a few times. I stare at it for a long time, wondering if this is what will fix things, but I can't bring myself to call them. I decide to send them an email. I write an opus. The essay goes on and on. I try to explain myself, my doubts about my abilities to parent, my fear and jealousy of children, my reasons for messing them around. What is it that I want them to tell me? And more importantly: it's not them I should be talking to. It's Emma.

No. It's Adrian.

I delete the email without sending it. I go into my drafts folder and make sure it's deleted there, too.

I don't want to see Emma either. I don't want to have to explain myself to her, flagellate myself for her dispassionate observance. How could she possibly still be on my side after I've done something like this? I'm not sure she ever was on my side. It's a professional relationship, after all. I pay her. It's absurd to think she cares about me.

And I don't want to think about what I've done, discuss it ad nauseam, pick it apart, analyse it to death. The examined life might be the only life worth living, but it's also excruciating to get through. What's wrong with a bit of distraction and denial? A bit of booze. Stronger meds.

I text Emma to tell her I'm not coming in for our sessions for a while.

*How long*, she wants to know.

*For the foreseeable future*, I text back.

She tries to call me. I stare at her name on the screen of my cell-phone vibrating in my hand, the little white circle with a green phone icon in it: slide to answer. I wait for Emma to give up. She tries again.

*I don't think this is a good idea*, she texts.

*Sorry.* I turn my phone off. I tell myself it's so that I can concentrate on work.

Liam waits two weeks before texting. It's something innocuous and sweet, like, *Hey boy, just checking in to see if you're okay*, but the message comes through while I'm sitting right next to Adrian on the couch, watching a series, and my body seizes up. I delete the message immediately, without reading it properly. I saw the name. I saw the affectionate 'boy'. I am suddenly very hot and flushed, and my whole face feels damp, but Adrian doesn't even look away from the TV screen. I suppose it's the one and only perk of our culture of constant digital distraction that my phone could have vibrated for any number of notifications. DMs, retweets, posts getting likes, reminders, someone commenting on a Goodreads review, family WhatsApp messages, texts from people you slept with. Adrian trusts me, still. About this kind of thing, at least.

'Do you want some more wine?' I say.

'Sure.'

I get up. He pauses the show and takes out his own phone to scroll through his feeds. In the kitchen, I lean against the countertop and wait for my heart rate to slow and the sweat to evaporate from my clammy face. How do people have affairs? How do they live with this kind of feeling in their bodies?

I pour a full glass of wine – almost to the top of the glass ('an Eastern Cape fill', my friend from Port Elizabeth calls it) – and down the whole thing before filling both my glass and Adrian's to the respectable level. I return to the living room.

I wait another week before responding to Liam. I don't want to respond to him at all, but none of this is his fault and I don't want to be an asshole. I spend ages crafting the perfect message that sounds friendly but final. When I am finally satisfied he can't read anything into it, I press send. He reads it but does not respond. It should be a relief, but it just makes me feel even more disgusted with myself.

# 26.

Sibs is waiting for me when I get home from work on Tuesday. She's changed out of her work clothes. She's looking beautiful, again – elegant in her headwrap, tank top and jeans. She sits on a bar stool at the kitchen counter. Beside her, a neat row of empty plastic bottles – surface cleaners, dishwashing liquid, wood polish, a tub of laundry detergent – all the household products I'll need to replace before her next visit. She uses this lineup system instead of a list.

'Are you okay, Sibs?'

She's usually gone before I get home. It's early evening, now. Nearly six p.m. I'd imagine. I glance at the time on the microwave. 02:14. Not the time of day, but the time since the last blackout. Every day now, the rolling blackouts. Stage two. Stage four. There's a schedule, an app. Our cities are divided into load-shedding zones and we've learnt what zone we're in so we know when to expect the power to cut out. The blackouts are so normal now, so frequent, that I don't bother to tidy away the candles or the flashlight. Adrian and I leave our camping head torches on our bedside tables, for reading at night, and there's a box of matches left out beside the gas stove. The clock on the microwave starts up again every day when the power comes back on, optimistic, ready to count upwards from 00:00 into the future, but the oven display has given up. It flashes four white dashes. Blank. Empty. New. This kitchen says a lot about the state of the country, I think, the state of my mind, the smallness of a life. It reminds me of a line I read in a Don DeLillo book, once: 'American kitchens'.

That's it. That's the line. I remember thinking at the time, He must think this conjures a whole setting in the mind of the reader. Wooden cabinets, maybe. Mid-century. Windows above the sink looking out onto a lush, hot garden. But all it did was make me think about cultural hegemony. The audacity to assume we picture anything at all.

If I wrote the line 'South African kitchens' and left it to readers to fill in the rest, what would they see? An open-air wood fire, a cast-iron tripod pot, somewhere deep in the rural Eastern Cape? A sleek, modern penthouse in Sandton, with marble countertops and Smeg appliances? Peeling linoleum? Perhaps I'd see a stopped kitchen clock. A microwave display reading 02:14 when it's dusk outside. A line of empty plastic household cleaner bottles on the counter. Various shades of white, mint green and toxic pink.

Sibs beckons me to sit beside her. She tells me she wants to take out a restraining order against her husband.

'Does he hit you?' I say, and it's not the first time I've asked her this, but I never get an answer I can understand. I get indecipherable hand gestures, deflections, non sequiturs, ambiguous body language and feigned incomprehension, as if communicating in English is suddenly beyond her abilities. No, she says, she's worried about how he'll react when her ultimatum deadline expires. The 'no' is quick, possibly indicating that my question is beside the point, that's not why she wants the restraining order – rather than a definitive answer to the question.

'You mustn't stay there if you feel unsafe,' I say, and my words irritate me. They are empty. Where is she supposed to go?

I think about the vigilante justice she's told me about before, how the flasher she saw in the Company's Garden on the day of Buhle's birthday picnic would be beaten in the townships. Does that mean abusive husbands get beaten, too? It's comforting to think the mob will keep her safe. Life in the townships must be terrifying, but at least the population density means the neighbours can hear you scream. They'll tear down the door and drag her husband off her. Make sure he never touches her again.

But if it were true that neighbours keep each other safe, why do the stats show we have some of the worst gender-based violence in the world? Women are not safe in this country.

'I don't think we have restraining orders here,' I say. I've only heard of them in movies. Maybe they are an American legal invention.

'I already have an appointment with the judge,' she says. 'That's why I'm saying – I can't come to work next week. It's my court date. Why are you smiling?'

'I'm impressed, Sibs. You don't take shit from anybody.'

She shrugs. Frowns at me.

'Let me know how it goes,' I say.

She continues to watch me. 'So it's okay if I miss work next week?'

'Why don't you come in on the Wednesday?' I say, but then I change my mind. 'No, it's fine, you can come in the following week. I'll still pay you.'

I find her expression impossible to read. Quizzical, maybe. She's frowning at me but it's not an angry frown. 'You know what's even worse?' she says, and I don't think I want to know what's worse than possible domestic violence, friends who believe you should stay with your husband no matter how he treats you, no money and very few options for escape. I'm not strong enough for something worse.

'I'm pregnant,' she says.

I almost make a joke about it, say something like, At least you're still getting some – Adrian and I haven't had sex in weeks! I want to throw this conversation off me, this tar that is settling on my bones and dragging me down into the misery of the world. But 'getting some' could be part of her misery, too. My mind spins with all the ways that this might have happened. Pregnancy when she's given him an ultimatum, when she's unhappy with him. I remember Adrian joking at our adoption workshop about the inappropriateness of straight couples telling you they're 'trying for a kid' as if it's normal to discuss one partner dropping a load into another. Sex is not always funny and light and sassy, no matter how much I might want it to be.

'Congratulations, Sibs.' I stand up to hug her. She's a wooden statue in my arms. Rigid. She doesn't hug me back or lean into me or soften in any way. She waits for me to finish. I feel my cheeks flush and I let her go. I walk to the sink and pour two glasses of water. I hand one to her.

'I don't want it,' Sibs says.

I sip my water, slowly, and watch her. 'Okay . . .'

She looks down at her glass but doesn't drink. 'There's something wrong with me.'

'There's nothing wrong with you.'

'I am so angry.'

'That's understandable,' I say. I almost say, Emma would be proud of you. She's always trying to coax me into accepting my anger.

Her eyes flash up at me, white-hot. I've been trying to encourage her to open up, but I see now my interjections are just interruptions. I resolve not to say anything until she's done. She can feel this. She speaks again, and this time she keeps going. She tells me how angry she is that she allowed this to happen. She hates the man she married. She cannot stand him. Everything about him makes her skin crawl. She wants to get away. To be far away from him and never see him again, but she can't. She can't keep Buhle away from her father, and now there is a new baby on the way. Even more contact. More years before

182

she can escape. She doesn't want the baby. Sometimes, when she's lying in bed at night, she dreams about having a miscarriage. But she gets sick from the guilt and the shame of it. She doesn't want to hurt the baby. She would never do that, I mustn't worry. But why does she want to? Is she evil? There is something wrong with her. It's not the baby's fault her husband is lazy and useless. The baby is innocent.

'I haven't told him,' she says. 'I don't want him to know.'

'You won't be able to keep it secret forever. He'll see.'

She won't look at me. Neither of us speaks for the longest time. The clock on the microwave reads 03:02. I feel paralysed. I listen to Sibs's ragged breathing. Jerky inhalations. Heavy exhalations. She isn't crying. There are no tears in her eyes. I'm not sure what it is that she's feeling.

I catch myself thinking how strong she is. A surge of irritation. This trope about strong African women. Resilient, powerful, formidable. You strike a woman, you strike a rock. It's impressive, for sure, and it's true. They hold so many families together. They carry so much of the burden of this country. It's a more empowered cliché than the Western conception of femininity – incapable, overly emotional, irrational and weak – but it's a cliché nonetheless. No less dehumanising. Why must African women be strong? Why are they not allowed to fall apart, or rest, to be nurtured, to be the receivers of care rather than the dispensers of it? They are strong because they have to be. Because they never get a break. They can't rely on anyone else to pick up the slack.

I don't think I'd really felt how much grief and trauma there is in adoption until now. Adrian and I have only been thinking about the joyful side: the innocence and hope of a baby, the transformative potential in that moment of receiving a child – the homecoming day – to turn a couple into a family. The possibilities ripple outwards through space and time. Imaginings, or futures in the multiverse, happening already in some other dimension. Family holidays. Road trips. Baby food dribbling out and pushed back into the mouth. Dinner conversations about the child's day at school. Dance recitals. Music lessons. Quarter oranges dished out on the side of frost-covered soccer fields on Saturday mornings in winter.

But there is another side to all of this, too. A shadow side. For every child who finds a home, a mother who has lost it. A mother who could not make it work. Whose life was too stressful, too overwhelming, too underresourced, to allow her to hold on to that baby. Teenage mothers who made a mistake, or bowed to pressure from a boy. Rape victims. Battered women who were trying to leave their husbands and couldn't, who wanted restraining orders and got pregnant instead. Mothers who wanted the baby to have a better life than they could scrape together, even though they tried, they gave it everything they had.

'Sibs,' I say, and my heart is racing before the words can make it out of my mouth, 'do you want Adrian and me to take the baby?'

Shadow side of adoption

184

# 27.

'You did what?' Adrian says. 'Are you out of your mind?'

We're on a walk with Frasier in De Waal Park. Adrian catches himself shouting and lowers his voice to hiss at me – 'Are you serious?'

'I know it's weird,' I say.

'Weird doesn't begin to describe it.'

'Hey, it's sort of the adoption thing back on the table.'

He locks eyes with me. His nostrils flare again. He changes direction and accelerates away from me, towards the fountain at the centre of the park. Frasier chases after him. I'm determined not to run, to preserve some semblance of adult dignity in this huffy power-walk-slash-tantrum, so it takes me a few minutes to catch up to them.

Frasier is playing with a Boston terrier puppy by then, each of them taking turns chasing the other in and out of the water.

'Do you know how fucked up this is?' Adrian says, presumably to me, since I'm now standing beside him, but he won't look at me. He's smiling at the dogs. Smiling at the other owners standing around near the fountain waiting for their fur-babies to blow off steam. He waves at the old man we see often in this park. Dishevelled, with big Einstein hair, and a limping, greying Labrador to match.

'Why?' I say. 'It's what you want, isn't it? And it'll help Sibs out. It's win–win.'

'It's white saviour bullshit.'

'Again with this! It's the same as going through an agency.' Charity begins at home, I think, but I remember what he said to me about children not being charity.

Isn't this a kindness? Doesn't it make the world a little less brutal, in this tiny microcosm of our lives? Maybe that's all we can hope for. To change one or two lives. Our generation's burnt out. Exhausted. Why not settle for doing a little good, even if we've given up on changing the world? And these regimented societal roles are bullshit, anyway. The domestic worker. The adoption agency. The employer and the employee. We're all just people. We're all trying our best to figure out this thing called life in our own way, with our own unique pressures and opportunities. Marred in history and politics and class and race. And with so little time. I arrived in my thirties overnight. Our lifespans are a farce, in the sweep of history. We're fireflies, burning out in a day. If this is all over so quickly, why allow ourselves to get bogged down in How Things Are Supposed To Be Done, in propriety and precedent?

'You know it's not the same,' Adrian says. 'And don't tell me what I want, either. What I want is for you to stop fucking making these huge life decisions without me. I can't believe you still don't get it. It's not complicated.'

'I thought you'd be happy about this. I'm making up for my previous mistake.'

'Then why did you wait until we were in public to tell me?'

The sunlight reflecting off the fountain hurts my eyes.

'What did she say?' Adrian says.

'Who?'

'For fuck's sake. Sibs.'

'Oh.' I try to smile at him but it's all falling apart around me. I'm heavy, stuck, and there is something fluttering in my chest. This was a terrible decision. Another one. They're gathering around me like storm clouds. Am I trying to blow up my life? 'She said she'll think about it,' I say, and I can't swallow back the tears any more, 'but to be honest, she didn't look happy. It was very awkward.'

'Please will you take Frasier and keep walking for a bit?'

'What do you mean?'

'Do another few loops of the park or something. I'm going home and I want to be alone for a bit.'

I wipe my eyes and smile at another dog dad we often see at the park. I wave at him as he walks past with his Staffie. 'Okay.'

Adrian heads home and I linger for a while at the fountain. Frasier starts sprinting in circles with three other dogs, but he checks up on me every few minutes, whenever there is a natural break in play. He looks over his shoulder at me, or turns fully around to make sure I'm still there, that I'm okay. Even in his carefree romping, he is always aware of me, the gravitational pull between us. I am his planet and he is my moon.

He follows without question when I call him to walk down with me towards the yellowwoods at the far end of the park, near the hospital, although I mustn't read too much loyalty into this. I mustn't get emotional about it. He's only compliant because he's had plenty of time to play with his friends. If I called him too soon, before he felt ready to leave, he would ignore me. He'd look at me directly, and ignore me.

We named him Frasier after the TV show of the nineties – Kelsey Grammer as the bumbling psychologist with a talk-radio programme. Like all names, it just felt right when we stumbled on it, but the idea came from a few different directions at once. Part homage, part joke, with all sorts of meanings tangled together: the fact that it was a show that both Adrian and I loved, and felt slightly embarrassed about loving because it was already so dated by the time we discovered it. It wasn't new or cool, and it was very white. Still, we told ourselves it had aged so much better than other shows from that era. Even the gay jokes, which now make me cringe when I watch *Friends*, aren't offensive in *Frasier*. The gay guy is never the butt of the joke. It's Frasier or his dad or Niles. They're the fools who get it all wrong, or play along, or ham it up, or panic, depending on the situation with the gay cameo character.

It was Adrian's and my shared secret shame to re-watch *Frasier* together when life got tough in New York. When we were overwhelmed by the scale of the city, and the pace, and we felt homesick and like we couldn't make friendships that went beyond pleasantries. Frasier was lovable and pompous, like me, Adrian said. Frasier and I were neurotic and we were pedantic about the same things: language and grammar and what people really mean. But mostly we named our dog Frasier because the original Frasier is a psychologist, and our little Frasier would be good for our mental health. I didn't believe Adrian when he said it. I was ambivalent about dogs. Their neediness. Their lack of personal space. I hadn't grown up with animals, so I didn't yet understand how they free us from our own minds, and rekindle joy. I was right to trust Adrian on this.

I throw a stick a few times for Frasier and he chases it down with characteristic glee, but this time the heaviness will not leave me. I know something is wrong. Adrian is not okay. I've driven a knife into him and every time I try to pull it out, I only twist it and mangle more of his flesh.

He is waiting on the street outside our house when Frasier and I get home. He has a bag packed. A black canvas tog bag by the security gate. He is watching his phone in his hand – he must have called an

Uber – and he looks irritated that I'm back before he could make a clean exit. 'I was going to text you,' he says.

'Where are you going?' I feel numb. I feel as if it is someone else's dead voice coming out of my throat.

'I need to not be with you for a while.'

'Please don't do this,' I say. My hands are trembling as I try to touch him. He lifts his hand away from mine. 'I'm sorry,' I say.

'Ya, you keep saying that. But it doesn't change anything.'

'I'll tell Sibs the offer is off.'

'You can't do that.'

His car pulls up in front of the gate. A white, dented Volkswagen sedan. Adrian throws his bag onto the back seat, then walks over to the front passenger side.

'Where are you going?' I ask again.

'I'll let you know.'

He leaves the car door open and walks back towards me and I think, for a brief, beautiful moment, that he is going to hug me, at least, that we won't leave it like this, but he drops to his haunches and gives Frasier a kiss on the head. He holds Frasier's head in his hands while Frasier's tail thrashes behind him and he says, 'Bye, my boy. I'll see you soon.'

It's what Liam called me. Boy.

I stand in the street after he's gone. I don't know how long I'm there, unable to move. Eventually, Frasier's patience wears thin and he jumps up against my legs and starts pawing at me.

Adrian doesn't even know about Liam. I have managed to make him this angry, and this hurt, and he doesn't even know about Liam.

The next time I see Sibs, she acts strange. There is no music blasting from her phone when she arrives. No wig. Just short, natural hair in a popcorn style. She is tired and she barely speaks to me. I almost ask her, on my way out to work, if she's had a chance to think about my offer, but I suspect this withdrawal is her way of telling me without outright telling me. She's outraged I tried to take her baby from her, but she can't say so or she'll lose her job. Maybe, if I'm being generous, she is more worried about sparing my feelings than losing her job.

'Where's Adrian?' she says.

I have no idea how she knew. He's almost always at work by the time she gets here, so what could possibly be different? He didn't take all of his clothes – only what he could fit in that tog bag, the clothes he wears most often. Nothing looks out of place, as far as I can tell. It's as if she can smell the despair on me.

'He's staying with a friend,' I say.

She watches me for a while. Then she puts down the vacuum cleaner that she had been dragging to the plug point in the living room, comes over to me, and wraps me in a hug. 'I'm sorry, neh,' she says.

I let my head rest on her shoulder for a few seconds. It's probably unprofessional, but this is the only human touch I've had in the week since Adrian left. I feel my eyes sting and I blink them hard to stop whatever is rising out of me. I pull away and try to muster a smile.

'Please don't forget to sweep the courtyard,' I say.


Things are awkward between Sibs and me for weeks. Neither of us mentions the offer, and I become convinced I've done the wrong thing. Sibs regrets opening up to me, and she feels dirty because I took her doubts seriously. I am a constant reminder of her moment of weakness, her one unmotherly thought. I want to tell her, I know you didn't mean it, I know you don't want to hurt the baby, or give up the baby, I'm sorry I said anything, but talking about it will only make things worse, so I avoid her instead. I make sure I have left for work by the time she arrives in the morning, and I stay at the office until after sunset to make sure I miss her in the evenings, too. She has her own set of keys. She can let herself in and out. Maybe we never need to look at each other again.

Staying late at work keeps me out of bed, too. All I want to do is sleep, and it frightens me. I can feel myself slipping into that catatonic, broken state, and if I let it happen, how will I ever claw my way back to the world of the living?

How did I let myself become a man who takes his partner for granted? How boring and unoriginal. How embarrassing, when so much of my life has been taken up by trying to be nothing like those men, those absent fathers, those entitled, straying husbands. I get home to our empty house and my whole body aches for Adrian. Emma said to me, once, when I told her that her Freudian stuff around sex is too weird, that what it really means is that when you're a child, 'you love with your whole body'. I want to rest my legs on Adrian's lap while we watch series on the couch, his hands warm through the fabric of my jeans. I want our lazy Sunday mornings back. Coffee in bed. Reading until Frasier finally loses his patience and demands a walk. Our walks with Frasier.

When I message Adrian to ask how he's feeling, he tells me he's still angry, and I feel the earth give way beneath me. A yawning abyss, endless, bottomless and dark. Lonely as a distant galaxy in the vast emptiness of space. A universe of titanic forces, mechanical laws. Cold, lifeless, and without love. What if he never forgives me?

I message Liam and ask him to let me know if he's ever in Cape Town. He's in Cape Town the following weekend.

'I didn't really want to hear from you,' he says.

We're at a bar on Kloof Street and I'm buzzed, already. I made my-self a Negroni while I was getting ready at home – properly, this time. No frumpy, thirty-something-married-guy attire. I'm in a black T-shirt that fits well and hides the softness of my love handles. Layered over this, a blood-red button-down open shirt. Dark jeans. I'm on my third Negroni of the night – my second since entering the bar – and Liam is still nursing his mineral water.

'I'm sorry about how things went down,' I say.

I'm growing accustomed to apologising. It's not humiliating any more. I have no shame left to protect. Or is it pride? I am approach-ing the acceptance phase. It's almost enjoyable to give up. The pre-tence is exhausting. The act of being normal, well adjusted. I imagine drinking Negronis like this every day until I lose my job and the house. Then maybe I'll downgrade to box wine. Brown sherry. I imagine sleeping for weeks at a time, emerging from the sleeping-pill-induced stupor just long enough to refuel with a bit of food. I'll go live among the homeless people in De Waal Park. We can make beautiful, useless sculptures from car tyres and other people's aban-doned detritus. Who would I hurt, then? Who would even care?

Liam looks around the bar. 'I can never get over how white Cape Town is.'

'Yeah, sorry.'

'Like another country.'

'I actually chose this bar because it's usually more mixed. Must be a bad night.'

'Hey, you didn't make the city like this.'

I'm annoyed with the two of us. Even though I agree with him, what is the point of this virtue-signalling? We're not going to fix Cape Town by complaining to each other about it, trying to prove we're good whites who notice these things and care about these things. But Liam isn't done.

'One of my Cape Town friends,' he says, 'won't take on any more white friends. He has a one-in-one-out rule. He said to me, otherwise, if you don't try, you realise you're part of the problem.'

'Good on him,' I say, mostly because it's easier. I don't tell Liam I think curating friendships like that is tokenism or racial essentialism, I don't know which exactly, but it's icky. And I don't tell him that I'd take whatever friends I could get. It's impossible finding time to see people these days. Everyone's lives are being pulled in opposite directions. Kids. Jobs. Even the gay friends. Being in your thirties is lonely as hell.

'Say what you like about Joburg,' Liam says, 'the crime and the potholes yada yada, but at least we don't have to work so hard to make sure our friendship circles aren't straight out of apartheid.'

'What are you implying?'

'I'm not implying anything,' he says. Then he smiles at me, for good measure. That dimpled smile of his. It's dangerous to look directly at it – like a solar eclipse. 'So why did you want to meet up?' he says.

Whatever I do with my face will seem lecherous, so I fix my gaze on my hands resting, without intent, on either side of my Negroni glass. 'Adrian and I are taking a break.'

Liam lets out a breathy groan and rolls his head back. 'Ah man, I'm sorry to hear that. Because of me?'

'No, no. It has nothing to do with you. Not directly, anyway.'

'What does that mean?'

'Nothing. This isn't your fault.'

He nods. Leans back on his barstool. 'I'm sorry. You guys were so good together.'

'Are you for real?'

He laughs, then, and holds up his hands in surrender. 'Okay, I don't know you guys well, sure. I'm just saying it looked like you were happy.'

'Is anyone happy?'

He rolls his eyes, but it's playful. 'Comfortable, then.'

'Don't wince! It's not a bad thing. It's not boring to be comfortable. Or maybe it is, I don't know. Maybe I'm ready for boring. I'm tired of the streets. I tell you, maybe it looks glamorous from the comfort of your relationship, but the streets are rough. It's exhausting; I'm exhausted.'

'Great pep talk, Liam.' I manage to wink at him when what I really want to do is shout at him. 'How do you know I'm not the wronged party?'

'Are you?'

I call over the bartender and order another round, except Liam doesn't want another sparkling water so it's just a drink for me. Liam watches me down the last of my Negroni in preparation for the next one.

'I think maybe you've forgotten how important it is to have someone who has your back. Who's always on your side.'

'What the fuck are you doing, Liam?'

'What the fuck are *you* doing? Why is it me here instead of Adrian?'

The room has lost the gentle softness I worked so hard to achieve. It no longer drifts when I turn my head, like some underwater place. It is in sharp focus. Illuminated by adrenaline. And rage.

'I shouldn't have come,' Liam says. 'I think I'm still angry about what happened last time.'

'Pick a number and stand in line.'

'Do you know how sad you looked?' he says. 'After we'd finished. You looked so unbelievably sad and full of regret. Then you couldn't get out of there fast enough. It might surprise you to know that it wasn't the best feeling in the world for me.'

'You knew I was married.'

An ugly, high-pitched laugh. I realise it's coming from my own throat. What a ridiculous play I've found myself in. This tired old script. The cheating partner looking for someone to blame.

'I'm gonna go,' Liam says. He looks in his wallet for cash but who carries cash any more? So he tries to flag down the bartender to ask for the bill so he can pay his portion with a card, or his phone, but I stop him. I can't bear this and anyway, he only had mineral water and I might not be done drinking. 'I'll get it,' I tell him.

Liam gives me an awkward half-hug – one arm around my shoulder – I think because he's also surprised by how bitterly this ended, and he also doesn't want to be the bad guy.

Later that night, when I finally fall into my bed, fully clothed but for my shoes, I wrap Frasier in my arms. He resists me at first. He struggles to get away, maybe out of a sense of loyalty to Adrian, maybe because I reek of alcohol and other people, but I won't let him leave me. I lock my arms around him as he writhes and pushes against me, but eventually he gives up. He lets me hold him. I slacken my arms slowly, to test him, and still he doesn't leave. I try not to move too much when the crying starts. I don't want to disturb him or make him uncomfortable with any shaking. I lie dead still, and let the tears run silently into the fabric of the pillow. Water from a leak in a pipe.

# 28.

I don't leave early for work on Tuesday. I want to see Sibs. I can't bear this avoidance any more. I make myself a strong cup of coffee and I wait for her in the living room. A cartoon villain in the half-light.

Yet again, no tinny cellphone music announces her arrival. No sound from the street but the squeaking hinge of the security gate, and then her key in the lock. It's been so long since her characteristic exuberance, it's beginning to feel as if I imagined it. How can this meek, defeated thing be the same person who shouted her views at me over gqom or amapiano? The woman who arrived in a flurry of dramatic wigs and bold earrings and fashion. Frasier runs to the door to greet her.

'Fa-jee!' comes an excited squeal from the hallway. She's brought Buhle with her.

'Sorry,' Sibs says when she sees me step into the hall. 'I didn't know you would be here.'

She has no make-up on. No jewellery. When she straightens up from greeting Frasier herself, the face she shows me is not hers. Dark circles under her eyes. She looks as exhausted as I feel.

'It's no problem! Buhle's very welcome. I'm just worried she gets bored.'

'No, she likes it.' As if on cue, Buhle sits down on the hallway floor to let Frasier climb all over her. Frasier licks her face and she squeals with delight and giggles and says hayi – no – over and over again but she doesn't mean it. She doesn't make any attempt to stop him.

How could I have ever believed Sibs would want to give up her child?

I watch Buhle as she leans so far back she ends up flat on the floor. She squawks. Frasier stands beside her head, licking her chin, her forehead, her ears. It must mean something that Sibs didn't want to leave her at home with the father.

'Sibs,' I say, 'did you get the restraining order?'

She sighs and dismisses the whole affair with a hand gesture.

'I'm sorry.'

Adrian would say, what can I do to help, but I hate that kind of question – offered so soon after bad news. We can seldom do anything meaningful in the face of life's misfortune, and whenever it's asked of me all it does is add to my stress. Now I have to say no, I'm fine, there's nothing you can do, and so it's actually just more work at precisely the moment when I have the least capacity to take on more work. Not only am I overwhelmed, but now I also have to reassure the people around me that they're good people, they're good friends, they asked if they could help.

'How is the pregnancy going?' I say.

The skin tightens ever so slightly around her eyes. She doesn't want to talk about the baby with me. I shouldn't have asked. I feel dirty for asking. She doesn't want to give the baby up, that's obvious by now. Why am I not getting the hint, she must think, and I want to shake her and tell her I *do* get the hint, but we need to keep going, we need to get to the point in the conversation where I can release her from all of this. I'll take it all back. I think I've figured out a way to do that without sounding like I've changed my mind. Rejecting her or her baby would only make things worse between us.

'It's fine,' she says.

'Have you been getting morning sickness?'

197

'What?'

'The baby. Are you feeling sick from the pregnancy?'

'Not really,' she says, 'I'm just hungry all the time.'

'With strange cravings?'

Sibs furrows her eyebrows. She laugh-exhales, then moves past me into the kitchen. Am I using words she doesn't know, coming off as ostentatious, or is it something else?

The kitchen is immaculate. It has been since last night. I'm extra thorough with the cleaning the nights before Sibs comes, as if sparkling countertops might make up for the random cruelty of fate; that she was born into her life and I was born into mine.

She opens the dishwasher and starts removing clean plates to stack back in the cupboard.

'Sibs,' I say, 'do you want some toast and an egg?'

I open the freezer and take out a frozen, sliced loaf of brown bread. I remove a butter knife from the drawer and insert the blunt tip of the blade between frozen slices to break one free, and then another.

'I'm fine,' she says.

'What about Buhle?' I say. Sibs hesitates. 'I'm making for myself, anyway.' I've already eaten but I can force it down if it's what needs to happen to get them to eat.

Sibs straightens from the dishwasher and turns to face Buhle, who is sitting cross-legged on the living room floor, next to Frasier's bed, stroking him. Sibs fires off some isiXhosa at Buhle and Buhle fires back. I'm amazed at the dexterity of Buhle's tongue. Complex, multi-syllabic words, uttered at speed from her usually mute mouth.

'Yes,' Sibs says, 'she would like that. You can also make for me.'

I drop three slices of bread into the toaster. I fill a small pot with water and bring it to the boil. I lower four eggs into the boiling water.

'Buhle loves Frasier, hey?' I say.

'She loves him.'

'That's sweet,' I say. 'I was scared of dogs when I was small.'

'No but Frasier is very gentle. You can see. He would never hurt anyone.'

'Sibs,' I say, 'I feel so strange about saying we would take your baby—' She tries to interrupt me but I can't stop now. I can't let her stop me; I need to get this out. 'It wasn't fair. You were overwhelmed and it's ridiculous to think that you meant what you said. Everyone has doubts. It's normal. You're not a bad mother and I know you don't want to split your family or give anyone up.'

I'm running out of steam and now that I wouldn't mind being interrupted, Sibs is all ears. I can't read what she's thinking.

'I have a better idea,' I say. 'What if you and Buhle move in here for a while? And the baby, when it comes.'

Sibs narrows her eyes. Am I still somehow managing to insult her?

'It'll still be your baby! And it would just be for a few months. It's up to you. No pressure. I just know you're getting divorced and you might need somewhere to stay. I wouldn't charge you rent or anything. It would be free.'

The timer screeches on my phone and I've never been so relieved to take an egg out of boiling water. I turn off the gas and spoon each of the eggs onto a side plate. I pour the boiling water down the drain. When I gather the courage to look at Sibs again there are tears streaming down her cheeks.

'For how long?' she says.

'As long as you like! It's just me kicking about in this place now.' Although already I'm thinking, maybe this will bring Adrian back.

Sibs's expression is stern, unsmiling (I see where Buhle gets it from), but then she steps forwards and wraps me in a hug. 'Are you sure?' she says.

'Absolutely.'

Over my shoulder, Sibs shouts a string of words at Buhle and Buhle says something in return. All of it is lost on me.

'Yes, it's fine,' Sibs says.

I peel the four eggs, place three of them on three slices of toast, which I've buttered and smeared with Bovril. 'Here you go.' I hand Sibs two plates, for her and Buhle, and I drop the fourth egg into Frasier's bowl. He leaps out of his bed and runs towards the kitchen, leaving Buhle behind. She sticks out her bottom lip – a caricature of a sad child. Sibs calls her to come sit at the table.

I wasn't expecting them to join me at the table. It feels comical, the formality of sitting down to eat our toast together in the dining room, on the clunky, old-fashioned wooden table that's child-friendly and ready for family. I remember sitting alone at the dining table when I was a boy, eating my supper in silence while Patience waited in the kitchen for me to finish. I'd call through the door when I was done, and she'd clear my plate, remove my mother's untouched food from the warming tray on the sideboard, wrap it in cellophane and put it in the fridge. Sibs wipes her cheeks dry and starts cutting up Buhle's toast. She smiles at me. We eat our breakfast while Sibs tells me about her friend who works for a Norwegian couple in Clifton, and how those people have fish for breakfast and it makes her friend sick, the smell of it, have I ever heard of anything as strange as eating fish for breakfast, and her friend's been sick so many times in the bathroom there but her employers don't know, she's always smiling at them and she uses a room deodoriser and so the other day, her employers even gave her a big cut of salmon to take home. In the background of Sibs's booming voice: Frasier, guzzling his egg in the kitchen like a gremlin – grunting and smacking his lips and trying to dislodge bits of yolk from his palate. He pushes his metal bowl all

200

over the room, trying to lick every last atom of flavour from the edges. The bowl clangs against the skirting board of the kitchen cabinets over and over again. And now Sibs and Buhle are both laughing. Sibs, a thundering, chest-heaving laugh at her own story about her friend, and Buhle's a high-pitched giggle, probably for no reason other than that her mother is laughing and it makes me want to cry, all of this noise and life. What a weird, sweet little family we would make.

# 29.

I allow myself to hope that Adrian might take the news well. He might think it's less of an aggressive proposition than taking a child away from Sibs. But yet again, I haven't asked him. The one thing he wanted, to be included in my decisions. Are you supposed to ask someone who's no longer around?

He agrees to meet me for coffee at the little café at the end of our block. We came here for breakfast before work sometimes, and would often pop in for a coffee after a walk over the weekend. I take a seat at the small round table in the corner, right in the window, with an uninterrupted view of Devil's Peak. This was our table, too, if we got here early enough on weekdays, before the scores of mysteriously-never-at-work-but-with-plenty-of-money-to-spend people decamped to the café for the morning.

Adrian has shaved off his beard and the effect is unsettling, like I'm meeting him again for the first time, years before we were married. I don't know if it's his clean-shaven youthfulness that makes me feel this desperately sad nostalgia for what we were like back then, before New York and my dad dying and my anxiety getting so out of control, before I started hurting him, before we lost whatever it is that we have lost – or if it's the fact that he is closed off to me now. It's a subtle shift, and not unkind, but it's there. The protective barrier that separates all exes. A glass wall between us.

Is this what we are – exes?

'These are for you,' I say as he sits opposite me at the table. I've brought him a small bunch of pincushion proteas – his favourite.

We talk for a while about work, about mutual friends. He tells me, at last, where he's been staying (with his friend Ettienne in Sea Point). I am trying to muster the courage to tell him the plan with Sibs, but I need to ease into it. First I tell him about how much Buhle loves Frasier, how we all ate breakfast together the other day and it was really lovely, like some strange hybrid family, how sweet he would find Buhle at the moment, but he doesn't want to hear it.

'I'm glad you called,' he says, cutting me off, 'because I have some news.'

I watch the mountain out of the window because there's really only one thing that can follow a sentence like that and I don't want to hear it, and I can't look at him while he says it. He's met someone and he's here to tell me that our marriage is over.

'I've applied for a job in London,' he says.

'You're kidding.'

'Listen, before you have a meltdown, I don't know if I've got it yet. It's early days. One interview down, and it went well, but there are two more – you know how these EdTech companies are. They like to think they're nimble and agile, that they're all about startup culture, but they're just like the huge corporates where you need approval from about a hundred people to hire someone. But I wanted to keep you in the loop.' The 'unlike you' is implied.

I ask him about the role, but I may as well not have bothered because I don't listen to anything he says after that. He talks and talks, and I get the sense, which surprises me, that he is nervous about this conversation, too. Something to do with building better systems for distance learning, developing bespoke software for tertiary education institutions. It's a lot of jargon. There are words I recognise, phrases

I remember from our life together, from his current job, but all I can think about – and it isn't really a thinking thought but a feeling – is that I set this all in motion and I don't want any of it. I don't want to lose him.

'And we have so many friends in London,' he says.

'I guess we do.'

Our coffees arrive and I force myself to take a sip. I think my hands are trembling so I use both of them to bring the cup to my lips and keep it steady. The foam is lukewarm; the texture of soft citrus fruit succumbing to mould. I keep going until I reach the hot fluid beneath. It scalds my tongue. I can't taste anything.

'Do you . . .?' I start, but I can't beg him. If I beg, it'll only push him further away. Everything I do these days seems to push him away. My face is very, very hot.

'Good luck, I suppose.'

Adrian clears his throat. He's blushing a little. 'I wanted to say,' he says, 'that the invitation is open. If you wanted to come with me.'

'What do you mean?'

'I think we could do with a fresh start. Or maybe to forget this one.'

'No thanks!' I say, trying to joke about this, but he jerks his head back like he's been slapped. I change my tone. 'I just mean . . . London. You know how I feel about that.' He does remember, doesn't he? We used to mock them together, the white South Africans fleeing to the UK. Good riddance, we said. Bunch of racists. They were disloyal and we didn't need them. We needed believers. People who were willing to muck in. Adrian must remember the fights I had with my father about the future of this country. The writing's on the wall, he loved to say. He and that awful British wife. He was delighted to have met a British woman, a ticket out. Mom would never have gone. 'We'll be here to turn off the lights at the end,' she said. I guess she

204

didn't anticipate the lights would turn off on their own, that the power utility would crumble.

My skin crawls thinking about how he tried to ingratiate himself into British culture. His little creeping Britishisms once he moved over there – his 'mum' instead of 'mom', his feet instead of metres, the way he turned up his nose at our wines that he'd once loved and only ordered French. It was all so obsequious and embarrassing, to try to fit into a culture that wasn't yours, that viewed itself as superior to yours. Grovelling at the feet of the old colonial masters. And yet he believed it was his. An ancestral connection. It undermines everything. Gives legitimacy to all the detractors of English-home-language South Africans, who believe we have split loyalties, dual citizenship, a traitorous lack of national pride. Even in New York, people would ask me 'But where are your parents from?', because they could not accept that I am as South African as they are American. As many hundreds of years under the belt. How many generations does it take before people accept that you belong?

'Don't be one of those, Adrian. We promised we would never be those people.'

'Who are we trying to prove it to?'

I think about going out in London with my brother, on a trip when we were visiting Dad, and how we ended up in an Aussie bar, and it was full of white South Africans, white Australians, white New Zealanders. A natural fit, everyone seemed to think. Honorary antipodeans. Is it a more natural alliance than, say, with Ghanaians and Kenyans? What kind of community is that? I don't fucking want it.

I make my voice nasal. 'This country is going to the dogs!' I whine, parroting all the emigrants we used to hate.

'That was different. Things were different.'

'How?'

He lets out a short, sad laugh. 'Because in those earlier waves of emigration it wasn't going to the dogs. It was just becoming more black, and they thought that meant the same thing. That's what was despicable. Now things are actually starting to fall apart.'

'What do you mean?'

'Do I really need to spell it out? You read the news. The power outages. The crime rate. The unemployment rate. The corruption. The stagnant economy.'

I can't believe it's Adrian saying all of this to me, itemising our failures on his fingers.

'We were supposed to be a miracle country,' I say.

'We were. Maybe no one can live up to that kind of pressure.'

'Look at Brexit,' I try, changing tack. 'Look at Trump! Everywhere's falling apart.'

'Do you know how much worse your anxiety is here? Can you not see that? You lie awake every night when the power goes down, waiting for the alarm system to come back on, listening for footsteps and whispers. You don't walk to work any more.'

'So, what? This job will sponsor you a work permit?' At least Adrian has no access to a British ancestral visa. I couldn't have dated him if he had.

He nods. 'And I just want to say that, I don't know if I'll get the job, but if I do, I'm taking it.'

'So this is an ultimatum?'

'Call it what you like. Actually, you know what? Forget it.'

'No, no,' I say, 'please. I'm sorry. Just give me some time to think about all of this. It's a huge bombshell.'

He winks at me. 'I learnt from the best.'

I take another sip of my coffee. Press my palms into my eyes. 'Sibs is moving in,' I say.

'That's nice of you.'

'No, you don't get it. Like, indefinitely. I was going to ask if you wanted to join us.'

Adrian makes an 'O' with his mouth a few times before finally speaking. 'So, like a live-in maid? Like our parents all had in Joburg in the eighties?'

Is he mocking me? Trying to hurt me? I speak slowly, aiming for a neutral tone: 'Exactly the opposite of that.'

He narrows his eyes and I can't decide if he looks quizzical or incredulous. I hope he's thinking what a generous gesture this is, what a cool attempt to disrupt the ossified race and class relations of this country.

Then he does the last thing I expect. He starts to laugh. It's a deep belly laugh, the release of months of tension. 'What a fucking mess,' he says, wiping his eyes. 'Good luck with that.'

# 30.

I spend the rest of the weekend in bed. It's a choice, at first, because I choose to climb under the covers at eleven a.m., after leaving my meeting with Adrian. I'm just so tired. Just a little nap to release me from this exhaustion. But then the sleep takes on a life of its own. It possesses me. A shadow-figure I can't throw off. He's waiting for me at the end of the bed whenever I wake for an hour to stare at the ceiling. He makes my eyelids grow heavy. 'Just a few more hours,' he whispers, and 'then you'll be rested.'

On the third brief emergence into wakefulness, I begin to worry, but I'm too tired to really expend any energy on the worry. It's more of an abstract exercise. A dilemma in someone else's life. It's not normal to sleep this much, is it? It's not healthy. I feel as if I've been drugged. Is it a problem with my heart? My thyroid? Is it cancer? My body must be shutting down. Organs failing one at a time.

I remember how hard my father fought to stay awake at the end. His determination to talk and joke even as his eyelids would not stay open. The might of his will, no match for the creeping darkness. I think of my mother's darkened room.

I pull Frasier into me. I don't need to hide this from him. He curls into my arms and rests his chin on my bicep. He gives me one small lick on my cheek. This is okay, he's saying. I'm here with you.

I allow myself to sink back into dreamless, black sleep.

I wake in the dark and let Frasier out into the courtyard to relieve himself. I give him his kibble. Order myself some soup and stare at the blank screen of the TV while I wait for it to be delivered. I return to bed after eating.

I spend Sunday like this, and Monday, too. I call in sick to work.

I text Emma to ask if I can come back. She will have filled my slot by now, I'm sure of it. Some new sad sap to whine on her couch. I'm bitter about it already. Why did I ever trust her or think I was important to her?

*You're welcome back whenever you're ready*, she replies.

I'm furious when I arrive, and I'm late – no apology. I'm dressed in old grey tracksuit pants with bleach stains on them, and a moth-eaten beige T-shirt I've had since university days. She must see what she's done. She must look at me like this. I want to rub her nose in it.

'This was supposed to fucking help me,' I say, 'not make everything worse.'

I'm scowling out of the window, and it's difficult to speak because I keep sobbing and it was easier when all of this was locked down. Tight and pressurised and secure.

'I thought, okay cool, let's try this. Let's stop avoiding the feelings and let them come. Let the sadness come, because maybe if I feel it I'll realise it's survivable. It's finite. It will run its course, if I'm not running away. Drain out of me like pus from a wound and eventually I'll be empty. But there's no end to this. It's bottomless. And you've disabled all my fucking defences.'

An image flashes across my mind. A small, pink creature writhing in the dark. A crustacean, maybe, shrimp-like, but his shell is missing. The carapace has been ripped off. He's soft and tender, wriggling, trying to coordinate his little legs to protect the parts that have become exposed, his stomach and heart. I think he's blind, too. Too young to know how to protect himself. Anything could crush him. I turn my head to see how Emma's taking this, but she's as impassive as ever. Calm, alert. Ready. She could remind me that this is what I wanted, that this is exactly how analysis was described to me by my friend who first recommended it. It's intentionally relentless. To get past your defences. But she doesn't say any of that.

'And what's the point of unlearning all my childhood coping mechanisms if there's nothing to replace them? There's nothing better. Just not coping.

'You've fucking made me like this. You let me relax into this. Made me think it's okay to trust people, to be vulnerable and weak, to be this fucking mess who needs other people to put him back together or hold him together. It sounds great, sure, to allow yourself to rely on people who love you, to let them see your shadow side. Your sadness. But it doesn't work. Adrian is gone.

'I've pushed him away. Everything I do at the moment pushes him further away, even as I've realised how much I need him.'

'That need frightens you,' she says.

'And so? I cheat on him. Bravo. Well done. Very clever. How is this healing?'

I tell her about Liam, and the cancelled adoption plan, and Sibs. Who cares if she still likes me when I'm done?

'I think,' she says after a long pause, 'that what you've been doing is a last-ditch attempt to protect yourself. What you call messiness, and some might call relationship, is dangerous to you.'

'Ya, well. Fuck. Now he's gone.'

'You were trying to prove to yourself that he would go.'

On Tuesday, I'm woken by the sound of generators in the lane. I have to get up, anyway, because it's the day Sibs comes to clean and the only thing strong enough to get me out of this bed is the imagined shame of lounging under the covers like some collapsed Victorian woman while Sibs cleans the house around me. I have to get up. But where do people find the energy to get up, day after day after day? I lie in bed listening to the sound of the generators. There are at least three of them nearby. The guesthouse on the corner has one, and two of the neighbours. The rumble is deep – I'm surprised I can't feel it in my sternum – and calming, like how a car's rumbling engine helps an insomniac baby fall asleep. I could close my eyes and imagine I'm in Harare or Maputo or Lagos. Those cities all sound like this – the gentle rumble of state collapse. Blackouts as part of normal life. Unremarkable, expected, that citizens can't rely on the state to provide basic services. It's only a few hours a day, and the timetable is scheduled, but Cape Town is starting to sound like every other African city. The end to South African exceptionalism. Good, maybe, to let go of our superiority complex when it comes to the rest of the continent, but enraging, too. This isn't poetic or quaint even if it reminds me of scuba diving holidays in Mozambique, road trips through Zimbabwe. This is backsliding, and it's what every reactionary said would happen at the advent of democracy. I start to argue with my father in my mind, haranguing him that this wasn't inevitable, but he never cared what I thought. He emigrated anyway. And it's impossible to win an argument with a dead man.

When the blackouts started again a few months ago, I bought a stove-top kettle. It's not as much of a concession to decline as a generator, and it means I can at least make myself coffee. No electricity required. I put the kettle on the burner and light the gas with a match. It whistles when it comes to the boil.

Sibs arrives while I'm still drinking coffee in bed, so I down the dregs and get into the shower.

'Are you sick?' she says when I emerge from my bedroom, even though I think I'm looking quite normal after the shower. Presentable, even.

'I'm just very tired.'

'You're late for work, neh.'

'I know. I'm going now.' I'm not going to work, though. I can't face writing cheerful, meaningless copy for corporations that pretend to care about the planet and the people on it, mostly because the agency I work for advised them to care about those things, because it's good branding, but really all they care about is making money. I'm helping them greenwash and I don't have the strength for it today. I know how capitalism works. I know I'm replaceable. If I don't do it, someone else will. Well, let someone else do it today.

'Are you excited about next week?' I say.

Sibs's smile is wide and bright. 'Are you sure?' she says.

'Of course.'

'My husband is going to help me move. He has a friend with a bakkie.'

'Are you still speaking to him?'

'No he must help me. He owes me.'

'Okay,' I say, forcing a laugh because part of me thinks that's really funny – the image of bossing around a soon-to-be-ex-husband against whom you've tried to take out a restraining order – but that part of me is buried beneath the part that's dead and heavy. 'I'll see you then, roomie!'

I contemplate booking a hotel room so I have somewhere to go sleep, but it's a ridiculous thought. I think of my girlfriends who have babies – there's no shortage of them at this stage – because they won't be at work on a Tuesday morning. I call up Jess and ask her if I can come over for tea.

# 31.

'Oh, Jesus, I'm sorry, honey.'

Jess has a second baby now – Roxanne. And she's small and immobile enough that I can pick her up without worrying she'll wriggle free and fall out of my arms. Roxanne is a blob. No muscles to twist away from me. No opinions of how dull my company may be. I know enough to know I must support her head. I cradle her in my lap and she stares at me with huge, unsullied eyes.

'Yup. London. Can you believe it?'

'I really thought your separation was going to be a blip.'

'Would you guys ever think about leaving?'

'You know what they say about Cape Town?' Jess says. 'It's the top deck of the *Titanic.*'

'Your mom's got jokes,' I say to Roxanne. I give her a finger to squeeze but she isn't very good at it. 'Will the lifeboats be seated according to class?' I say, very chuffed to remember that line from the movie.

Jess laughs. 'I hate to say, but yes, we are thinking about it.'

'But you guys love it here!'

'We have to think about the kids,' she says. Her voice is flat, as if she's been told by Johan that this is the line, and she must repeat it. I remember that first taxi driver saying to me, the day Adrian and I moved home, that the only white people who ever talk to him about kids are the ones who say they want to leave the country. In spite of everything, Jess is a type. Maybe Adrian is, and I am too.

213

I tell Jess she isn't helping my mood. So she goads me instead: 'Come on, it's not so bad. Aren't you seventy-five per cent British, anyway?' She's amusing herself. She has that wide-eyed mischievous grin she gets when she wants to laugh.

'Fuck off,' I say, 'you know it was forty-five per cent.'

I should never have told her about having done the DNA test. As if the results could ever have validated me. I wanted so badly to be part black, or part Middle Eastern – anything but all-white. There was that show on TV when I was younger, where they tested a bunch of famous South Africans - Mandela, Marc Lottering, Pieter-Dirk Uys – and most were surprisingly mixed. I suppose my results had felt like something, at least. To be less than half-British. To be descended from Jews and Scandinavians and the French. I had to settle for white, but at least I wasn't only descended from imperial power and domination. There were more humble, ahistorical migrations in there, too.

I don't even believe in bloodlines. It's a specious, divisive way to view the world. Great for rousing armies and stirring up nationalistic senti-ment. Great for identity politics. But we're not defined by our blood. Isn't that what trans people keep telling us? And adopted people?

Home is where you grow up. It's the people who love you and the places that hold your earliest memories. It's the culture that shapes your thoughts and your vowels, your sense of humour, your references – and culture is not coded in our genes. It's an ever-changing group effort, pulled this way and that by insiders and outsiders, compatriots and immigrants, literature and song and conversations in the park. It's an argument passed down through the generations across every kind of family. It's not about ancestors. Our ancestors are strangers to us.

'Don't you have a British passport, anyway?' Jess says, and she's really amusing herself now. She topples sideways on the couch to giggle and to get away from any swings I could take at her.

214

'Don't make me throw this baby at you.'

'I'm kidding. I'm really sad about it all, too. We've been to three farewells in the last month. Three!'

'Fuck.' I cover Roxanne's ears, but Jess laughs and waves the concern away with her hand.

'She's too young to know what anything means.'

'Nick?'

'Where is Nick?' She calls his name repeatedly and loudly over her shoulder until Nick comes teetering into the room with a small plastic racing car in each hand. 'Oh, there you are, honey. I just wanted to check you're okay. You can go play.' But he doesn't go play. He sits beside his mom on the couch and leans his head against her shoulder. He stares at me for a period of time that would be inexcusably rude if he were an adult, and then shifts his focus to his sister in my lap. Emma would say I'm projecting onto him, that loneliness I see in him, but not everything can be a projection, surely? People are lonely, everywhere you look.

'He didn't get much sleep last night,' Jess mouths at me. 'You were saying?'

I appreciate her attempt to keep the conversation going, to bring it back to the adults and not pivot everything to her children, the way mothers can, but I don't really want to talk about what we were talking about.

'It doesn't matter.'

'No, it does,' she says. 'It does. Sorry.'

I wait a beat. 'I feel like this is about more than Adrian getting a job. It's part of my identity. I don't really know who I am if I give up on this place.'

Jess says nothing for a while. Just looks at me the way you look at a sad child, mouth downturned in sympathy, or pity. Maybe it's com-

215

miseration. I get the sudden sense that we are both long dead, and I'm looking back at us from some distant future point. We are forever sitting in this room, suspended in a faded and grainy old film. Look at these people, in these clothes of the late 2010s; emblematic of a particular time, a particular history. What happened to these far-flung, forgotten remnants of empire, those left behind by the retreating waters of European colonisation? Was their fate the same as the Romans in England, the Chinese in Malaysia? Did they integrate or isolate or trickle away in quiet waves of emigration? Stay tuned for a hundred years to find out.

I pinch my left hand. These abstractions are a kind of dissociation. Why do I do it? Does trying to find how my life fits into a larger narrative help me understand it better? I've been doing it for as long as I can remember. Calling my school years 'homophobic', part of the global story of queer suffering although hopefully towards the end of its arc through history – but does that explain away my experience? Does the term 'toxic masculinity' do anything to convey into another's consciousness what it was like to be trapped, cowering under my desk? I can label my uncertainty about the future and my shifting sense of self as symptoms of the democratic transition, or decolonisation, but that doesn't make it feel any less painful to let go of a dream, to think maybe all my idealism only gets in the way. Why does it matter so much to me how this country fares, how my generation contributes? I am not the story of white South Africa or childhood trauma or homophobia. I am not a symbol or a microcosm or a sociological experiment. This is my life. It is particular and individual. It's the only one I'll ever get.

'Don't think of it as giving up on anything,' Jess says. 'You have to just try to live your life. To do what's best for you.'

'Even that's hard to figure out.' My tone is flippant and she laughs.

216

Jess is a trooper. She's trying to pay attention to me but it's difficult. She's distracted by her children. Nick has now started rolling his little plastic car up and down her leg and Jess seems to have that sixth sense, all mothers have it, that Roxanne is getting antsy in my lap. Roxanne is hungry, and the signs appear first in Jess.

'You know,' she says, 'I could remind you that you said you were coming home to have a baby.'

We smile at each other. 'Same thing,' I say. 'Fixing the country. Adopting a baby.'

She lets out a snort. Playfully rolls her eyes. 'What did Adrian say about calling a baby a project?'

'Not to do it, sure, but it's a stupid thing to say, because unless we're going to fall pregnant by mistake, it obviously is one!'

Roxanne has now caught up to her mother's intuition and has realised that she's hungry. She contorts her face into a pained expression, the precursor to a wail. Jess removes her from my lap and bounces her up and down for a bit as she paces the room. 'So what are you going to do?' she says.

'I don't know. I have Sibs and Buhle and the baby moving in next week.'

'But that's not permanent, hey? You can tell them it's for a few months until Sibs is back on her feet, and then you can go join Adrian in London.'

'I had kind of thought it was going to be permanent.' My voice is irritating me. Whiney and nasal.

Jess returns to the couch and starts breastfeeding Roxanne. I don't think, in all the years we lived together as flatmates, that I ever saw her areolas before.

'This is home, you know? Wherever else we go, we'll never be at home.'

She offers me a conciliatory smile, but she's not invested in the conversation. It's surface-level for her, trying to be a good friend, but she isn't really present. She just wants to be with her children.

I want to leave but instead I try the opposite. I lean in. Maybe I am the reason there is this glass barrier between the world and me, this blunting of the connection I feel with anyone. 'I keep trying to build a home,' I say, 'and it keeps failing. I finally figured out that I was also the one tearing it down, so that I'm in control of the process, I'm not the unsuspecting victim, but now that I'm aware of it I've been really trying not to sabotage anything, and it's falling apart all the same.' I surprise myself by crying here, not just in front of people but in front of children, who pounce at the first sign of weakness.

Jess looks stricken. She has no idea what to say to this sudden outburst.

'Sorry, let me get out of your hair,' I say. 'You've got things to do.'

'No, don't go,' Jess says.

I stand up and wipe my cheeks dry. I smile at all three of them like some kind of awkward salesman who's been rebuffed.

'Please stay,' Jess says. 'I love having you here.'

I can't keep talking about this, though, and I can't bear the thought of talking about anything else.

'Thanks for the tea.' I take our two mugs into the kitchen and place them in the sink. Jess follows me to the front door, cradling Roxanne against her breast, which would have been much more comfortable had I just let us stay seated in the living room.

'Please take care of yourself,' she says.

'You too.'

'And take it one day at a time. Don't even think about the big stuff. Just the day in front of you. And think about Buhle!' she says, eyes wide with remembrance. 'Think about Buhle.'

And so that is exactly what I do.

# 32.

The cot is still in the guest room. That stupid, shameful cot that I used to break Adrian's heart. I want to smash it to pieces against the wall, but Sibs will need it when the baby comes.

I buy some coloured pencils and crayons for Buhle. Notepads with unlined white paper. Coloured card. What else might she enjoy?

I walk down to the indie bookshop on Roeland Street that I adore, and I buy more books for Buhle. She's already got all the Xhosa-language children's books that I bought her when we started lessons with Sibs. Now I buy my old childhood favourites. *The Very Hungry Caterpillar. Where's Spot? The Wump World.* Some Roald Dahl, even though I suspect he's been cancelled for something or other by now, and she's too young to get started on them just yet. I think back to some of the books that I was read as a little boy, still in print in the eighties. *Little Black Sambo*, with his parents, Black Mumbo and Black Jumbo. There were Golliwogs in *Noddy*. The eighties weren't even very long ago, and all of that was normal. There's better stuff, now, at least. Stories written for little black girls from Africa. Stories with zebra protagonists and lions and giraffes. Stories with black girl pro-tagonists, and little black boys. Villages that look like Africa, rather than the kind you find in Europe. Then there's the gay propaganda. I buy Buhle that contentious story of the penguin with two dads that set off a culture war in America.

'You have to start the brainwashing young,' I say to the sales clerk who rings up my books at the till, but she doesn't know I'm joking, or she's too nervous to laugh in case I'm not. I suppose I'm dressed like an ordinary mid-thirties straight guy, not queer enough to pass as queer in today's queer idiom. Maybe she thinks I'm a bigot.

If Adrian were here with me, he'd find my comment funny. He'd build on the joke, come up with some even more heinous thing that Republicans like to say about gay people and quote it at me, dead-pan, like he believed it. We're grooming kids. We're recruiting. I hate that I'm doing this alone. I feel my eyes prickle when I think about Adrian being here with me – how much he would have loved this, choosing books for Buhle – but I've always known this was how it was going to go. We end up alone. Love can't be trusted and no one sticks around. I think I've been waiting for Adrian to leave me since we met, and there's a relief that it has happened. No more, the agony of waiting. I don't need to be on high alert for warning signs. I don't need to anticipate the moment when he will have had enough of me so I can try to delay it.

I deliver the books back home, then I have a second surge of energy. I run to the hardware store and buy some blackboard paint. I brush three coats of this over one of the walls in the guest bedroom, and when it's dry, I draw a scene on it in chalk, to get Buhle started. A little girl with big solemn eyes, her narrow, dazzling smile. I surround the blackboard Buhle with daisies, and I draw a big rainbow arching across the sky.

That night, I take one of the books I bought her to bed, and I read it from cover to cover. Not to practise, so much as to refresh my memory of the story. I want to be able to do it right with her when she comes. To let her snuggle under my arm and to read it with feeling – all the voices and animal sounds and everything.

# 33.

I've taken another day off work the day Sibs and Buhle move in. My boss is starting to worry about me and my plummeting productivity, but she's aware of my mental health issues – even though I never told her quite how bad things got in New York – and she's always very nice to my face about it. This leave was booked in advance, anyway, and my colleagues are excited about the social experiment. My phone is littered with messages by the time I wake up.

*Good luck today! Let me know how it goes!*

*Is it too soon to ask you to bring Buhle in to work with you? Do you think she likes choc cake or vanilla? I can make carrot too?*

*Hey dzaddy, how's it going?*

I have arranged all the soft toys that I bought for Khanya on the bed in the guest room. I went back to Jess's yesterday to borrow a wooden train set and some plastic stacking toys and wooden blocks. I've lined these up on the bookshelf above the cot, next to the illustrated books I bought this week, organised by height. I bought arum lilies yesterday afternoon, and I've arranged them in a vase on the mantelpiece in the guest room. I've rolled up two bath towels the way they do in hotels, and left them on the bed. It was Sibs who laundered the towels, but I hope it's still a hospitable gesture. The room catches the early-morning light. It's homely and warm.

I pace the living room and check my watch a few times. Eight-fifty-five. Eight-fifty-eight. I'm not even sure what's making me nervous – that Buhle might take against me for no reason? That Sibs's soon-to-be-ex-husband might drop them off and he'll scream at me for interfering in their private lives? Who the hell do I think I am? Maybe I'm worried I'll find this living arrangement untenable, and I'll have to admit to myself that I'm a fraud. I don't care about people as much as I like to think I do. I want my own space. I want the poverty and suffering of others to be out of sight. I'm no better than all the other middle-class people in this country.

Sibs has not arrived by nine-fifteen and I'm not going to call her. I'm not going to be that clueless, privileged employer who imagines it's easy getting from the townships to the city bowl before nine a.m. I know about delayed and cancelled trains, over-full and unreliable taxis. There's probably a taxi strike on at the moment. There always seems to be a taxi strike on.

I can't stomach another coffee, so I decide to take Frasier for a walk. We head up the oak-lined lane, bursting now with the luminous, highlighter-green leaves of early summer. These oaks were planted in the nineteenth century and at first glance, they are magnificent: tall, gnarly, thick-trunked. Squirrels jump from their branches onto the roofs of the houses below. But the longer I've lived here, the more disease I've noticed. The jagged remnants of torn, rotting branches. The sticky film that covers the paving beneath the canopy. It coats my car, clouding the metal with a black patina. All the oaks in the city are diseased, a tree specialist told me when he came to trim the branches back from my gutters. They are overwhelmed with aphids, I think he said, or mould, little microorganisms anyway that the oaks can't shed every winter as they would in Europe. It doesn't get cold enough here for these northern hemisphere deciduous trees. They lose their leaves in autumn, but not all of them. Some of last summer's leaves hang on throughout the winter, brown and scraggly, just enough to keep the colonies of parasites alive. These microorganisms will spread their sickness quickly over the new spring growth, but for now, at least, for the next few weeks, the canopy is bright and healthy.

Frasier loves these walks, even if we're not going to the park, and he pulls hard on his leash, straining against his collar. I keep my eyes on his back as we go; it's impossible not to feel a little of his relentless optimism, his conviction that this is going to be the most joyous walk yet. He checks over his shoulder to make sure I'm still there – big, sad eyes looking back at me. Sometimes I think I might burst, looking at him. All this pure, untainted, unwithheld love. His smallness is too much to bear, his vulnerability, the beating of his tiny heart in his chest. I can feel it through his little ribs when I pick him up from a precipice on a hike, or lift him away from an aggressive dog's snarling. He doesn't know what's coming. He doesn't even try to protect himself from loss. He loves with his whole body, freely, even though I'm powerless to save him from anything that matters, anything bigger than a fall or a fight. Cancer. Ageing. The gradual erosion of sight and smell and touch, every pleasure in life. And then finally, the end of all companionship. I can't protect him just as I can't protect Adrian or my mother. At the end of the day, what's the difference between love and grief? Love is holding their hand at the side of a hospital bed, watching them slip away.

Today, Frasier's innocence feels like a revolutionary act.

'You know what he represents,' Emma said to me before. 'He's your inner child. You want to protect and nurture him to heal something in yourself.'

'That's what clueless parents do with their children,' I said. 'The ones who aren't self-aware.' I meant for her to laugh, and I think I heard her laugh, but her point was taken. His helpless vulnerability doesn't infuriate me the way it does when I detect it in myself. I don't find

223

him weak and contemptible for needing love and offering it so freely.

My metaphorical inner child sniffs the corner of an ugly, face-brick apartment building, then pees on it.

We ascend the steep incline of Upper Orange Street towards the lower slopes of the mountain. This view never gets old, never fails to calm me. This enormous, flat-topped mountain, remnant of an ancient range that once dwarfed the Himalaya. This grey-green wall of rock towering over our little lives. Its stability feels eternal. Larger than any human history or despair.

But the city squabbling at its hemline is always changing. Shattered glass lines the pavement in front of me, and again on the next block. Broken car windows, glittering in the sunshine like fallen galaxies. There are 'For Sale' signs everywhere I look. On small terrace cottages and grand houses, at the entrances to blocks of flats. For Sale. For Sale. For Sale. I remember when the exodus reversed for a while, when it seemed like the city was brimming with people who'd recently returned from Australia and Britain and America.

I turn left onto one of the quiet residential roads that follows the contour of the mountain. Frasier stops to smell and pee on another property wall and, while I wait for him to do his business, I glance through the metal gate into a garden.

It hits me with unexpected force. A memory dislodged by this overgrown oasis. Clivias in bloom at the base of an old milkwood tree, deep in the shade where the sun cannot reach them. The inflorescences are bright and beautiful. Red and orange explosions above dark, strappy leaves. They are the only plants I know that flourish in such darkness and, thinking that, my chest is suddenly tight, my hands shake, and I see her: my mother, walking among the clivias in her nightdress, her long, sandy-blonde hair wild and protruding in tufts. Her eyes

224

ringed with red. 'They're so beautiful,' she says, 'don't you think they are beautiful?' She runs her pale hands over the leaves, careful not to disturb the blooms, and I should be happy that she's out of bed, that she's finally awake, but this is just as frightening as her endless sleeping. She's barefoot in the bushes, roaming down here like a madwoman. I have no idea how long she's been here, in this dark, forgotten corner of the garden. 'They're beautiful, Mom,' I say, and she smiles at me and there are tears streaming down her cheeks, and I see, perhaps for the first time, how desperately she is trying to claw her way back to life, how hard she is fighting to find beauty again, to find anything worth living for. She's putting all of her strength into this, to come back *for me*.

She's so ghostlike and pale it can't be real. It can't be a memory. It must be a dream, and yet would a dream press down on my chest like this? There's something beneath my arguments with Adrian and Jess and my father about my responsibility to make things right in this country – and it's not political. It's not even articulate. It's pre-verbal. A yearning. If I leave, I'm abandoning her at the bottom of the garden, with these improbable, defiant blooms. Clivias grow wild in the shade here, and only here, in southern Africa. Every time I see them I think of her, that first crack of joy in the endless darkness. How can I ever give up that hope? How can I ever give up that love?

Sibs has still not arrived when I get home. I try to call her on the most recent number I have for her. It does not connect. I try another number, the one she used before this one, I think. An old woman answers. She shouts into the receiver, her voice gravelly and deep, and I don't understand a word she's saying. She's speaking isiXhosa but too quickly for me to make sense of it. She hangs up, and I try again just to be sure the number is correct. The same woman answers and hangs up. My first reaction is irritation. Why is it always so difficult to get hold of Sibs? Why does she go through numbers like this? I remember teasing her about burner phones once, but she'd never heard of them, and didn't know what was funny.

I send her a WhatsApp message asking if she's okay. No response. The message does not deliver. She's more than an hour and a half late, now, but I try not to worry. These things happen. There's always some bizarre and unforeseen reason why she does things the way she does. She's probably lost her phone again, and she'll call me later to explain why she couldn't come in.

By lunchtime, I've accepted she's not coming. I try a few of the numbers I have for her. None of them work except the gruff old lady. I phone her again and try my slow, haltering isiXhosa.

'Molo, Mama. Ndicela ukuthetha noSibongile.'

She releases a stream of rapid-fire language, far above the level of my Introduction to isiXhosa course, or any of the storybooks we read.

I try to be more direct: 'Uphi uSibongile?'

It's no use. The woman is agitated. She's shouting again – probably asking me to stop calling this number, to leave her alone, to learn to speak goddamn isiXhosa properly. I send a second message to Sibs's WhatsApp: *Let me know when you get this. I just want to check you're okay.*

# 34.

Sibs hasn't called back after two days. No voice note, no missed calls. My WhatsApp messages have not delivered.

I've been trying to cope with this on my own, not to burden Adrian with it because it's my mess, and he wanted nothing to do with it, but two days is a long time to go without explanation. I message him about it and immediately feel less panicked. He's going to talk me down, tell me this is just my anxiety, she's fine. There's a simple explanation for it. She's lost her phone.

*That's not great,* he texts back. *Sibs isn't usually rude.*

*I know. It's very weird.*

*Please let me know if you hear from her.*

*I will. Maybe she went to the Eastern Cape?*

*I guess we have to wait and see.*

I try to focus on the website copy I'm writing for a wine farm. It's a decent wine. Tasty. I enjoy it. And the owners have a whole skills development programme for the farmworkers. Free schooling for farmworker children. They've set up a profit-sharing initiative with their workers, and I should feel excited about it. These are some of the good guys. The industry is notorious for its terrible labour practices, stretching all the way back via the dop system to the days of slavery. This client of ours is trying to correct for some of this heinous history, and yet I can't concentrate. I can't muster any passion. I struggle to find the words for anything.

My phone vibrates in my pocket. It's Adrian, again: *Didn't Sibs ask for a restraining order?*

Still no contact from Sibs on Day Three. I don't know the names of any of her friends, or aunts or cousins or anything. I don't know who her other employers might be, the people she cleans for on the days she's not with me. She mentioned that friend of hers who works for the Norwegian couple in Clifton, once, and an employer who tried to help her get medical attention a few years ago in Claremont, but that's all I've got to work with. No names. How would I find them? How do I know so little about her? She knows almost everything about my life. Which underpants are mine and which are Adrian's. The books I like to read. She asks about my mom and my brother. She remembered Khanya's name, even when Khanya was just an idea from years before.

I don't even know her husband's name.

Adrian and I are texting again. He messages every few hours to check on me, and to hear if I've heard anything. *Let's not panic,* he says now. *Let's see if she comes next week.*

I imagine Sibs arriving. Loud and glamorous and laughing. Bright lipstick and a completely new hairstyle. She's sorry she didn't get in touch. It was a silly misunderstanding. She had to go to the Eastern Cape for a funeral, last minute. No, she lost her phone and had no money for a replacement SIM. We'll all laugh about it and I'll feel ridiculous for having worried.

I don't think I can wait until next week.

I start phoning clinics. I call the hospital in Khayelitsha, the clinic in Philippi. I even try the private hospital near my house, though if anything happened to her, the private hospitals would have turned her away.

None of the clinics in the poorer areas will give me an answer, anyway. They won't give out patient information, and besides, how do they know if they have a patient by that name. Don't I have a last name for them? Do I know how many Sibongiles there are in Cape Town?

I send a group message to the residents and homeowners in my lane. It's a group I try to avoid because of the crime hysteria, the reactionary politics, the thinly veiled racism. I ask if any of their domestic workers know mine. Sibs must have had friends working nearby. She knew that Adrian and I had returned from New York almost as soon as it happened.

No one in the group can help me. None of their cleaners know anything.

I send another message to her phone, as if my increasing desperation will make the message deliver this time. I suppose I'm hoping she's avoiding her phone, screening her calls. I do that too when I'm feeling overwhelmed.

Along with the creeping panic: guilt. She didn't want to move in. She felt obliged because I'm her boss and she thought she couldn't say no to me. It's like all those hideous sex scandals in Hollywood, the sexual predators in high schools – the power imbalance in our relationship is so extreme that she must feel like she has no agency. She will agree to anything I say, even if she doesn't want it.

*Maybe the whole thing was just too weird for her*, I text Adrian. *She realised she can't go through with it?* While I see that he's typing a response, I try to imagine her angry at me. Livid that I expect her to be grateful for something she never asked for. To play the smiling servant all day long, every day. But I can't keep the image in my mind. She knows that's not what I wanted. That's not how our relationship works. I couldn't have been clearer that no was an option, could I? She could have said no.

The person I keep imagining angry is her husband.

But is that a stereotype?

I go to the police on the fifth day. The police station on Buitenkant Street is an imposing behemoth of reddish-brown brick. Four storeys tall, as wide as a city block, with tiny windows like an old colonial fortress, which it probably once was. The ground-floor windows are impenetrable, screened with thick metal bars. I wait in a short queue in a room that smells of sweat and floor polish. The constable behind the counter is a large man, bored by his job, who addresses each of the people in front of me with eyes at half-mast. When it's my turn to speak, he tells me I can't file a missing person's report if I'm not related to them. I have no idea if that's the law; I try to google it on my phone while I argue with him, but he tries to wave me away so he can deal with the person behind me. I tell him that Sibs had gone to court to ask for a restraining order.

'Did she get it?' he says.

He can read the answer on my face before I'm able to lie.

'This is ridiculous,' I say. 'What if something's happened to her?'

I'm shouting now, making a spectacle, and I can feel my cheeks burning, the eyes of all the people in the queue behind me. He tries to tell me that I shouldn't get involved in domestic issues, that what goes on between a husband and his wife has nothing to do with me. I start quoting nonsense statistics at him, the high femicide rates in this country, the levels of domestic abuse. The gist of what I'm saying is all true, even if the numbers are made up, and he's focused on me now, his eyes more alert than they had been. I can't tell if he's thinking of throwing me out, or hearing me, and then a female constable comes over from the other end of the counter. She looks irritated with her colleague. He busies himself with some papers until I move away from him.

230

'Bhuti,' she says, 'what do you think has happened?'

'I don't know, but I'm worried about her. I haven't heard anything in five days.'

'You don't think she resigned?'

'I hope that's what it is.'

She sighs and starts to write in the open book in front of her. 'Okay, what's her full name?'

I give her the first name and wait for her irritation. 'I don't know her last name.'

'Her ID number?'

'I don't know.'

'Address?'

'I don't know.'

She sighs again, rubs her eyes. There's almost nothing in her book. 'Do you have any friends or family members we can contact?'

I try to conjure the husband's name, again, but nothing comes. Did she ever tell me?

'Do you have a photo of her?' she says. Finally, something I can offer her. Sibs will have a profile pic on her WhatsApp. I find our most recent conversation on my phone. An endless stream of one-sided messages from me, undelivered. *Sibs, where are you? Is everything okay?* I tap to enlarge the small circular pic. It isn't her. Who the hell is this woman? But whoever she is, she's dancing in front of an old blue couch with a child. The child is Buhle. My eyes fill with tears.

'This is her daughter,' I say.

The constable nods at my phone. 'Why don't you print that out and bring it back to us.'

It strikes me that maybe they want the picture to help identify bodies. My eyes blur again and I wipe them with my palms.

This constable isn't uncaring. She has kind eyes. 'What I suggest,' she says, 'is that you wait until next week. If she doesn't come back again, then we know she has gone. Come here, and we will open a case.'

'That's a long time,' I say.

'Hopefully everything will turn out to be fine.'

I hover. Hope doesn't do much, I want to say. 'In the meantime,' she says, 'if you are worried, try to find out more about what might have happened. Where she was last seen, what she was wearing – these are the kinds of things that are helpful. Who she was with. See if you can find any of that out for us, or maybe you can find someone who knows her. Come back with that. And the picture. You can ask for me. I'll remember you.' She gives me her name, and I thank her, even though I don't know what I'm thanking her for.

What did I expect? I haven't provided any information the detectives can use. It's the haziest sketch. An idea of a person. Do I really know so little about Sibs? We've shared jokes and stories and birthday cake. I know her daughter is frightened of white dolls. I know she never wanted to marry Buhle's dad. I know what music she likes to listen to, how she snorts so loudly to clear snot from her nose that I can hear her from the street. I know she changes her hairstyle every week. I know what she thinks about dogs and children and men who expose themselves in parks and that she loves Buhle more than anything in this world, and she'll love her new baby too, even if she didn't want it at first, even if she's scared and doesn't know how she's going to manage it all. Yet the police form is almost blank. I'm reporting the disappearance of a stranger. In the heat of this dimly lit room as I make my way out, in this rancid, pungent smell of sweat, I'm cold. Am I finally losing my mind? Is Sibs someone I've dreamed up?

I take the day off work again on Tuesday to wait for her. My boss knows the story – that it's a semi-missing-person situation – so she allows it, but this has got to stop. No more, she tells me. She'll have to speak to HR if this happens again. Maybe issue me a formal warning. I'm grateful for the labour laws of this country. I would have lost my job ages ago if this were New York.

The line I tell myself now, when I can't sleep at two a.m., is that Sibs forgot she was supposed to move in last week. She got the dates muddled, that's all. She missed work, and that's a bit out of character, but it was a workday just like any other. Maybe she also needed to cry, or sleep, or generally try to hold herself together in this hellscape of late-stage capitalism.

She's not in by nine a.m. I make myself wait until ten a.m. Then I'm in the car. I start driving towards the police station, but my hands steer me onto Philip Kgosana Drive, the wheel turning as if some other consciousness controls it. This is the freeway out of the city and into the townships. It's completely stupid – I don't know where Sibs lives – but is it any more stupid than going to the police station again? Letting them humiliate me with their questions and my answers. Even if they did open a case, it would be to humour me. To get this persistent white guy out of their hair. It felt pretty clear that they won't look for her. I think about the American and British crime shows I've watched over the years, and how unrealistic they have always seemed to me. The expectation that a criminal will be hunted and caught. The satisfying narrative shape of justice, as if people ever find the perpetrators. Crime does not get solved. It merely gets reported. I can't leave Sibs and Buhle to the indifference of the police.

I pass the hospital and curve away from the mountain towards the sprawling townships. I can do this. I have some information to go on. I know they live in Philippi, which narrows the search. It's not the whole vast slum that stretches to the Stellenbosch mountains that I have to search through; it's one discrete section of it. I know she lives in a 'hokkie', whatever that means. Either a shack or a lean-to or a backyard structure, but it's not a house, so I don't need to trawl the streets with proper brick houses on them. Maybe I'll recognise the street from that video she showed me in winter, the sewage and stormwater flooding between the homes, swallowing everything.

I drive between two luminous green golf courses, the Black River shimmering beside the freeway for a moment in the morning sun. I pass the old, abandoned power station on my left, the convergence point of three apartheid-era residential boundaries: black, white and coloured. White Cape Town is behind me now, coloured to my right, black to my left. The transitions from one to the other are still painfully obvious in spite of the new housing estates and the deregulated ownership laws – the way the greenery falls away almost immediately, the sharp downgrading of homes from leafy suburban to humble and tightly packed and then, at last, to tiny, derelict structures interspersed with shanties. I normally find it depressing going past the townships, to be reminded of how cheap black life still is in this country, how little has changed for so many people, but today it's not depression I feel. It's not nerves either, though my nerves are heightened – I'll never shake the nervousness of being a white guy in the townships. But above all else, today I am enraged.

I want to drive my car into a building. I want to set fire to something. Punch someone in the face. But whom would I punch? Whom can I blame for this? Hendrik Verwoerd? Cecil Rhodes? My father, with his comfortable disinterest in politics? Every foot soldier of colonial dispossession, every apartheid-era bureaucrat? Even the police in this hard-won democratic state. All of us who turn a blind eye to this. We're all complicit. I'd have to punch everyone I've ever met.

234

I take the offramp just before the airport and turn right into the dusty streets of Nyanga. I've never been here before. The only time I've been into the townships was to go to Mzoli's once, the shisanyama in Gugulethu that became a famous tourist attraction, and I felt so proud to be supporting a township business, to be immersed in township culture. I'm ashamed of it now. The arranged transport. The warnings to be out before nightfall. I was too frightened to walk more than a block in either direction of my 'authentic experience'.

I swear the pedestrians on the side of the road are watching me. I remember Sibs telling me that Buhle has never seen a white person. 'She's seen me!' I replied, affronted, but that didn't count.

According to Google Maps, I'm heading in the right direction.

When I get to the shanty section of Philippi, I pull over. There are people everywhere, and they mostly ignore me, but that doesn't shake the feeling of being watched. I get out of my car and I approach a woman, who walks faster to get away from me. 'Uxolo, Sisi, do you know Sibs?' She shakes her head and continues on her way. I ask another woman, older than me, and friendlier than the first, but she doesn't know anyone by that name. I ask an elderly man, three teenagers, a few more people in their twenties. I feel tears coming on. It's hopeless, but I can't give up on her. I take out my phone and pull up a photo of Sibs that I got off Facebook. I finally found her on there last night, after hours of trawling through Sibongiles on the app. She hasn't posted in months, and she didn't respond to my message, but at least I have a picture of her now. And her surname. I'll take both to the police when I'm done.

I'm aware of holding an expensive phone out in the open, but I won't let fear sabotage my mission. I approach a young man in a threadbare red T-shirt and black cap. He seems irritated to be approached but he waits for me to speak. When I show him Sibs's picture, he thinks he knows her. He calls over a friend, another young man watching me from the doorway of his shack. The two of them argue about whether it's the right person. The first guy says he will take me to find her.

He shakes my hand and introduces himself once we start walking. His whole demeanour has changed since I first asked him about Sibs and it makes me nervous. He is warm and friendly. His eyes are soft and crinkled above his smile. He has the kind of face that's impossible not to trust, but maybe that's part of the trap. He didn't seem like this when I approached him. Was that real, or is this? Maybe he's seized on the role of winning me over and luring me away from safety? I think about the neighbourhood WhatsApp group that I hate, the endless suspicion, and how I want no part of it. The Ones I Will Never Be Like. But I also remember the man who threatened me with a knife. He was handsome enough to make me almost drop my guard for a second.

The pathways between the shacks are too narrow for cars. I walk beside this man into a maze of sheet metal and wood. The ground beneath us is white and sandy and hot, a buried desert. He asks me about my life, tells me about his plans to start a mobile bar business which seems, given the resources in a place like this, an unrealistic dream and part of his plan to butter me up before what comes next. Like the thieves on Long Street who walk beside you telling you how much they like your shoes, no matter how old or ugly your shoes happen to be – where did you get them, what size do you wear, do you like mine – while their friend slips a hand into your jeans and removes your phone and wallet. I hold on to my phone in my pocket. The dread claws at my throat as my car disappears from view behind us. Not for what the car is worth but what it represents. An escape.

This was a stupid decision. I could be murdered in broad daylight in this maze and no one would ever know; no one would find me. The police would shrug the way they did when I tried to report Sibs's disappearance. What was he thinking, going somewhere like that alone? The residents wouldn't do anything to help me. And I get it, I understand why, but understanding doesn't make it less frightening. There was that famous case of the tourist couple who came here on holiday a few years ago. The wife was murdered while they were touring a township, and everyone said how fishy the story sounded from the start – what were they doing there at night in the first place? No one would be stupid enough to do that, even for an organised tour; the husband must have wanted her dead, must have planned it to look like an accident.

I take out my phone again and, shielding the screen from his eyes, I drop a pin for Adrian to find me. A live location tracker, though who knows how useful those are. It'll be turned off the moment something happens to me. I try to regulate my breathing. I try to deepen my voice and keep it steady and masculine. Am I walking like a straight guy would? Someone he wouldn't fuck with. How do I slip into conversation that Adrian knows where I am? Without making it obvious I'm gay, and maybe less able to defend myself in a fight. Should I say loads of people know where I am? I live in a commune. I work for a gang. How did I end up here without telling anyone where I was going?

Adrian tries to call me but I ignore it. Let my phone vibrate until it goes quiet. We turn left and right and right again, zigzagging through a hundred lives. Metal walls crowd me on both sides, radiating heat from the morning sun. There's the smell of smoke, the heavy, sweet smell of pap. I'm being watched. I can feel the malevolence even though the people we pass in these narrow alleys wave at my new friend, they greet him. If his charm is an act, the purpose of this act is not to trap me. He's charming with everyone.

We find the place. A shack just like all the others. It has one square window and a door. Walls made from roofing material. Rusted, unpainted corrugated iron. Sections of flat metal coated in some kind of streaked, fibrous brown substance. Strips of wood in the gaps. The whole thing must be about the size of my living room. But that's enough space for a group of violent men to sit and wait. He knocks on the door and nothing happens. They ready themselves inside for the ambush. Maybe the strongest of them hides behind the door, ready to pull me in when it opens. The heat is overwhelming. I think I might be sick.

A woman opens the door. She looks at us with stern eyes and a heavy line in her brow.

'Is this her?' my friend asks, his face buoyed and bright.

I can see the resemblance – the high cheekbones, the full lips, the shape of her nose.

'Uxolo, Sisi,' I say. I'm so relieved not to be abducted or killed that it takes a second for my hope to wither. This isn't her. I'm no closer to finding her.

The woman exchanges a few words with my companion, and her forehead smoothes over. 'Let me see the pic,' she says.

I show her the photo of Sibs on my phone and she looks at it for a long time, thinking. She shakes her head. 'I don't know her.'

'I'm sorry, my man,' my guide says.

I apologise to the woman again. I give her an awkward wave as we leave. On the way back to my car, I try to make up for my earlier distrust by being extra talkative and interested. He took time out of his day to help me, and it makes me quite emotional now, in retrospect, for him to have cared so much about my plight. Sibs and

Buhle's plight. I keep imagining Buhle's wide, solemn eyes watching me. Watching from a hiding place behind the bed as her father beats Sibs unconscious. Would he spare her? Did he even think about her, or was he too busy cursing Sibs for trying to leave him, for thinking she's too good for him, too good for this life? Did he pin Buhle down on the bed, arms behind her back, and scream at her to shut the fuck up, stop crying? Stop crying. Those big, solemn eyes of hers, her irises dark, her pupils drinking in all the sorrows of the world. Stop fucking crying.

'You've been so much help,' I say when we get back to my car.

'Good luck. I hope she's okay. It's nice of you to look.'

I think about giving him some money. I don't want him to be insulted and I also don't want to take out my wallet and then find I don't have any cash in it, after he's been waiting for me to look. I get into the driver's seat and close the car door. I wrap both hands on the steering wheel to calm my shaking.

It's hopeless. I know it's hopeless, but I try again at a second spot, and then a third. When I eventually give up for the day, I'm sunburnt and dehydrated and dizzy. I'm exhausted from the adrenaline and the fear and I'm exhausted from the war that rages in my head. The belligerents in this mental war: self-hatred on both sides. For persevering (classic white saviour complex. Sibs is fine. She's avoiding you. You're not respecting her agency) and for giving up (classic white privilege. Just run away when things get tough, back to your little bubble of nice homes and gentle walks and armed response). I can't stop thinking about the first time I met Buhle. She was so shy and serious. She hid behind her mother's legs and pulled herself close. She'd be helpless if something happened to her mom. I can see her trying to nurse her mom back to health, watching over her as she sleeps. Lying next to her in bed and listening for her mother's breathing.

Would the neighbours have heard something? Would they have intervened?

I start the car and head back towards the freeway. There's smoke up ahead, but I think nothing of it. Trash fires are common in the townships. There are often towers of smoke like this visible from the mountain. When I get closer I see the road is closed. Rubber tyres burning in the middle of the street. A protest. Flames lick the air and turn the people behind them into rippled, ethereal beings in the heat. Protestors dance and sing. To my right, in a section of the slum I drove past about an hour ago, the authorities are evicting people from their shacks. Uniformed officers in black riot gear. Trucks parked on the kerb. The crowd shouts at them, waves their arms in the air, films them on their phones, but no one dares touch them. I slow to a stop, acid rising in my throat. The officers are tearing down a shack. The structures are flimsy, easy to pull apart. How easy it is to destroy a home.

One of the officers yanks at the sheet-metal wall of a shack and the nail holding it down resists once, twice, then gives way. He hands the wall to his partner who confiscates the material, throws it onto the back of one of the trucks. A third officer kicks against the corner wooden post. The roof caves in. The walls collapse inwards and a woman rushes out of the shack holding a young child against her chest. She screams at the officer but she is invisible to him. He is indifferent to her tears, her volume. She is not a human being to this man, but a pest to be eradicated. I watch from my car as the whole shack comes down and the walls get carried away to the truck. Officers swarm onto the next shack like stinging ants. The woman is no longer shouting. She tries to console the baby on her hip by bouncing it up and down and kissing its forehead. She turns away from her possessions, exposed in the hot November sun. There's a square footprint where her shack once stood. In it, her mattress. A carpet. A kerosene gas cooker and pot. It's the sky-blue babygrow laid out on the bed that finally heaves the acid up and out of my stomach. I open the car door and puke onto the street.

I'm up, and I'm running, and whatever else is happening in my body, I'm no longer small. I reach the officer who delivered the terminal kick to this woman's home. He stops pulling at the wall of his new victim's shanty and he straightens up to face me. Every cell in my body is screaming at me to back off, run away, but I'm done listening to that fear. There's something else in my blood, too, something hot and fast, that quickens when I glance back at the baby boy on his mother's hip. His little sky-blue babygrow in the sun. I'm swelling like the bone-dry reservoirs after all these winter rains. I am strong. I am huge. If that mugger attacked me now, he'd meet his match. He is not the only sorcerer. He is not the only underworld being with the power to empty the streets.

'What the fuck are you doing?'

He's startled. Eyes wide. Then he notices the vomit on my chin and his face twists into a snarl. 'What?'

I wipe my face. 'Leave these people alone.'

Two of his colleagues have joined him. 'No,' one of them says, 'we are evicting them.'

'I can see that. Why?'

'They can't be here. It is private property. They are squatting.'

A laugh escapes my mouth, and then I exaggerate the laugh. It is loud and false and I hate it, but I can't stop rubbing their faces in it. Private property? Who would own land like this? Who would want it?

I step forwards and I push one of the officers hard on his chest. He stumbles backwards. The power that floods through me is new; it is electrifying. All of the rage that I've spent so long pushing down,

241

wishing away, medicating into subservience, it swirls and it swells and it is going to consume me but for once, I am not afraid of it. I want it. I am entitled to it. The impact of the shove travels through my hands, my arms. It ripples back through time, to a cowering little boy. He pulls himself upright; stands tall. He looks his tormentors straight in the eye. How fucking dare you treat me like this? His whole body tingles. He is no longer just a mind, a receiver of experience. He is made of bone, and muscle, and heft. He forms a fist and he swings it, with all of his strength, at the ringleader. If need be, we can fight to the death.

My opponent is stunned for a second, then lunges at me. The two others grab hold of him and pull him back before the blow he had aimed at my head can connect. I yell at them: 'What is wrong with you? Look at what you're doing. Look at that mother. What if that was your mother?'

And then it hits me, how much more likely it is to be one of their mothers than it is to be mine. These men might live somewhere just like this. Forced to carry out this violence for meagre wages to keep their families safe and fed for another month. Their mothers might live in flimsy shelters like this. The woman with the baby is watching me. She is not falling apart. She doesn't have the luxury of falling apart. Her eyes are angry and hard. She doesn't need rescuing by me.

And these men are restraining themselves from turning the full force of their violence on me because I'm white. It's why none of these soon-to-be-homeless residents have dared to get as close to them as I have. They will not be spared. It is this knowledge, at last, which extinguishes my fight. I am not helping. This can't be stopped. I am just another white guy trying to boss a black man around. The woman turns away from me. Her baby is screaming, sobbing. She wanders off, trying to shield its eyes from what is happening.

Back in my car, my scalp tingles. I shudder and wipe away the last of the vomit from my lips and I see it, clear as a religious epiphany: how the trauma of this country contaminates everyone. Violence everywhere, unresolved and ongoing, rolling on through the years, the generations. It victimises the powerless and kills something in the powerful. I think of my father conscripted to that unholy war in Angola, forced to kill for an evil, racist regime. The pressures on those boys at school, to be men, to be tough, to never show weakness or compassion. Don't be pussies. These officers tearing down people's homes will not sleep well tonight. They'll be angry, irritable. They'll snap at their wives and their children. Maybe they'll beat them. They have lost something of themselves here, just as they have taken something from these people who have nothing to give.

And where does the trauma go? I remember Emma saying to me that you can't wish it away. You can't push it down.

The eviction team has almost destroyed a third shack when I put my car in reverse. I drive as fast as I can. I take a different route out of the township. Adrian phones me again when I'm almost home. The call comes through the speaker of my car.

'Are you okay?' he says.

'I'm fine.'

'What the hell were you doing in Philippi? Fuck. I was so fucking worried about you. You just dropped a pin and then disappeared.'

'Sorry.' I'm laughing with relief, but I'm also shaking, and my eyes are wet and I can still smell the puke in my mouth. I'm a mess, and I want to go home and shower for a very, very long time. I want to scrub my skin raw under scalding-hot water. I want to be alone.

But that isn't true.

That is the pattern that repeats.

A voice in my head: the puppy trainer, when Frasier was a baby.

'Dogs are a social species,' she said. 'They hate to be alone.' She said it with absolutely no judgement. It was simply the reality of their biology. We're a social species, too. Emma has told me before: hyper-independence is a trauma response. It sounded clever when she said it. It even sounded wise and true. But that was an intellectual exercise. Easy to agree with the theory; difficult to act. To let myself depend on people. It's the thing I swore I would never do, way back in my bedroom when I was eight. But pursuing total independence has not protected me from getting hurt. It has only made me feel alone when I am surrounded by love.

'Actually,' I say, 'I don't think I am fine. Can I come over to you?'

I don't even think Adrian takes a second to reply, but in that second, all my hope crumbles. It was stupid to reach out. Of course he doesn't want any part of this. He can't bear my neediness. Who would?

'I shouldn't ask,' I say. 'Sorry. I know we're separated.'

'Are you kidding me?' he says. 'Come over as soon as you're back in town. I'm still at work, but Ettienne can let you in. I'll be home as soon as I can.'

# 35.

I move in with Ettienne and Adrian for two weeks. I don't want to be alone in the house and Adrian isn't ready to move home with me until we work some things out between us, so I just stay with him in Ettienne's guest bedroom. The decor is very Ettienne – charcoal walls, black-and-white photography, golden side table lamps, but the room smells like Adrian. It feels safe.

It's amazing how quickly the arrangement feels fun – like a holiday, or a return to our twenties. I don't stop thinking about Sibs – and I come to an agreement with my boss that I'll work from home, on Tuesdays, so I can return to the house and wait for her – but all the other weight of my life peels off me. I've always liked Ettienne, even though he's more Adrian's friend than mine, and living together like this feels delightfully unserious, like rewinding to a happier time before everyone paired off. We're flatmates, albeit temporarily, and I remember how to live like this. It comes back to me. The constant company. The laughter in the kitchen. The venting about work. Three is less pressure than two, conversationally. It reminds me of living with Jess, except Ettienne won't touch a carb so we order in more than we cook, and each of us gets to eat whatever we want while we binge Netflix and shriek at the TV. Instead of *Friends* reruns and *Survivor* it's *RuPaul's Drag Race* and *Real Housewives*.

Ettienne has also managed to maintain a wild sex life even as all our other single gay friends complain about the tiny pool of available men in Cape Town. I think it's because it's summer and Ettienne likes to hook up with tourists and swallows. Adrian and I have maybe every third night alone together.

Ettienne suggests we put out missing person alerts on social media. I've taken a few different pictures of Sibs from her Facebook profile – when her wigs are always changing, it's hard to find a picture that will be instantly recognisable to someone scrolling past it in their time-line – and I add the details about when she disappeared and my contact info. I don't care so much any more about being seen as a meddling white guy. I can take the embarrassment. If she's fine and just decided not to move in and I should have taken the hint, then let someone tell me that. I'm not relying on hints. I need to know she's okay.

People are good about sharing the posts. I put them up on Face-book, Instagram, Twitter. I get thousands of retweets and dozens of shares. Hundreds of replies, too. And I check them every day, read-ing through the comments, the thoughts and prayers, the well wishes, the insults, following any leads and tagged accounts. But nothing. No definitive answer.

I don't know what to make of that. Previously, I would have as-sumed it meant the worst. But if her husband had killed her, there would be a record, surely? Maybe he just forbade her from contacting me ever again. Maybe they left Cape Town. But imagining her trapped somewhere far from here with a man who threatens her when she planned an escape isn't much of a comfort. Nor is knowing that maybe I precipitated this.

Adrian tells me he got the job in London, but it doesn't feel like an ultimatum this time around. I'm too burnt out for adrenaline, may-be, or maybe he's softened. We discuss it without defensiveness. We

246

talk about what it means to do something for someone else rather than yourself, whether that's your partner or society at large. The perceived judgement of leaving; the perceived service of staying. Is it really a service? Does it really make a difference to anyone whether we stay or go? Countries need their middle classes, sure, but do he and I matter that much? One couple out of millions. Sibs's salary made a difference, maybe. And we paid for Buhle's creche and were planning on paying for her schooling, and the baby's. But beyond that – we have good intentions and not much else. Do intentions transform a country?

We might have made things worse for Buhle. Khanya may resent us for growing up separated from 'her culture', even if we perfected our isiXhosa, even if we tried as hard as we could to make sure she never felt out of place.

What do we do with our generational frustration? Social transformation has been so slow since the transition to democracy, maybe even stalled. Post-racialism has been done so badly, and hypocritically, and it's been co-opted to mean we don't need to change, everything was resolved in 1994 — but is that enough of a reason to give up on it? To yield to racial determinism and stop trying to find common experience, common humanity. I'm not ready to give up on that dream just yet.

And yet life is short. Must I offer mine up to a dream? To a belief system? When do we start living for ourselves? Perhaps a selfish, individualistic life is what Emma would see as growth. To be central in my own life. My own protagonist. But to give up on ideals? Where does meaning even come from if we're not part of anything?

Adrian tells me not to be so melodramatic. Nothing is permanent until we're dead. Look at Chimamanda Ngozi Adichie. She left Nigeria and moved back, many times. Look at the exiles who returned after liberation. It calms me to think of black people who've left and come home – it makes his talk of leaving feel not quite so traitorous – and I almost tell him this, but I know it will provoke him, and even though I'm trying to be messy and enmeshed and not keep him at arm's length, I think I'm still allowed to keep some thoughts to myself. We can sculpt this marriage in any way we choose. No roles. No assumptions.

'So should I take the job?' he asks me.

'I thought you said if you got it, you were taking it.'

He's grinning at me. 'Maybe I was bluffing.'

I try to imagine a fresh start. Another city in the global north. Green parks. Walkability. Theatre. There were things I liked about being an expat. I want to say to him, sure, let's try it, but I can't do it just yet. 'Can you give me some more time?'

Another thing I'll never tell him: what happened with Liam. It would only hurt Adrian to know about it and it would destroy this fragile rapprochement – and for what? To finish the work of sabotaging my life? It wouldn't change my resolve. I will never let it happen again. And this is another exercise in trust, maybe, to trust that Liam won't use what happened to destroy me. I can relax about that, and have faith, almost. I can't control every outcome, but I can try not to always imagine the worst.

We even have sex again. It's nothing like Ettienne's stories that we hear at breakfast or after work, and sometimes hear first-hand through the wall from his bedroom. But it's something. I'm in the shower one morning. Adrian is still in bed. I hear the front door of Ettienne's apartment opening, and slamming shut. His cleaning lady is here. Frasier runs to the front door, howling in excitement or warning – I'm not sure which.

248

Adrian leaps out of bed and locks the bedroom door. 'Hi, Zanele!' he shouts through the door, then he joins me in the shower.

'I'm almost done,' I say, but he doesn't wait for me to get out. He steps into the small space with a devious grin and an erection. 'Are you kidding? We don't have time for this.'

We haven't showered together in years, since maybe before we were married – it seems almost absurd, now, the kind of thing that young people do because their hormones are out of control and sex is still new. The urgency is all made up. And yet the hot water, the slipperiness of his naked body, his proximity. It's all very good. I feel myself growing hard and there's a split-second surge of shame, as if I'm back in the showers at boarding school and this is going to reveal my perversion.

'Exactly,' Adrian says, grabbing my soapy hands and rubbing them on his chest, 'there's no time to shower separately.'

'I'm almost done!' I say again, but I'm laughing and I feel the closest thing to happy that I've felt in a long time.

He turns his back to me, reaches behind and pulls my arms around his chest. I hold him close, press his body against the wall, stepping into the warm flow of water. He takes the shower gel from my hand and lathers a generous dollop into his ass. He tries to direct my erection, but I can take it from here. I push the head of my cock into him and feel him tense around it. 'Is this okay?' I say.

'Yes.'

'Do you want me to stop?'

'Keep going.'

He pushes back onto me and groans, and suddenly I'm inside him. He is tight and this feels amazing and I begin to slide in and out and there is something deliciously powerful about this, something dangerously verging on force, but it isn't force. He moves back to take me deeper into him and I am picking up speed, now, thrusting as if it's the most natural thing in the world to express attraction like this, and maybe even love. 'Shhhh,' I say, because his groaning is getting out of hand, 'you have to be quiet.' He arches his back, turns his head to kiss me. I wrap an arm around his neck and pull him close as we kiss. Then I place my hand over his mouth and he moans into it and I push him back against the wall and I feel my whole body flush with warmth. A tingling in the pit of my stomach; a ball of fire gathering. I think I'm going to orgasm inside him, and I've never done that before, I've never been able to get past the numbing effects of the anxiety medication. I've never been able to get past the feeling that this can't be about me, sex can't be about me, or my pleasure, it is purely for someone else. And yet this doesn't feel like it's about pleasure, either. This is cosmic, what is happening. This gathering fire. I am about to pour my soul into him.

But the moment doesn't come. The ball of fire subsides. I keep going for a while, but I've lost it. 'Sorry,' I say, 'I can't stop thinking about the water.' I turn off the taps because the dams aren't full yet and this is so wasteful. Adrian rolls his eyes at me but he doesn't mind, not really. He's accepted this about me by now. And he's also conscious of climate change, and drought, so he smiles and tries to resume where we left off, but now the sound of my pelvis slapping against his ass is so loud without the falling water to muffle it that I start to go soft. I wiggle free.

'She'll hear us,' I say.

Adrian sighs. 'Okay,' he says.

'Sorry.'

'No, you're right. Will you get out and let me shower?'

He's only mildly irritated, but I hate that I've ruined it.

'Aw don't look so sad!' he says. 'Hang on, I've got another idea. It's *quiet.*' He whispers the word at me. He drops to his knees.

'No, man, gross,' I say, so he makes a show of pouring a lake of shower gel into his hands and he cleans my now only semi-erect penis thoroughly, then turns on a brief downpour of hot water to rinse us both off. Then he teases the tip of it with his tongue. I grow hard again when he wraps his lips around me and sucks. I try to relax. I place my hand on top of his head.

Zanele knocks on the bedroom door when I'm close – I've been quiet, but he must recognise the rhythmic pulsing of my stomach muscles because he speeds up – and I call out to her, 'We'll be out in a second!'

He pulls me deeper into his mouth as I come.

It was maybe a little bit awkward, but I kind of love that it was awkward. Not sexy in the way porn is sexy. Not sexy, probably, in the way that Ettienne's sex is sexy. No choreography. No pouts or smirks or perfect muscle. It's humourless, that kind of attraction. It's nothing like friendship.

'Wow, thank you,' I say.

He stands up and winks at me. 'No problem, stud.'

# 36.

Adrian moves home with me after two weeks, but it is short-lived. I can't go anywhere in the house without seeing Sibs and Buhle. The picture nail in the wall beside the guest bathroom, where Sibs used to hang her wig while she worked, makes me so sad I decide to hang a picture on it, but that makes me feel worse, so I take it down again. I move Frasier's bed to a different corner of the living room, because I can't stop seeing Buhle sitting on the floor beside him, stroking him while he tries his best to ignore her. I eat breakfast standing up in the kitchen, but still my gaze drifts to the dining room, and that strange, sweet breakfast the three of us ate together, only a few weeks ago, as a kind of family. Watching Sibs cut up Buhle's toast the way my brother does for his kids.

I have to go into the guest bedroom to throw out the moving day flowers, long rotten and stinking up the whole house. I open the window to air out the room. I look at the picture I drew of Buhle among the giant daisies on the wall, white chalk on blackboard paint, and it makes my stomach heave. A sob or vomit, I can't tell. I can't make sense of my body. The somatic expressions of emotion. I'm going to stop trying to make sense of it, to rationalise everything. I'm going to try to let it express whatever it wants.

I take the chalk and draw Sibs into the picture, too. It's sentimental and I should feel embarrassed about it, but it feels good. It feels right.

I try leaving their bedroom door open all the time, hoping it will start to feel bright and ordinary, a bedroom for out-of-town visitors, the room as it was before Khanya, and the baby, before Buhle. I try leaving it closed so I don't have to look at it. Nothing works. We need to get out of Cape Town.

Adrian suggests a road trip before we join my family for Christmas.

'Matatiele?' he says, and my body pushes something else up and out of my eyes. I hug him for the longest time. 'You've always wanted to go,' he says.

The only way out of the city is east, through the townships and slums that connect the peninsula to the mainland. Adrian talks incessantly as we drive – about a book he's been reading, about a new project some of his colleagues are working on at work to help improve literacy for primary school learners. I try to listen. I know why he's talking like this, on and on without a break, without waiting for a response. I have nothing to say except thank you, and that wouldn't make any sense. I'm so grateful for him right now. Grateful and irritable in equal measure. For not letting me brood as we pass Philippi, where I tried and failed to find them, where one of these hokkies either holds or once held their whole lives.

It's a violent place, I try to remind myself. Maybe it's a violent world. Countless people are trapped in unhappy lives. I have no control over that.

Eventually the shacks peter out, replaced by soulless strip developments that flank the highway near Somerset West – car dealerships and lighting warehouses and a gym with its plastic signage sun-bleached pink.

We rise into the uplands of orchards and vineyards and forest, apple country and wine country, then descend again into a patchwork of tan and green and yellow, gently undulating farmland that goes on for hours until we rejoin the coast. We pass old farming towns with white-steepled Dutch Reformed churches from the seventeenth century and ugly, orange-brick and concrete Dutch Reformed churches from the 1960s. We cross over wide, lazy rivers, the mountains a grey-flecked green, always to our left. We spend the first night of the trip in Knysna, the traditional first stop on this, the Great South African Road Trip that I must have done thirty times in the last fifteen years, ever since my mom moved to a small town on the east coast. She left Johannesburg as soon as I finished high school – her maternal duties done, her youngest child no longer a child – and I've driven this road every year since then, except the years we were in New York. Christmas holidays, Easter holidays, escapes from break-ups and breakdowns. But this time, we're going well beyond where my mother stays. Deep into the rural hinterland near the border of Lesotho.

The road from Knysna is hugged by heavy forest. Dense and dark, it looms over the car, its magical branches straining to close us in. I love this stretch through the Tsitsikamma, one of the last small vestiges of indigenous rainforest left in the country, but it doesn't last long. Soon the pink-blossomed keurbooms and enormous, ancient yellowwoods give way to endless pine plantations, many of which have been recently harvested and stand barren of any trees. We cross over into the Eastern Cape. The vegetation changes again. Aloes and euphorbia. The survivors of unreliable rainfall. The mountains fall away around Kareedouw and the horizon recedes, a tension going slack.

Wind farms with vast white turbines rise from the landscape and it feels, for a moment, like we're three hundred years into the future and we all got it right. The energy is clean and we're no longer angry and panicked. Maybe we're no longer even corporeal – just calm, kind minds and benevolent technology. But then we dip into the Gamtoos Valley and I can't help but think about Saartjie Baartman back in the 1700s, born here and taken to Europe to be exhibited in freak shows. She was tormented and ridiculed. She died young, in misery, so far from this sunny valley, and I think about how all the Khoi in this area were treated, in all the areas where Europeans encountered them, hunted for sport, and I think about the wars of dispossession of the Xhosa and how that legacy still lives on in land ownership and access to resources – I see it, in the complexion of the farmers who pass me in their bakkies, and the complexion of the labourers who stand in the open cargo beds at the back, holding on to the bars so they don't fall out – and I think how history is always just the butchering of the powerless by the powerful and it's maybe less extreme now, but it's mostly just better disguised.

The freeway after Port Elizabeth is wide and bone-white in the heat. The light is different in this part of the country, though I know that's not scientifically possible. It must be a trick of the mind – my memories of summers here overwhelming my senses – or maybe there's dust in the air from the dry interior. Particulate matter filtering the sunlight, turning it golden and warm, both brighter and somehow softer than the light in Cape Town. The freeway follows the coastline for a while. Indian Ocean to our right. Hitchhikers to our left. There are so many hitchhikers at this time of year and I love to see them, the joy and the promise of journeys home, even if we never stop. They stand on the shoulder of the road with their hands outstretched. Ten-rand notes, bright green in the sunshine. Twenties. Cardboard signs made from old boxes with destinations written in blue pen. *Grahamstown. Cradock. East London.* People are leaving the city to visit family for Christmas, to return to the rural areas and ancestral homes. I look for Sibs among the hitchhikers, and I see her. A kind of Schrödinger's Sibs, both here and not here. She's from the Eastern Cape and it's possible – possible – that she escaped. That she's happy. It feels good to imagine her here, making her way back to some rural village. Buhle holding her hand and waiting with her in the sun by the side of the road. Smiling, even though she never smiled, because look at all this space. Look at all this green. She's never been to this part of the country before. She's never seen farmland and wilderness. She's never seen her mother so carefree. I imagine the rondavels waiting for them in whatever village they are heading to. The ancient makhulu. The wood fires and umqombothi.

Hazard lights flicker on the car ahead of us, a red Toyota Camry with tinted windows. It pulls over. Someone extends an arm from the back window and waves over a group of heavyset, middle-aged Xhosa women in bright clothes who'd given up on us and the Camry as potential lifts. As we pass, the women are gathering their bags, holding their headwraps, running to the car. They are laughing and it makes me smile – I can't help it – even though I have no right to share their joy when I would never stop for hitchhikers.

We spend the second night in East London and I take Frasier for a long walk on the beach. He sprints in wide arcs, full speed but always coming back to me, relishing the feeling of warm sand on his paws, the new smells, an ocean that is so much warmer than at home. Indian, not Atlantic.

The last leg of this pilgrimage is seven hours on poor roads. We leave East London early and head inland, north towards Lesotho, through the achingly beautiful, achingly poor former Transkei. It's the kind of Africa tourists imagine – rolling hills dotted with small

villages. Mud huts and small round houses, cattle and goats, dirt roads and the sounds of roosters and echoed voices in the valleys. This is a place of chiefs and poor cellphone signal, where young men paint their faces with white clay during the initiation season, and old women do it too, and it looks, at first sight, to be untouched by modernity. Peaceful. But I know from our friend who works in the non-profit sector that this land is contested. Tribal communities are fighting for their lives, against unscrupulous chiefs and administrators who sell the land out from under them, offering mineral rights to mining conglomerates. Activists disappear. There are political assassinations. Evictions are common. Environmental impact assessments are approved in return for a little sweetener, no matter the environmental impact. There is no escape from modernity, even here.

Matatiele is a small town in the foothills of the Drakensberg. There's nothing here, really. No reason to come unless you have an existing connection to the place. My connection is tenuous. I've never been here before, but Matatiele is where my great-grandmother grew up.

It's been bothering me more and more that I don't know where my father is buried. It shouldn't mean anything. I know that a body is just a body – his would have rotted down to bones by now – and I can choose to remember him however and wherever I like. But I'm tired of arguing with myself about how I should feel. Maybe it's sentimental to want a place to go to, or maybe it's borrowed from movies, this idea of finding peace while visiting a grave, but so what? Feelings aren't rational and maybe it's okay to be irrational. To be an animal, not a computer. To let myself yearn for something. I want to feel held by my family. I want to be anchored to this earth.

It is not just grief bringing me here, I know that. I've been unmoored ever since we returned to South Africa. Less sure of my place. Less sure of anything. Reverse culture shock, maybe, but that's only part of it.

This is the wrong side of my family, anyway – the roots of my mother's people are here, not my dad's – but it's the best I can do. My parents grew up in Johannesburg, like me, and that shapeshifting city is too volatile, too quick to be an ancestral home. Most of the places my father loved aren't recognisable any more. Torn down and replaced. And besides, whom can I ask for the missing details? He was an only child. His parents are long dead. Which house did he grow up in? I have no idea. The one I was born in is under a shopping centre, now, and the home Mom and I lived in after the divorce was razed to the ground to make way for a gated townhouse complex. I don't know much about his family, and there's nothing I can do about that now. But I know the stories of Matatiele. My maternal side is large. They believe in family, and family lore. They have reunions. It's like a great African family, with that original matriarch as the source. I know about the old farmhouse with its stained-glass window and its copper bath on the stoep. My mom and her sisters had to bathe there when they came down from Joburg to visit. I know about the party-line phones, when phones finally came to this place, and how each farm had a different ringtone so you knew who should pick up. Three longs and a short, I think was theirs. And it became something that visitors hooted from their cars, when cars were invented, when the descendants of that original couple, my great-great-great-grandparents, came to visit the family farm. They'd hoot as they approached the farmhouse, three longs and a short. A reconstitution of the clan.

I asked my mom where the farm is, and she couldn't tell me. She visited for the last time when she was a girl. Her grandmother moved to a little house in the town when the farm was sold, she says, but she can't remember the address of the house either, so we drive up and down all the streets of Matatiele – there aren't many – looking for an old stone house with a red door. I send my mom pics of a few of the contenders, but she can't pinpoint the one. It's been a lifetime since she was here, and anyway, that wasn't the house that held her childhood memories. She remembers the farmhouse, when her grandmother was in her prime, not the place 'in town' the old widow moved to when she was ninety.

She does remember the old church, and the family graveyard, and she directs me over the phone to a small stone chapel in a dry field outside of town. The grass is overgrown in the churchyard, almost the same burnt-ochre colour as the church itself, a low building with a humble belltower and a corrugated sheet-metal roof. The church is abandoned. The windows are broken. The main doors are missing a hinge, and they sag to the right. They are wooden, painted a dull uniform brown that has fissured like winter lips. Across the doors, a locked metal security gate, olive green.

It's a depressing place. Tranquil in the way that all churchyards are tranquil, especially rural churches with distant mountains, but it is falling into ruin. The overgrown weeds, the rusting roof. It's the security gate that depresses me most of all. It stops even the entropy from being graceful. This isn't Venice or Angkor Wat. It's prosaic. Just an old building left over by people long gone, locked so no one can get in and steal whatever remains.

Adrian calls me back to a corner of the graveyard close to where we came in. He's found my mother's family, a whole family tree laid out in the earth, graves going back a hundred and fifty years. My father isn't there, but many of these people knew him. They liked him, I know that. They commiserated with me when they were drunk, pulling me into a quiet corner at large family gatherings to tell me what a shame it was that my parents had split up. What an interesting man my father was. And funny.

There must be thirty relatives there. Great-aunts and uncles, long dead cousins, great-great-grandparents. I think, for a second, of one of the first things I said to Emma when I started therapy – that if you're chosen to be a sangoma, the ancestors torment you until you open yourself to them. If you don't listen, you'll lose your mind.

Well, ancestors, I'm here. And I'm listening.

My mother's branch of the tree is all collected in one place. Plaques on a large stone cross. My grandmother, returned to her parents. Her siblings are here, too, those I remember and the names of those who died before I was born. She was one of twelve, born before the invention of reliable contraception, and suddenly more stories come back to me, seeing all these names. Jokes about my great-grandmother throwing herself down the stairs to try to lose yet another baby. Her discovering, while already in labour, after already having birthed a child, that it was twins. Someone said to her (I don't know if it was a doctor in those days or a midwife or just her husband), 'There's another one in there,' and she replied, 'Well, I'm not having it.' She didn't want twelve. Twelve was too many. With twelve children, how could she hold on to anything in her life, keep anything of herself, that wasn't the role of 'mother'?

There should be eleven small plaques beside my grandmother, but there are ten. I find her youngest sister on a different face of the stone cross – alone, looking out towards the mountains.

'Do you know why they did that?' Adrian says to me.

'They ran out of space?'

'They did it for suicides. Did she kill herself?'

I trace my finger across the smooth, cool surface of her plaque. Ruth. She did kill herself, in 1968, in Durban. She was gay, I remember that.

The first gay person I ever heard about. Spoken of in hushed tones, the scandal and tragedy of it all. She was the reason my grandmother loved Evan so much, I think. The reason she leaned on his arm and laughed at his stories at her eightieth, when those other relations hissed that he shouldn't be allowed near the children. Gran got so tearful when I came out, too. She called me the night of my matric dance to say she was proud of me for taking a boy as my date. 'I bet you both look gorgeous,' she said, and then she choked up and cut the call. Ruth had been Gran's favourite sister, my mom explained. She hadn't known about the girlfriend until Ruth was dead.

Adrian is seething. 'It's sick,' he says, 'the way they treated suicides. Where is the compassion? What kind of person says no, she can't be with her family because she sinned?'

I hadn't thought, before, about how many suicides there have been in my family. My great-aunt. My uncle. Two of my cousins. Who knows how far back it stretches. Mental illness runs through us all like a recessive gene, inarguable as the colour of our eyes. Although I have to hope, for the sake of my own sanity, that it's not genetic. Maybe the culture of the family was toxic, a lineage of bad coping mechanisms, bad communication and callousness in the face of despair. We repress our emotions until they overwhelm us. Until they make it impossible to breathe.

I can't do anything about my genes, but if it's the culture I've inherited, I can change that.

I sit in the long, dry grass, facing the stone cross. Frasier climbs onto my lap and I hold him so tight he starts to wheeze. I loosen my grip, but he does not leave. He folds himself into a ball in my lap. Rests his chin on my knee.

I'm surprised by how much the names on the cross affect me. The lives running backwards to that old, original matriarch at the top.

There was a patriarch, too, I suppose, but I don't know anything about him. The men are invisible on this side of the family. They came via my mother, and her mother, and her mother, and hers.

What made that first great matriarch come here, to this dusty town in this remote part of what was then an empire? The promise of a better life? The promise of quietness?

I imagine her standing here in this churchyard in 1872, short and unsure of herself, a young woman with a small frame and a large hat. Maybe she missed her parents back in England. Maybe she thought, what the hell have I done? Something new creeps into my blood, a lightness that makes it easier to breathe. They were ordinary people, I realise, not the monsters I've long believed I was descended from. Colonialism was so violent, so outrageous, its legacy is so pervasive and evil that it's always been difficult for me to comprehend how it happened, other than to believe there is something inherently evil in white people, some malice that I carry in my heart. But there is no malice in the stories I know of these women. There were no great campaigns for domination in this family. They weren't foot soldiers fighting for the expansion of an invading power. They were just people.

I used to fight with my parents about apartheid when I was younger – how could you let it happen? How could you stand by and do nothing? I was desperate to believe we weren't terrible people, but every response they offered sounded like an excuse to me. A cop-out. 'We didn't know how bad it was,' they said. 'You can't imagine what it was like without the internet, without TV, with press censorship. No one knew what happened in the townships.'

'You could see there were no black people in your school,' I hissed. 'You knew your domestic worker lived in a small room at the back and needed to carry a pass.' It enraged me, this wilful ignorance and cowardice. But I was frightened in Philippi. I was surprised when I

looked into that shack. How much of Sibs's life did I know, even with the internet and TV and a free press? Without apartheid laws to keep our lives separate? You don't need to wish harm on others for there to be suffering all around you.

Hating my ancestors is easy. It's more difficult to grapple with their humanity, to allow the possibility that they were not especially bad people. They may have even been caring people, thoughtful and kind in their own small lives, and yet an evil system flourished on their watch. Maybe it's more useful to ask: how do these systems flourish when not everyone is a villain? How can I use this unearned privilege for good, rather than berating myself for having it?

The sun is low on the horizon. The shadow of the overgrown hedge that entombs the churchyard creeps towards me, then washes up over me, cooling my skin. Dappled golden light in blotches on the dry earth, the dead grass. These last remnants of warmth fade quickly. The sky in the east is darker than dusk. Storm clouds are rolling in.

'We should get going,' Adrian says. 'Are you ready to go?'

'Sure.'

'You don't want to do something? Like a ritual or something?'

I smile at him. What is there to do? My father was an atheist. He believed there was nothing on the other side of death. He'd be appalled to see me praying at a graveyard, talking to myself as if he were here. How stupid, he'd think, to cling to the idea of souls or ancestor spirits, to believe that any part of us survives the brutal shortness of life. There's nothing here but what we can see.

But you can't see love, and you can't see power, and I'm not ready to give up hope just yet. Besides, I let Adrian drive us across the country for this. I can't leave without some semblance of a ceremony. A stroll through the graveyard isn't going to cut it.

'Can you give me a moment?' I say. I hand Adrian the car keys and he takes Frasier with him out of the churchyard. I hear the car unlock on the other side of the hedge. The back door opens and closes. The front passenger door opens and closes.

I get down onto my knees in the dead grass, and I close my eyes.

'Hi Dad', I start. I think I'm going to laugh at the absurdity of this when, instead, I start to cry.

'How was that?' Adrian says when I climb into the car. Frasier is asleep in his bed on the back seat, snoring loudly.

'Thanks for coming with me.'

He squeezes my hand. 'Of course. Anyway, it's been a beautiful trip.'

'I wish we could have brought Khanya,' I say, and immediately I regret it. I'm the reason we don't have Khanya. We'd have been a family by now. One of the mothers would have picked us. But Adrian doesn't glare at me or sulk or lash out or remind me of any of the ways I've fucked up in the last year. He reaches back between our seats and wakes Frasier up by ruffling the fur on his head.

'We brought our baby!' he says.

# 37.

I've been thinking, since visiting the graveyard, about my parents as young people. Before the fighting, and infidelity. Before the war at the border, and the strictures and disappointments of marriage. Their eyes were bright that day they met each other on the steps of the university. Hers would have been clear, ice-blue, glistening in the sunshine. She would have been squinting against the glare. His, the colour of dark roast coffee. A big, raucous group of his friends on those steps, and yet his laughter was quieter, softer, for her. She laughed easily, too. They recognised something in each other. Already, a language that was theirs and theirs alone.

I can't shake the idea that, maybe, what really happened was that I was born from love.

We arrive at my mother's house on the afternoon of Christmas Eve. It's later than she wanted, nearly a week after my brother and sister-in-law and their kids arrived from Joburg, and Mom's greeting is inflected with hurt.

Frasier runs into the garden with Lily.

I set our bags down in the upstairs guest bedroom and join Mom in the kitchen. My brother hands me a glass of wine, and I am quickly set to work.

'I haven't started on the vegetables yet because you always do such nice things with them,' Mom says.

'I'd go mad if I didn't,' I say, 'living with a vegetarian.'

'How are you two?' she says, her voice quiet and conspiratorial. She knows all about the botched adoption, the separation. She doesn't know about Adrian's ultimatum.

Adrian steps into the kitchen and kisses her on the cheek. 'We're good, Laura.'

'I got all the things you said to get. Whatever they had available in the shops.'

She's made her famous slow-roast lamb. The air in the house is thick with the scent of it – garlic, rosemary, rich meaty earthiness – and the oven has warmed the whole kitchen. I get to work slicing discs of red onion, chunks of butternut. I toss them in olive oil, salt and pepper, and slide them onto the shelf in the oven beneath the lamb. I start working on a lemon tahini dressing. I'm focused, aware of the time constraints and the roast pear and walnut salad I promised on the phone last week, and I'm enjoying myself, but Mom pulls me into her for a long hug. She's feeling bad about having been aloof with me when I arrived. It was a punishment she's now decided I did not deserve. To be a few days late is better than not being here at all.

'I'm so happy you made it,' she says.

'I was always going to come, Mom,' I say and then, when that seems to chastise her, 'I'm happy to be here.'

At dinner, my brother asks me: 'Did you ever find out what happened to your maid?'

'Domestic worker,' I say. Hilton rolls his eyes, and I think, not for the first time, how irritating it is that he managed to marry someone coloured. He thinks it proves he has no prejudices. It gives him licence not to question his assumptions or interrogate his word choices. A badge he can point to if ever the conversation drifts into the uncomfortable territory of privilege or complicity. I don't even like the term 'domestic worker' – it's got an anonymising proletarian ring to it, like 'office worker' or 'factory worker', and it still retains some of the servitude of the word it replaced. But it's better than 'maid', surely? All of these job descriptions feel like violence. We are not our jobs. We are not what we are forced to do. 'And she wasn't mine, either.'

Hilton takes a deep, exasperated inhale.

'Come now, you two, stop bickering,' Mom says.

I smile at her and turn back to Hilton. 'No,' I say. 'We have no idea.'

'That's wild,' Mia says. She holds her glass of wine on the table, but she doesn't pick it up. Her eyes have an unfocused, faraway look. 'I can't believe people can just disappear like that. In today's age!'

'You have to assume the worst, I suppose,' my brother says.

'Rubbish!' Mom declares. 'She might have gone home for a family emergency. Anything could have happened.' I look at her and feel a rush of warmth and gratitude. All these years later – she's let her hair go grey, now – and still her impulse is to protect me. I squeeze her hand on the table.

'Maybe she got a better job,' Adrian says, smiling to encourage my mother's line of thought.

'Have you got someone else?' my brother says. 'Or are you going to wait a bit?'

I catch Mom's eye for a second. She gives a tiny, almost impercep-tible headshake, then looks down at her food. He's not trying to be insensitive, I think she's saying. He's not saying Sibs is replaceable. Mom hasn't told my brother I asked them all to move in.

'I suppose it'll be awkward if you offer the job to someone else and then she does come back.'

'I paid for Buhle's nursery school next year,' I say. 'So I'll know if Buhle doesn't turn up in January.'

'Shame, man,' Mia says. She turns to Lily, beside her, and tells her she has to eat some of the roast pear. She mustn't only eat the meat. 'Your uncles put a lot of work into that,' she says.

Lily glares at me and stabs a wedge of pear. She shoves it into her mouth with melodramatic fury, but then her face softens because she quite likes the taste.

'You don't have to eat that, Lily,' I say.

'Yes, she does.'

I take a sip of my wine and think about that old home video Mom had converted to DVD a few years ago. We didn't have a video camera when I was growing up, as far as I know, so there isn't much footage of our early lives. Just the one tape, I think. An ad hoc montage of vignettes, decades apart. They must have been filmed on borrowed camcorders, or by other people. My parents' wedding, my grandmother's eightieth, and that one huge family Christmas we hosted, the year before Dad moved out. It was the early nineties, in what I now know was a scary, uncertain time in this country, but in the video I'm not concerned with politics. I don't even know about politics. I'm probably a year older than Lily is now. Bowl haircut. Giant front teeth. There are so many people in our house we couldn't fit them all in one room. Long trestle tables in the living room and the hallway and the dining room, all done up with festive trinkets and brightly coloured, mismatched tablecloths. In the video someone calls out to me that Father Christmas is coming and he won't leave presents for me if I'm awake.

The boy in the video leaps up from the table so fast he knocks his plastic cup of juice into a candle. He runs upstairs whisper-shouting *no-no-no-no* and disappears. Moments later, he runs back downstairs in his Care Bears pyjamas, eyes wide, to find his mom and ask her how he's going to fall asleep in time. He can be heard saying: 'But he'll know if it's fake. He'll know I'm lying. I can't fall asleep that fast. What if I'm too late?' And I can't hear her response over the giggling of whoever's holding the camcorder, but she takes pity on the boy, strokes his head and leads him back upstairs.

The video troubles me because that boy is panicking. It's before his father left and transformed into a cold, distant man. It's before his mother succumbed to her grief. He didn't yet know he was gay and would be hated for it. And still, he's distraught. He is so sure he's messed up in some important way he hadn't foreseen and doesn't know how to fix.

Maybe I'll never find the original cause I've been searching for, that dark, sparkling trauma in the deep recesses of my mind. Maybe it will always be an amorphous feeling, an unnameable dread, and no explanation will make it go away. Maybe it wasn't a single event, or even a handful of them, but the accumulation of countless small experiences, all internalised in the wrong way. The world is dark and malignant. You're not strong enough to withstand it. You can't trust anyone to help.

'Do you think you'll get nice presents?' I say to Lily. There are only six of us at the Christmas table this year. No overflow trestles in the hallway. No distant cousins.

Lily takes my hand and looks deep into my eyes. 'Uncle Benji,' she says, 'of course I will.' She releases my hand, sits back and sighs. She's cool and confident as a bubblegum-popping teenager. 'I've been very good.'

In the morning, we watch Lily and Simon rip through their presents. Simon is too young to know what's happening, and the sense of being on stage, watched and cheered by a couchful of uncles and parents and a grandmother, sends him into a fit of inconsolable wailing.

Mia gives Lily a small parcel to give to Frasier. Lily waves the present, obviously a ball, gift-wrapped in silver paper with white stars, in Frasier's face and he ducks away from her. 'Bring him here,' I say, and she hefts him with both arms and stumbles over to me. I make room for her on the couch between Adrian and me, and I put Frasier on her lap.

'Is this for Frasier?' I say and she nods, solemnly. 'Can I unwrap it for him?'

'I'll help you.'

We each take a side and we tear at the paper, and a bright, new tennis ball falls out onto the carpet. Frasier jumps from her lap to pick it up. 'You see,' I say, 'he loves it! Thank you, Lily.'

'I chose it,' she says.

I catch Mia's eye and stifle a laugh.

'Thank you,' I say again. I hug Lily and mouth my thanks to her parents over her shoulder. Mia winks at me and smiles. Her eyes have the kind of misty, sparkling quality I know from watching parents watch their children when the children are being sweet. I know the feeling from watching Frasier and it hits me, suddenly, that the love I see in her eyes isn't just for Lily. It's also for me.

'Shall we go play with him outside?' I say. 'You can throw the ball.'

The little girl and the dog run into the garden and I follow them, grateful to get away from the pile of toys and discarded paper and forced merriment. Lily shrieks with joy as Frasier lunges at her hand and she tosses the ball deep into Mom's bloukappies. Frasier tramples the flowers in his path to retrieve it, so I redirect the game into the driveway. A long stretch of running space, concrete pavers and moss, walled in by the bougainvillea on one side and a hedge of hibiscus on the other. Lily and I throw the ball to each other, with Frasier running his fastest between us. Lily holds the ball and runs with it in her hand so that he chases her.

Within a few minutes I find that I'm chasing her, too. I tickle her under her arms and run after her as she squawks. I growl at her as if I'm a big wolf and it's fine, this silliness, I don't care how it makes me look. I'm able to be playful with her the way I'm playful with Frasier when it's just the two of us, no one else around. I remember those women at my gran's eightieth saying gay people shouldn't be allowed near children, and I remember the boys at school who told me I run like a faggot, like a girl, and it's fine, now, to do this anyway. They aren't here. Lily isn't judging me. Frasier howls at us, delighted and overwhelmed by all of our movement.

'Benji,' Adrian calls from the house, 'you want a mimosa?'

'Yes, please!'

I'm out of breath by the time Adrian finds me. My cheeks are flushed and Lily is sitting on top of my shoulders. She places a sticky hand on my forehead. Why the hell is it sticky?

The moths in my mom's garden are the size of birds, and the birds are the size of insects. It's paradisiacal on this remote stretch of coast, even with the daily water cuts and the power cuts. Mom has rainwater tanks for drinking water, at least. We know when the municipal water comes on so we can plan our showers accordingly. I'm sure it won't be long before there's a scheduling app.

Adrian offers me the mimosa, and I tell him I'll come inside to drink it.

'You two look like you're having fun,' he says in that clownish voice people use for children and dogs.

'You three,' Lily corrects him from above. 'There are three of us, Uncle Adrian.'

'Yes, sorry, Frasier too!' Adrian says. He sips his mimosa and he smiles at me. His beard has almost grown back, now. His eyes are crinkled and soft. Quietly, in his adult voice, he says to me: 'We're not going anywhere, are we?'

'Yes we are!' Lily shouts. She drums her sticky fingers in my hair. 'We're going to the beach.'

# Acknowledgements

Benji might not like to say it, but it takes a village to bring a book into the world. I am so grateful for the team I've had. Special thanks to my publisher, Stevlyn Vermeulen, for believing in this project from the very beginning, and to everyone at Kwela/NB Publishers, especially Helené Coetzee and Gys Visser. Thank you to Claire Strombeck and Angela Voges for your thoughtful edits and kind words of encouragement, and to Damon Galgut for your advice on the manuscript.

This novel was born in the anxiety and isolation of the Covid lockdowns, so I relied heavily on my writing group, 'The Waterberg Set'. Thank you Alex Matthews, Erin Conway-Smith, Louietta du Toit, and the more ad hoc (could we say flaky?) members: Sarah Khan, TJ Thorne, and Gareth Langdon.

Thank you Mike Wilter, for being so generous with your time, for sharing your insight and experience of adoptive parenting with me, and for suggesting useful books to read on the subject. Thank you Arlene Joffe, for holding my hand and helping me find my way through the shadows.

To my readers – you made writing this book much more difficult than writing the first one! I had to let go of the illusion that this was just between myself and the flickering cursor. But you have also made it all worthwhile. I have been truly moved by your messages, by conversations we've had at book events, and I feel honoured to have been allowed a space in your consciousness for a while.

Thank you to my friends and family, for your unwavering support. I have been very lucky in love.

To Reggie, the didn't-even-really-need-to-be-fictionalised pup who cracked open my heart and let the light in, and Oscar, who had a very tough act to follow, but still manages to make me laugh.

Michael, my first reader, biggest cheerleader, and companion in life and love, thank you for everything.